HOT SEAL DEVOTION

HOT SEAL Team - Book 8

LYNN RAYE HARRIS

The Hostile Operations Team® and Lynn Raye Harris® are trademarks of H.O.T. Publishing, LLC.

Printed in the United States of America

First Printing, 2020

For rights inquires, visit www.LynnRayeHarris.com

HOT SEAL Devotion
Copyright © 2020 by Lynn Raye Harris
Cover Design Copyright © 2020 Croco Designs

ISBN: 978-1-941002-53-7

Chapter One

SOMEONE WAS WATCHING HER.

Kayla hurried down the sidewalk, carrying two bags from the diner that contained lunch for everyone at *Hair Affair,* and told herself she was being paranoid. The Kings of Doom motorcycle club was done, busted up and scattered to the winds by her soon to be brother-in-law Alexei Kamarov and his SEAL buddies. They'd rescued her sister and stopped her psychotic ex before he could harm Bailey.

And before James could sell Kayla's baby—his *own* child—to an adoption agency. Kayla shivered as she quickened her steps. Little Anastasia was secure in her playpen in the salon, watched over by Chloe, Avery, and JoJo, and life was good. Kayla had been working at the salon as a shampoo girl since the previous one left a couple of months ago. Before that she'd been answering phones at a real estate office and contemplating getting her license, but she didn't like

1

the idea of meeting clients alone at strange houses. It wasn't likely anyone would kidnap her and turn her into a sex worker like the Kings of Doom had done to so many unsuspecting girls, but knowing it had happened—*still* happened, since trafficking was a thing—made her supremely uncomfortable with the idea of being alone with anyone she didn't know.

But then Chloe had suggested she replace Milly the shampoo girl, who was moving to another state. Avery—the salon owner—had agreed, and Kayla had been there since. She liked working at the salon. Chloe, Avery, and JoJo were sweet to her, and they'd started encouraging her to think about cosmetology school. She would love to learn how to be a stylist, but she didn't have the time or the money.

Someday. Maybe.

Right now she had to work to take care of her daughter and provide for the future. James was in prison, and even if he weren't, he wasn't the kind of guy you asked for child support. A man who'd been planning to sell his own daughter to an illicit adoption agency damned sure wasn't going to pay money for her care.

Kayla was nearly to the salon when a car pulled up beside her and slowed. Her heartbeat quickened and sweat popped up on her skin, but she didn't turn her head.

"Hey, baby," an oily voice said. "Where you goin' in such a rush?"

Kayla gripped the bags tighter and didn't reply.

She cut her gaze sideways, trying to see the man without being obvious about it.

"I'm talking to you, baby," he said again. "You too good to talk to me?"

The salon was just ahead. She could taste safety even if she wasn't there yet. She walked faster, unwilling to break into a run—and unable to anyway with the wedges she'd worn today. Her stomach twisted with fear.

Keep walking, Kayla. Don't look at him. You're almost there.

She heard those words in Bailey's voice because her sister had been the one to take care of her when she was a kid, to protect her from harm and make sure she had food and shelter. Bailey had been more mom than sister, and when Kayla needed to be brave, she thought of Bailey's strength and determination. If Bailey was the one in her shoes, she'd stop and tell the asshole to piss off.

But Kayla didn't like confrontation. She didn't want attention, and she didn't want anyone to notice her or remember her. Not beyond the few minutes it took for some sexist asshole to catcall her on the sidewalk anyway. That was pretty impossible to stop with men being what they often were.

The man revved the engine. "You're gonna get what's coming to you, bitch!" he yelled before peeling out in a squeal of rubber.

Kayla stumbled up the steps and into the salon, her heart racing. Chloe looked up from where she was sweeping around her chair after her last client had left. Something must have showed on Kayla's face because Chloe dropped the broom and hurried over.

"Hey, honey, what's wrong?" Chloe asked with her sweet Southern drawl, putting her arm around Kayla as she took one of the bags from her hand.

Kayla pulled in a deep breath as hot shame flooded her. It was stupid. She was stupid.

"It's nothing. Some idiot tried to pick me up."

Chloe reached behind her to twist the door lock and flicked the switch for the neon *Open* sign so that it went out. "Oh, honey. I'm sorry. I heard that jerk squeal his tires. Was he the one?"

Kayla nodded. She was still trembling. Why? It wasn't like she hadn't been harassed by a man on the street before. But this one had just seemed so… deliberate. "Yes. I didn't look at him, and he got pissed off about it."

"Men are jerks. Well, not all of them. Not even most of them. But the ones who are—lord a mercy, girl, they really make you want to scream."

Kayla knew Chloe'd had a bad relationship before, but she didn't know *how* bad because Chloe hadn't said. To her way of thinking, Chloe had one of the good ones now. Ryan Callahan was a Navy SEAL, like Alexei, and he was so totally in love with her that it would have made Kayla jealous if she didn't like Chloe so much.

Besides, Ryan wasn't the SEAL she wanted. The

4

one she wanted mostly treated her like she was his little sister.

Except for that one time.

Once, Zach "Neo" Anderson had let down his guard and lost his famous control. It had been the most glorious sexual experience of Kayla's life, being the focus of all that gorgeous male attention and skill. She hadn't known what she'd been missing until that moment. All heat and fire and pleasure so intense she'd wanted to sob with it.

But when it was over he'd gone right back to treating her like his little sister. Worse, he'd treated her with more distance than before. Maybe it was her fault for running away the next morning, but she'd panicked. She'd awakened in his bed when the sun was just starting to peek over the horizon, her nipples aching from how much he'd sucked them, her pussy still throbbing with memories of his mouth and cock, and she'd known she couldn't be there when he woke up. She couldn't face him like that, when the night before was fresh and raw and her sheer neediness embarrassed her.

When she'd seen him again a few days later, he'd been so cool that she'd realized nothing had changed. He didn't want a relationship with her. And why would he? She was a mess, and she had a baby. There weren't many men who wanted to start a relationship with a woman who had a baby.

"Come on, honey, let's go eat," Chloe said. "You'll

feel better once you cuddle that cute little girl of yours and get some food in you."

"You're right. Thank you."

They walked toward the back of the shop and the small break room where they took their lunch. Kayla loved that they ate together every day. Working in the salon made her feel like she was part of a family. Like she was accepted. She'd told them bits and pieces of what had happened to her, but not all of it. She didn't want their pity or want to feel like she was nothing but a living and breathing tragic figure.

JoJo was holding Ana. Avery stood to help with the food when Chloe and Kayla walked in. Ana's little face broke out into a grin when she saw Kayla, and Kayla's heart melted. She'd never known she could love anyone as much as she loved her baby. She would do anything to keep Ana safe. *Anything.*

Ana reached for her. JoJo kissed her on the head before handing her over. "You want your mama, little girl?"

Kayla stretched her arms out and took her baby girl. Ana cuddled into her, smiling so big and wide as she wound her fist into a lock of long blond hair that had fallen from Kayla's messy bun.

"How's my little love bug?"

"Some jerk harassed Kayla on the street just now," Chloe said as they sat down to lunch.

Avery and JoJo looked furious. And concerned. Kayla's heart warmed. She'd always had Bailey, but now she had these women too.

"It's okay," Kayla said. "I overreacted. It was just some guy in a car trying to pick me up. I don't know why men think that hollering *hey baby* out the car window to a woman they don't know is ever anything but creepy."

She didn't tell them the part where he'd said she was going to get what was coming to her. She didn't know what it meant—if it meant anything—but it bothered her more than the catcalling had.

"It's totally creepy," Avery said as she flipped open the Styrofoam container to reveal a club sandwich.

JoJo speared some green beans from her container. "You'd think somebody would tell them. Or that the lack of a positive reaction might clue them in."

Chloe snorted. "You'd think, but those types aren't all that bright. Not to mention, I think they *do* know. It's not really about getting a date so much as it's a power issue. Assert your dominance over the poor little female and make her cringe. It's what my ex would have done."

Kayla didn't know a lot about Chloe's background, but she knew there'd been some sort of clash with her ex where Ryan had to get involved. Now they were living together and planning to get married and the ex was dead. Chloe had been hurt in the exchange, but she was fine now. One day, Kayla might get the courage to ask her more about it. She felt like Chloe of all people would understand what she'd been through with James Dunn.

But no matter how nicely these girls treated her, she had a lifetime's worth of trying to protect herself emotionally to overcome. Logically, she knew they wouldn't judge her. She knew Chloe would put her arms around her and hug her tight if Kayla told her about James and the Kings of Doom. Still, she wasn't ready yet.

Kayla ate her lunch with one hand while holding Ana with the other and bouncing her up and down. The women talked about a mix of things, from men to clients to the party Chloe and Ryan were having this weekend at their place. Chloe promised to fry up a bunch of chicken and make a Southern feast. It sounded delicious.

"I've got a perm coming in this afternoon," Avery said when they were finishing up. "Mrs. Flynn at three."

"Bailey is swinging by at two to pick up Ana," Kayla said.

Avery reached out and tweaked Ana's nose. "We don't want this precious little girl breathing those nasty fumes, do we? No we don't," she added in a baby voice.

Ana giggled. Kayla was so grateful to Avery for letting her bring Ana in whenever she needed to, but Avery was firm about making sure Ana wasn't around when they were dealing with strong chemicals. Which Kayla very much appreciated.

"So Chloe," JoJo said. "Tell me more about that yummy SEAL who came in with Ryan yesterday."

Kayla's skin prickled. Zach had been with Ryan yesterday. They hadn't stayed. Zach had said hello to her, but that was it. There'd been no emotion in those green eyes as he'd looked past her after their brief exchange. It hurt, though it shouldn't. They'd been friends who'd slipped. Nothing more.

Even if she wanted more. Even if that single night had been unforgettable in so many ways. She fantasized about life with a man like Zach—strong, honorable, protective. She still worried that James would come for her some day. With Zach in her corner, how could James succeed?

"Zach?" Chloe asked. "They used to be roomies until Ryan moved in with me. Zach still has the house across the street. I don't know if he's looking for another roommate or what."

"Is he dating anyone?"

"I don't think so. But why do you care? Didn't you tell me you had a hot date this weekend?"

"Well, yeah—but you know me. More is always better."

Kayla nibbled the inside of her lip while she fed Ana a bite of mashed potatoes. She liked JoJo a lot. But if the woman started going out with Zach, Kayla knew she wouldn't take it very well at all. Not that he was hers or even very likely to be hers. But if he was going to date someone, she wanted it to be a person she didn't know.

Chloe shrugged. She didn't make eye contact with Kayla. Was it on purpose? Or was she imagining it?

"I don't think he's looking right now. I think he's hung up on someone."

Kayla's stomach flipped. Who was Zach hung up on? Not her, because he'd been coolly distant since the night they'd shared. It was over two months ago now, so *definitely* not her. Which meant he'd met someone—or maybe he'd already been hung up on another woman when he'd slept with Kayla, which made the whole thing infinitely worse. No wonder he'd been distant.

Her heart pinched to think about it. He'd slept with her but he might have been thinking about someone else. Wanting someone else.

Stop. You don't know that.

"Well she needs to step up then," JoJo said. "Because it's crazy to let a man like that go."

"I got the impression it was complicated," Chloe said.

JoJo snorted. "What's so complicated? The man is a US Navy SEAL—the best of the best, hotter than hot, and if he's half as good in the sack as he looks out of it, well, I am of the opinion this woman is a little nuts if she doesn't jump on him."

Kayla kept her head down as she fed Ana. She couldn't look at JoJo while she talked about Zach like that, and she couldn't let anyone see the anguish she felt inside. Zach was an amazing lover and a good guy. He'd be perfect to help raise Ana. But how could she ever expect him to do that? Ana wasn't his responsibility.

"Not everything is as easy as riding a guy like he's a bucking bronc, Jo," Avery said, her voice low and a little pained.

"No, you're right," JoJo said. She reached out and squeezed Avery's shoulder. "I'm sorry, hon. I know it hasn't been all that long since you broke up with Jimmy. I should be more sensitive."

Avery pasted on a smile. "I know you don't mean any harm, Jo. I love you—and I love that you're as crazy as you are. I get to live vicariously through your exploits."

JoJo smiled. "They're pretty good, right?"

Chloe snorted. "Epic."

They all laughed. Kayla had been a bit amazed at how open JoJo was about her sex life, but she couldn't help but listen to Jo's stories anyway. Aside from that one night with Zach, Kayla hadn't gotten any action in more than a year. Not that she had time for it with an eight-month old, but now that she'd been with Zach, she often thought about it late at night when Ana slept. About how amazing it had been. How wonderful to lie in his arms and feel safe for a while.

And now he was hung up on somebody. Her stomach fluttered and tumbled. Was that why he'd never mentioned it again? She hadn't either and maybe she should have. Maybe it would have been less awkward if she had.

You have a baby, Kay-Kay. Most men aren't comfortable with that.

Bailey had never said those words to her, but that's

how Kayla heard them. Bailey, always trying to shelter her and ease the blows that life dealt.

Kayla kissed Ana's soft, dark hair. Any man who wasn't comfortable dating a woman who had a baby wasn't a man she needed in her life anyway.

They finished lunch and cleaned up, then prepared to open the salon again. At two on the dot, Bailey arrived to pick up Ana. Kayla smiled at the sight of her sister bounding up the steps to the salon. Bailey's hair was long now, and she'd stopped dying it purple. These days it was blond. She looked so happy as she stepped inside. She glowed, and that was due to Alexei. Kayla loved that he made her sister happy, and she was envious too.

Bailey had never been so weak she took up with the first man to pay her any real attention, but Kayla had fallen for James Dunn's solicitousness from the first. She'd been aching for someone to love her, and he'd exploited her weakness as soon as he found it.

"How's my little Ana-banana-boo?" Bailey said, dropping to her knees in front of where Ana sat in her playpen with her toys. Ana rewarded her with a yell and Bailey stood and scooped the baby up with all the ease of a natural. It made Kayla smile when she considered how clueless Bailey had been a few months ago.

"She's had a great day with us," Kayla said. "Not a single tear."

Bailey bounced her. "Ana is a good baby. Aren't you a good baby? Yes. You. Are."

Kayla had already packed up Ana's diaper bag. Now she hurried to collapse the Pack 'n Play and stow the toys. "Thank you so much for coming to get her."

"Not a problem, Kay-Kay. Stay as long as you need to. I'm home for the evening."

Bailey knew that Kayla wanted the hours, and Kayla was grateful. Her sister was in nursing school and probably needed to study, but Bailey always worked it out somehow.

Kayla said goodbye to her sister and kissed Ana, then went into the back to take a load of towels from the dryer and fold them up. Her phone buzzed in her pocket and she answered it without looking at the screen. Nobody ever called her but the women in the salon and her sister. "What did you forget, Bailey?"

"I know where you are," a man said. "I know what you did."

Kayla's heart dropped into her toes as fear crawled up her spine. "Who are you? What do you want?"

The man laughed. "You'll soon find out. Oh, and nice shoes you're wearing today, Kayla. Not too good when you want to run though, are they?"

Her heart was a mad thing in her chest. Fear chewed her from the inside out. "Y-you followed me. How do you know me?"

"Your sister is still banging, too. Sweet tits on that babe. Too bad she got away. She'd have made a lot of money for us with that hot body. She's too much trouble though."

Her blood ran cold. He was one of *them*. "I'm hanging up now."

"Better not," he said casually. Menacingly.

She gripped the phone in both hands and forced herself to breathe. "What do you want?"

"What you owe the club, bitch."

"I don't owe them anything."

"I think you do. And you're gonna pay, one way or the other."

"I don't have anything of value. Leave me alone."

He laughed. "You have the kid."

Ice cracked inside her. "No way. Never. I'll call the police if you dare—"

"Really? An unfit mother like you? You sure you want the police involved? They might take her into state custody."

Outrage and fear flooded her system at once. She fell into a chair and gripped the phone tight. "Come for me and I'll kill you," she growled.

The line went dead. But not before he laughed again.

Chapter Two

NEO WAS NURSING A BEER WHEN KAYLA WALKED INTO Dirty and Chloe's backyard pushing Ana in her stroller. His senses snapped into high alert. She wore a pair of cut-off jean shorts that clung to her perfect ass and a breezy white cotton tank top that showcased her luscious tits. Her blond hair was in a ponytail, and his gut twisted at the thought of wrapping all that hair around his fist and tugging her head back so he could plunder her mouth and throat before burying his cock deep inside her pussy.

He shifted in his chair and turned away to get a handle on his reactions. He wanted to go to her, and he also knew he shouldn't. She didn't need the uncertainty of his life clouding hers. Kayla was a mother, and her baby was her first priority. God knew she'd been through enough with her ex and the motorcycle club he'd been a part of. James Dunn had manipulated her, imprisoned her, and tried to take her baby away. He'd put a haunted look in her eyes, and Neo wanted nothing more than to take that look away.

But he couldn't. He couldn't guarantee that he wouldn't put her through a different kind of hell if they got involved. It took a special kind of woman to put up with an operator's life. He didn't doubt that Kayla was special, but she'd been through enough.

"She sure is pretty," Corey "Shade" Vance said, and Neo's hackles rose.

"Yeah, but she's got a baby to take care of and no time for the likes of you."

Shade made a noise of disbelief. Neo turned to meet his gaze.

"I was talking about that one right there. The brunette."

Neo followed the jerk of Shade's chin to Avery McCarthy, Chloe's boss at the salon. She was also the woman who'd owned this house until Dirty and Chloe moved in together and made her an offer. She was a leggy brunette, dressed in a pair of jeans and a white button down tied at the waist. Polished compared to Kayla, with perfect makeup and hair.

Neo liked Kayla's messy blond locks, her simple clothing that often had spots from where Ana dropped food on her. Avery was an uptown girl. Kayla was the girl next door.

"She's pretty," Neo said. "And recently single."

"Yeah, I know."

"So ask her out."

Shade took a sip of his beer. "Too soon."

Neo didn't ask questions. He didn't really want to know why Shade cared how long ago the breakup was.

Ryan "Dirty Harry" Callahan and Alexei "Camel" Kamarov strolled over and flopped into chairs while the women gathered around Kayla and Ana, cooing over the baby and talking about whatever it was that women talked about at picnics.

"Man, I'm starved," Dirty said. "Chloe said ten more minutes. She's almost done with the chicken."

Neo couldn't wait to have Chloe's fried chicken. And her dessert, whatever she'd made today. Living across the street from Dirty and Chloe, he was the lucky recipient of her cooking quite often. He wasn't complaining.

Soon, Chloe leaned out the back door and yelled at Dirty to come help her. He shot upright and disappeared into the house. A few more minutes and they were carrying out fried chicken, corn on the cob, green beans, biscuits, and that strawberry pretzel dessert that made Neo's mouth water. He should have been faster to make a play for her back when she'd moved in. Instead, he'd let Dirty have her.

Which was the right thing to do because Dirty was head over heels for Chloe. Neo loved her, but not like that. He loved her because his buddy did, and because she was sweeter than the cakes she baked. Platonic love, nothing more incendiary.

Neo piled his plate high with chicken, knowing how good it was going to be when he bit into it. Fortunately, Chloe had made a shit ton of food. She knew who she was dealing with when it came to this crowd.

Neo was perched at a table and biting back a moan over the buttery biscuits when Kayla appeared beside him. She held a plate and a drink and she looked uncertain of herself. Ana was asleep in her stroller at another table, watched over by Bailey.

"How are you, Zach?"

Neo swallowed a bite of biscuit and worked at keeping his dick under control. "Fine. How about you?"

"I'm okay."

He'd found the only table in the yard that was small and had two chairs. He glanced at the empty one. "Did you want to sit?"

"I, um…." Kayla nibbled the inside of her lip. His balls tightened. "For a second, I guess."

He stood and pulled the chair out and Kayla sank down on it, keeping her eyes from meeting his. She tore off a piece of chicken and popped it in her mouth.

"Good, huh?" Neo asked.

"Oh yes. Chloe knows how to cook."

"She sure does. Dirty is a lucky bastard."

Kayla swallowed and nodded. "He is. Nobody in our house cooks like this."

He knew she meant the house where she lived with Camel and Bailey. She was in the in-law apartment that was an addition the previous owner had built. It had a separate entrance from Camel and

Bailey's house, as well as its own kitchen, living, bed, and bath. They'd bought the house with Kayla in mind, but they also knew they could rent the apartment if she ever moved out.

He'd been inside the apartment a couple of times. The night they'd spent together had been at his place though. He still thought of her every time he climbed into his bed. It was torture to remember the way she'd felt beneath him. Her silken heat gloving his dick, her perfect little tits in his hands and mouth, her tongue sucking his like she couldn't get enough.

Fuck. Stop, dude.

He was going to embarrass himself right here in the middle of the damned party with a hard-on that wouldn't go away if he didn't rid his mind of those images.

Kayla didn't say anything. Neo didn't either. He was too busy thinking unsexy thoughts. He ate in silence, wondering what she wanted and getting pissed that she didn't speak. Maybe she didn't want anything.

Except to torture him.

"How's your sister?" Kayla finally asked.

"She's fine, thanks. The kids are doing well, and she's got a new boyfriend." Maybe this one would stick. He hoped so. He hoped this guy was a good one.

"That's good, right?"

"I think so. I hope it is."

He'd told Kayla about Lesley and the husband

who'd abandoned her and the kids. He wasn't in a motorcycle gang or doing anything illegal, but he wasn't a prince either. Neo had thought Kayla needed to hear about someone raising her kids alone when he'd told her about Lesley. His sister was doing the best she could. Neo sent gifts for the kids. He'd tried to send money, but Lesley wouldn't take it. She was too proud, his little sis. She wanted to do everything herself. He had no choice but to let her, but he hated watching her struggle. If she'd ask for his help, he'd be there in an instant.

He'd left home to join the military when she was still in high school, and that's when everything went to hell. Their parents divorced, and Lesley got stuck with their narcissist of a mother. She'd gone a little wild, and then she'd gotten pregnant. She'd married the father, but teenage parents didn't stand the best chance of making it work.

"Zach, I…" Kayla set her fork down and clasped her hands in her lap. He waited. She shook her head and scrambled to her feet, grabbing the plate. "I'd better get back to Ana. It was nice to talk to you."

Neo watched her go, his gut hollowing out with disappointment as she reached her sister and dropped into a chair beside her. Dirty was at the next table over. He met Neo's gaze, eyebrow lifted.

Neo shrugged, though he felt anything but unaffected. Why did Kayla Jones twist his guts the way she did?

20

"Join us, Neo," Dirty called. "There's room. Drag that chair over here."

He started to say no. But why? He'd have plenty of time to brood over Kayla and her hot and cold reactions to him tonight when he was alone. He joined the group at the picnic table and did his best not to think about Kayla's perfect ass in his hands as he slammed into her hot little pussy and made her beg him for release.

———

KAYLA SAT in her car outside of Zach's house and gripped the wheel, thinking hard. The party had broken up a little while ago. Bailey and Alexei had taken Ana home earlier when Ana started to fuss. Kayla had insisted she could do it, but Bailey said, "It's okay, honey. Stay with Avery and Chloe and have fun. Alexei and I will put Ana down in the guest room tonight, so take your time."

Kayla let them do it because she needed to talk to Zach. She'd told no one about the phone call she'd gotten two days ago. She'd blocked the number. It didn't matter, though. The man knew where to find her which meant she'd been living in fear every moment since. He might have been the one in the car, though she didn't know for certain. The one in the car had gotten angry fast. The one on the phone had been cooler. More calculating. That's why she feared there was more than one of them.

And they were watching her. She didn't really think they wanted Ana as payment, but she wasn't taking any chances. She couldn't.

Kayla stared at Zach's place as if looking for a sign. An idea had begun to form itself in her head this afternoon at the party and she couldn't shake it. It was an outrageous idea, and yet outrageous was what she needed right now.

She didn't know who the man on the phone was, but he was one of the Kings of Doom. He had to know that she was responsible for the raid on their operation. They'd been scattered and broken up, but clearly not all of them had gone to prison.

What she didn't understand was why he'd called her. Why not just kill her? It's how the Kings had always operated. Revenge was sacrosanct in their world.

Settling scores. Sending messages. Nobody betrayed the club and got away with it.

So why let her know they knew where she was? Why not attack when she least expected it?

Kayla bit the inside of her cheek. They didn't come for her yet because someone wanted her to suffer. They wanted her scared. Or someone did anyway.

James? He was in prison, but that didn't mean he couldn't find thugs to do his bidding. He would know how to contact her.

Maybe she should tell Bailey and Alexei about the call. Just tell them and let them deal with it.

But how could she do that? It'd been months since the SEALs had raided the Kings of Doom compound and rescued Bailey. Months in which Bailey had gotten over the trauma, gone back to school, and gotten engaged. She was planning a wedding next month, and she was happier than Kayla had ever seen her.

Bailey had spent her life taking care of Kayla and her problems. Bailey was four years older, and she took her duty to protect her baby sister seriously. How could Kayla disrupt her life yet again? How could she take away the joy she saw in her sister's eyes every single day?

The man on the phone had seen Bailey. The threat was subtle, but it was there. Kayla wouldn't let her mixed up life drag Bailey down ever again.

And she damned sure wouldn't let it drag Ana down. Not her precious baby.

That's why she had to do this. Why she had to try. It was either this or run again.

She didn't want to run. She loved her job, and she loved the people she'd formed attachments to over the past few months. She didn't want to leave her daughter, either. Because she would have to. It wouldn't be safe to take Ana with her. She'd considered all the options, and this one was best.

Kayla wanted security. She wanted a bodyguard like her sister had. Like Chloe had. A big, bad, intimidating as hell bodyguard who would protect her and

Ana. Someone who could make a grizzled biker think twice before he came gunning for her.

A Navy SEAL.

Crazy.

She firmed her jaw. *Not crazy. Necessary.*

Even if he was hung up on someone else.

She couldn't let that stop her. She shook her head, sucked in a fortifying breath, and opened her car door. Then she climbed out, locked the car, and strode toward Zach's place. Her heart hammered, her skin grew moist with sweat, and her breath quickened.

She stood on the threshold and gathered her courage. Would he laugh at her? Would he tell her to get out?

Maybe. And maybe she deserved it.

It was a chance she had to take. If he did, she'd think of something else.

Maybe.

Or maybe she'd get on her knees and beg.

Determined, she pressed the doorbell. Zach had occupied the bottom floor while Ryan had the top, but now that Ryan was living with Chloe, Kayla didn't know what Zach's arrangements were. Still, she'd gone to the side door leading to the lower floor because that's where she'd entered the house that night.

Kayla swallowed. *That night.*

Yes, the night they'd gone out to dinner together, just friends, and then ended up back here where they could talk without loud music or other people.

And then, somehow, they'd wound up in bed. A little too much tequila on her part, too much Scotch on his.

Didn't change the fact it had been hot and amazing. Or that she still dreamed about that night and the way she'd felt so utterly cherished. Zach knew his way around a woman's body, and he'd made hers sing. They'd fucked hard, but never so hard that she'd been afraid. He'd drawn reactions from her body that she hadn't known she was capable of. He'd made her so crazy with need that her inhibitions fell away as she did whatever it took to maximize her pleasure.

Yet another reason she'd run away from him the next morning.

The door jerked open and Zach stood there in all his hard muscled glory. Faded jeans that hugged his narrow hips, dark T-shirt clinging to muscles sculpted during hard combat, bare feet. He was tattooed, but it wasn't overdone like the bikers she'd lived with. He had a tribal tattoo circling one arm, and she knew he had others on his back and chest. In the background, she could hear a car auction on the television.

"Hi, Zach. Can I come in?"

He hesitated. And then he stepped back, holding the door wider. "Yeah, sure."

She walked inside, twisting her hands together in front of her. Could she do this? She *had* to do this.

He closed the door and leaned against it, watching her with hooded eyes that glittered like emeralds.

What was he thinking? Probably that she wanted something.

He wasn't wrong.

In the background the auction continued as someone bid an astronomical amount for a car. She didn't know what kind of car. Wasn't looking. Didn't care.

"What did you need, Kayla?"

She should have expected that he'd cut straight to the chase. She pulled in a deep breath, let it out again. It was now or never. Her breath got tangled up in her chest, but she forced the words out anyway. He was a good man. She focused on that, not on the other stuff. The feelings and the raw sexual heat that still pulsed inside her. For him.

This was either going to be a disaster, or it wouldn't. She didn't know until she forged ahead.

"I need a favor, Zach. A big favor."

Her heart beat so hard she thought she might pass out. Her vision tunneled for a second. *Be strong, Kay-Kay. You can do this. For Ana. For Bailey. For you.*

"What's that?"

Kayla closed her eyes. Her throat constricted. She forced them open again. Willed him to understand.

"I need you to marry me."

Zach didn't move. Didn't blink. He was a mountain of hard muscle and he didn't budge.

Didn't say a word.

His eyebrows lifted, and her stomach went into free fall.

"What?"

Oh shit. Ohshitohshitohshit…

Kayla swallowed. She held out her hands, spread them wide. "I know. I know it's crazy, and you no doubt want to tell me to get lost, but please hear me out—"

His frown nearly undid her. But he didn't say anything so she continued. But what she said wasn't the real truth, only part of it.

"Ana n-needs a dad. She needs medical insurance. I lay awake at night worrying about what I'd do if she ever got really sick. How would I afford the medical bills?" His eyes narrowed and she swallowed. Maybe she'd lost him but she tumbled on anyway. "I know this is asking a lot. I know it. But I'm doing all I can, working as hard as I can, and I still can't keep her safe. I can't rely on Bailey and Alexei forever. Alexei is great, but Ana isn't entitled to his insurance. She can't be his dependent."

She hated that word, but that's what the military called family members. *Dependents.* A dependent was someone very specific who was entitled to all the benefits the military provided. Free insurance, tax-free shopping privileges, bargain groceries, educational opportunities—the list went on. Bailey would be Alexei's dependent when they married next month, but Kayla could never be. Neither could Ana.

Zach still didn't say anything. She hadn't expected him to. Not really.

His expression made it clear what he was thinking.

He didn't move. His body was a wall of hard muscle blocking the exit. Not that she was leaving yet. She couldn't. Shame made her skin hot but she didn't drop her gaze from his. She waited, knowing he was about to eviscerate her. Feeling like she deserved it and trying to plan her next move anyway.

"You're asking me to marry you for my benefits." Zach crossed his arms over his chest. Frowned down at her. She couldn't help but notice the way his muscles popped beneath his shirt sleeves. *So strong and sexy.* Those arms had held her close once, folded her to his chest and made her feel safe and protected. "As touching as this proposal is, I'm going to have to refuse."

Kayla's throat tightened. Her belly went into free fall. "I understand."

He snorted. It was a sound of disgust. "Then why did you ask? What the fuck, Kayla? You've barely talked to me in two months, and now you want me to marry you? What the actual fuck?"

Tears threatened. She wouldn't let them fall, though. She didn't have time to cry. Kayla tipped her chin up even though she trembled inside. "You're safe, Zach. Stable. It wouldn't have to be forever. You could still date other women. Ana and I could live upstairs, and you could do what you've always done—"

The fury in his expression stopped her. He closed the distance between them, put his face into hers. She could feel the heat of his anger rippling off him. If she touched him, would it burn?

"Are you fucking kidding me? You want to get married for my benefits and then you want to keep seeing other people?"

She spun away from him, the anger on his face too much for her. The disappointment.

He loves someone else….

She didn't want him to date other women. That was a lie. But she'd felt like it was something she ought to say. Something to sweeten the deal.

"I didn't say *I* wanted to see other people. I just want to provide for Ana and not have to worry if I can afford her next checkup, or an emergency room trip. Military insurance is *free.* And I'd pay for anything else she needed. I want stability for a change!"

The emotion of the situation got to her. The desperation of all she was feeling. She put her head in her hands. Shook it. Everything had sounded reasonable in her brain, but now it sounded like the worst kind of gold-digging. Except instead of money, she wanted his military benefits. Not much difference, she supposed. No wonder he was pissed.

She'd spent her life without stability. She didn't want that for her child. She hadn't realized how precarious her life—and Ana's by extension—still was until she'd gotten that phone call. She hadn't done anything that would prompt child protective services to take Ana away, but the suggestion had rattled her. Badly.

"Sorry, Kayla, but no. I'll give you money if you

need it, but I'm not marrying you. And I'm definitely not living like roommates instead of a married couple. Do you have any idea what Camel would do to me if I married you and kept dating other women?"

She shook her head.

Zach continued. "He's a sniper. A damned good one. And while I don't *think* he'd shoot my ass, he might. At best, we'd have to stop working together because he wouldn't trust me anymore. The team would fall apart and one of us would need to be replaced. Probably me since the rest of them would think I was a douche for cheating on you."

Kayla's shoulders slumped. "You're right. I know you are. I just thought…."

She'd thought of Zach because he was a good guy, and he knew what it was like for a single mother to struggle. He loved his sister and he'd do anything to help her. She'd thought he would understand. She sucked in a breath and bit the inside of her lip as tears clogged her throat. She would *not* cry. She never cried. She couldn't afford to show weakness. She'd learned that in the hell of the motorcycle club. A tear escaped and slipped down her cheek anyway and she slapped it away angrily.

Zach made a sound halfway between a groan and a sigh. Then he closed the distance between them and put his hands gently on her shoulders. Rubbed her arms lightly. "I'm sorry, Kayla. Really. But trust me, you don't want to marry me for my benefits. It's not a good reason to marry anyone."

His kindness undid her. That and the stress of everything she'd been feeling. The worry. Before she could stop it, the tears began to flow. He didn't say anything. Just took her hand and led her over to the couch. Sat her down and picked up the remote to mute the television. A box of tissues appeared. She tore several out and wiped her eyes, angry that she'd let her weakness show.

Weakness got you in trouble and she didn't need more of that.

When she looked up again, Zach was watching her, his handsome face set in a frown. Seeing through her flimsy excuses for marriage and looking for the truth. His words confirmed it.

"Why don't you tell me what this is really about, Kayla."

Chapter Three

NEO WAS STILL REELING FROM HAVING KAYLA IN HIS home, but he was reeling even more from what'd just happened. First he'd been shocked. Then pissed.

Now he was puzzled. Kayla sobbed like her heart had been broken, which meant there was more to her showing up here tonight than she'd let on.

There were definitely women who chased military men for the benefits—and the other way around since men were also capable of gold digging—and even more women who were SEAL groupies and would love a chance to snag one.

But he didn't think Kayla was one of those. If she had been, she'd have been chasing the single SEALs relentlessly until one fell for her. She'd certainly had every opportunity to do so, but she never had. It was just him and Shade who were single left on the team, but she had access to other special operators, not just SEALs. HOT was a joint service organization, which meant Marines, Air Force, and Army too. She was pretty enough to have her pick, but he'd never seen her flirt with any of them the few times they'd all been at Buddy's Bar & Grill together.

She pulled tissues from the box and wiped her eyes, blew her nose, and finally pressed the heels of her hands to her eyes when the tears didn't stop. He thought about calling Bailey, but he didn't think Kayla would thank him for it. Whatever was bothering her, if she'd wanted her sister involved then it would've already happened.

He figured he'd let her cry it out, find out what was bugging her, and do whatever he could to help her overcome it. He hated seeing her cry. Hated seeing any woman cry, really. He'd always had a visceral reaction to a woman crying and now was no different. It made his gut tighten with unpleasant memories.

When he'd been a little boy, before he'd realized that his mother's drama was manufactured, he'd always gotten anxious when she cried. He'd hovered and patted and doted, and that's what she'd wanted. Even now, he had a mixed response to tears. Part of him wanted to make them stop and part of him wanted to know what the angle was.

"Kayla," he said after a few more minutes had gone by, "you gonna tell me what's going on? Or do you want me to call Bailey and ask her to come get you?"

Fear crossed her features. She grabbed his arm in

her cold hand and gripped it. "No, please. Don't call her."

Just as he'd suspected. "Okay, but you have to tell me what's wrong. This isn't because I said no to your proposal."

She dropped his arm and shredded the tissue in her hands, her gaze on her lap. She sniffled from time to time. If her tears were fake, she was damned good at it. He didn't think they were, though. His mother wasn't a normal human being by any definition and she could whip up Hollywood-level hysteria at a moment's notice. Most people weren't that good.

"Kayla. You can trust me."

"I know," she whispered. Then she sighed as if she'd come to a decision. "I don't want Bailey to know yet. She went through hell for me, and her wedding is next month. I don't want to worry her when she's so happy. I want to take care of this myself."

He didn't like the sound of where she was going. He didn't know what it was, but he wasn't getting a good vibe here. Something was frightening her.

"If I can keep it between us, I will."

Her eyes were wide and wet. "Please, Zach. Please don't tell."

"I'll do my best, Kayla. I swear."

"On your honor as a SEAL?"

He didn't hesitate. "On my honor as a SEAL."

She pulled in a breath. Met his gaze evenly. "The other day, I went to get lunch for everyone at the salon. You know the diner on the corner?"

34

"Yes."

"I walked over there, picked up the food, and walked back. A man in a car slowed down and started talking shit to me. Catcalling. That kind of thing."

His gut twisted with anger on her behalf.

"I know that doesn't sound like anything. Just some asshole who saw a woman walking alone and wanted to harass her." Kayla pulled in a breath. "But that wasn't all. When I didn't respond, he said I was going to get what was coming to me, and then he squealed his tires and left. Which still might be nothing, I know that. Anyway, I told the girls about it and that was the end of it. But something else happened later, and I don't think it's a coincidence."

The back of his neck started to prickle with warning. He'd learned never to ignore that feeling during countless missions overseas and into enemy strongholds. It was that feeling, that tickle, that kept him alive. He wasn't the only one who had it. Every operator he knew—the good ones anyway, and HOT only had the good ones—had some version of that warning system.

"Go on."

"Bailey came to the salon a couple of hours later to pick up Ana. When she left, I got a phone call. I thought she'd forgotten something."

He waited for Kayla to continue. She shredded the tissue some more. Closed her eyes. He reached out and put a hand on her knee. Her bare skin was warm, soft. He ignored the way touching her made his cock ache and gave her a light squeeze for comfort before pulling his hand away again. She sucked in a breath and lifted her gaze.

"It was a man. He said he knew where I was and what I did."

The prickling intensified. "There's more."

Kayla nodded. "Yes. I asked who he was. I didn't recognize the voice. He said I'd find out—and then he mentioned my shoes, the ones I was wearing that day, and how hard it must be to run in them. He also talked about what Bailey looked like. I asked him what he wanted—and he said he wanted what I owed the club. He said I was going to pay."

Anger flared, scouring his insides with acid. Some fucking lowlife asshole from the motorcycle club had stalked her and scared her. He clearly wanted something from her. But what?

She swallowed. "I told him I didn't have anything of value. And he said… He said I had Ana."

Neo saw red. No way would he let that happen. No fucking way.

"I told him I'd call the police and he said…." She closed her eyes. "That I shouldn't do that because I was an unfit mother and she might end up in state custody."

Neo growled. "There's no way he can make good on that threat, Kayla. It's not a matter of making an accusation and they take your child away. There's more to it than that. He wanted to scare you. Fucker."

She looked pale. "I know."

"And you don't think you should tell Bailey about any of this?"

She shook her head. "No, not yet. Bailey already went through so much because of me. And it might be nothing other than some asshole from what's left of the Kings who wants to harass me. It might even be James making it happen from prison for no other reason than to scare me."

"If you believed that, you wouldn't be here."

Her gaze dropped again. "No, that's true. But if I tell Bailey, then what? What can she do? It was one phone call, and that was a couple of days ago. I blocked the number, but he could call again from a different phone. He hasn't so far. I haven't seen anyone watching me either. I make sure to check my surroundings thoroughly, and I don't go anywhere alone. It's work or home, and that's it. I only go other places when someone is with me, like today. But if I tell Bailey, then she'll do something drastic, like quit school or postpone the wedding until the danger is past. She'd upend her life to protect mine, like she always does, and I don't want that. Alexei would have to spend his time watching out for me and Ana instead of planning his future with Bailey. I'd like to prevent that, if possible."

Neo didn't like any of this shit. Someone was threatening her. But there was still a lot to unpack here.

"How will us getting married fix anything?"

Her pretty hazel eyes skimmed over his face.

"You're a SEAL. If we were married, whoever is out there would think twice about coming after me because it would mean trouble with the military. And I wouldn't be parenting alone anymore. I'd be married and Ana would have a dad. I could put her into daycare on the base since she'd be entitled to it then. She'd be safer there than at the salon every day. When she isn't in daycare, she'll be with me and you together. She'd be safe all the time, and I wouldn't be as scared that something might happen to her. I also don't think child protective services would be as likely to take her. If they did, the military would help us."

Now he understood. She wanted to protect her baby. She was terrified that whoever'd threatened her could make good on the threat to have Ana taken away. He didn't believe it was likely, but he didn't need to. She did.

He also understood why she'd want Ana in base daycare. The base was a fortress guarded by military dogs and armed military police with automatic rifles. No one who wasn't supposed to be there was getting in. Camel couldn't get Ana into daycare before because she wasn't his, and he wasn't marrying her mother.

Which, if Bailey got involved, he might. Temporarily, and so Kayla and Ana could have his military benefits until such time as it was safe for them to divorce so he could marry Bailey instead. It wasn't all that far-fetched either, because Camel would do anything for Bailey. If she asked him to protect her sister, he would. Even if he had to marry her to do it.

Shit, what a mess. It made perfect sense why Kayla had come to him. She knew what her sister was like. What she would sacrifice.

"You know that I'll have to deploy, right? My job isn't nine-to-five, five days a week. I can be gone for weeks at a time. I can't guarantee I'd be here with you all the time."

She twisted the remains of a tissue. "I know. But I'd still feel safer because Ana would be on the base during the day, and we could stay with Bailey when the team deploys."

Neo rubbed his forehead. The whole thing stunk, but he understood why she didn't want Bailey to know. She was happy, planning a wedding, moving on with her life. Still, Camel was his teammate and Neo wasn't going to be able to keep this from his brother-in-arms. Not for long anyway.

Kayla reached out and cupped his face in both hands. It shocked him enough that he stilled, waiting for whatever she wanted to say. Her hands were cool, but his skin still sizzled where she touched. His cock twitched to life at that reminder of what it had been like between them.

He'd owned her hot little body once, and he'd wanted so much more. He'd wanted to drown in her. He still wanted it.

"You want to tell Alexei. I know you do. I get it—but Zach, if we're married, then Bailey won't worry as much about me once she finds out about the threats. She'll know you won't let anything happen to me because she knows how safe she is with Alexei. She won't quit school and she won't postpone her wedding."

"Or suggest that Camel marry you instead."

She made a soft noise and then nodded. "Right. She's capable of that. Just for a while, just to protect me. But what would that do to her happiness to watch the man she loves marry me so I can have his military benefits? I won't do that to either one of them. I'd run away first."

She sounded so fierce that he believed her. He turned his head, pressed his lips to her palm. She didn't snatch her hand away. She might have whimpered. He didn't know why he did it, except he wanted to taste her again. He wanted to taste a lot more than her palm, but that would do for the moment.

They were only inches apart. He could smell her scent, that combination of lavender and baby powder that had permeated his sheets and pillows before he'd stripped the bed and washed them in detergent and bleach in an effort to erase her from his dreams.

He could tell Camel about the threat she'd gotten. They'd go to Viking and Ghost, and they'd start digging. Find out who was harassing her. Find him and make it clear as crystal that if he came near Kayla or Ana, he'd suffer in ways he'd never dreamed.

Yet, what if it wasn't that easy? The military had no authority when it came to domestic crime. When they'd gone after the Kings of Doom before, they'd been temporarily assigned to Ian Black, who didn't run a military outfit. The Kings were officially done, so how did Neo and his team go after stragglers in any official capacity?

They didn't, which meant it *would* be better for Kayla to be married and safer for Ana to go into daycare on base. He could also apply for base housing, move onto the facility with Kayla and Ana. It would take a couple of months, probably, but once it happened they'd be secure when he deployed. Living on a military installation was like living in the most secure gated community in the world. Everything Kayla would need was there. Hospital, commissary, Exchange. She wouldn't have to leave the base at all when he was gone.

And if he deployed before they got on base, he could arrange for some of the guys on other teams to watch out for her and Ana. He could keep them safe from afar.

Neo blinked. Was he really considering it?

Yeah, he was. He told himself it was for his teammate, so Camel wouldn't end up marrying her instead. But that wasn't the whole truth. He was also thinking of Lesley and how fierce she was when it came to her kids. She'd do anything for them, and he loved her for it. She was nothing like their mother, and she was determined to give her kids the best life she could.

Kayla was cut from the same cloth as Lesley. She'd had a rough time of it, but she loved her child—and her sister—fiercely. She would do whatever it took, including run away again, if that's what she thought would save them both from harm. It was in his power to prevent that. If Kayla ran, she'd never stop running. She'd never be free.

"If I agree to this, we have to iron out a few things first."

She nodded. Her hands dropped to her lap. He hated that she wasn't touching him anymore. Yeah, that was another reason he was thinking about it. Bastard that he was, he liked it when she touched him. He'd like it even better if they were naked when it happened. That wasn't a reason to marry anyone, but his dick didn't think too deeply about much of anything that wasn't physical.

"What kind of things?"

"If we're married, and I'm responsible for you and Ana, then I'm not living downstairs and dating other women. I want us to have the kind of relationship married people have."

If he was getting married, it wasn't going to be a marriage of convenience. He only knew what that meant because Lesley had liked romance novels growing up and told him about them whenever she could make him listen. And he wasn't doing that shit. If he was giving up the single life to protect Kayla and Ana, then he wanted more from the relationship.

"Sex, you mean."

Awareness flickered hot. "It's more than sex, Kayla. We've done that once, and we know it's good. I'm talking about making a real go of it. I don't want to live separate lives and pretend that's normal. If we get married, then we get married. If it doesn't work out for some reason, then we'll figure that out when we get there. But I don't want to go into it thinking it's not going to."

She nibbled her lip, her cheeks reddening. He wanted to bite that lip. "Honestly, I want Ana to have a dad she can count on. And I want to know before she's old enough to miss you if it's going to work out or not. I wouldn't want to stay married if we're miserable."

"Neither would I."

She frowned. "Zach…. Chloe said something the other day, and I need to know if it's true. It won't change my mind about marrying you, but I want to know…."

"Okay." He couldn't imagine what Chloe had said, but if he could ease her mind about something, then he would.

"She said you were hung up on someone and it was complicated. Is that true?"

His gut twisted. Chloe said that? He didn't have to wonder where she'd gotten it. Dirty had told her.

"No, I'm not hung up on anyone," he said. And

he wasn't. Yeah, he thought about Kayla a lot. Wanted her. Dreamed about fucking her again. It didn't mean he was hung up on her, no matter what Dirty thought. "There's no one in my life right now."

She dropped her lashes. "I'm sorry for asking. I just wondered."

"What about you?" he asked, and her head snapped up.

She blinked. "Me?"

"Are you hung up on anyone?"

Color flooded her cheeks. "I, um, no. Of course not. You're the only man I've been with since Ana was born, and that was only once. I don't have time for men."

"Fair enough." He hesitated, wondering about the pink in her face. "If we do this—make a real go of it —I'm not saying we have to share a bed right away. I'd understand if you wanted to ease into that part of it."

Her eyes widened. "You mean we'd date first?"

"If that's what you want."

Kayla ran her palms over her shorts. Her hands were small. Her body was small. She was lovely and vulnerable and he found that he desperately wanted to protect her. Like a frigging caveman.

"Okay, that's fair."

He sat back and raked a hand through his hair. On the television, they'd moved on to another car. Somebody else paying astronomical amounts of money for a classic automobile. Must be nice.

He'd pretty much made up his mind, but there was a little more to discuss. "If I say yes, you still don't want to tell your sister the real reason?"

She shook her head. "Not yet. Not until she has her wedding if at all possible. I don't want to ruin her happiness. I just want her to have a lovely wedding and honeymoon, and I don't want her worrying about me and Ana."

"Do you think that's fair, Kayla?"

She thrust her chin out. He recognized it for the stubborn gesture it was. "Yes, I do. It's temporary. Only until she and Alexei get married. I've caused Bailey enough trouble over the years. For once I want to solve my own problems and take care of her, even if it's just letting her think everything is great for a while. Her knowing the truth won't change anything, so keeping quiet for another few weeks won't hurt."

He wasn't so sure, but Bailey wasn't his sister. And he wasn't getting between them. "Okay, but if I have to tell Camel so he can protect her, then I will. You need to understand that. I don't keep secrets from my teammates if they need to know something important."

"He'll tell her."

"He might not. He might agree with your reasons not to. Did you ever think of that?"

She shook her head.

"He loves her and wants her happy. Same as you. You need to trust him."

"Okay."

The word came out as a whisper and he knew she didn't like the idea of Camel knowing. He didn't think Camel needed to know just yet, but if he did, then Neo wasn't keeping it from him.

"One more thing. If we do this and you don't want your sister to know why we're really getting married, then we'll have to sell it to her. That means we have to pretend to be in love."

She reddened again. "Agreed."

He'd never been in love before, but he'd been around enough of his teammates who were that he was sure he could pull it off. Plus, it wasn't a stretch to physically want her. He'd told Dirty a couple of months ago that he thought of her like a little sister, but that had been a lie.

A big fucking lie. Dirty saw through it, but Neo hadn't been about to admit what he'd really wanted to do to Kayla Jones. How badly he'd wanted to taste her pussy again. If he married her though?

Yeah, Dirty would give him hell. So what? He'd still be the one who got to strip her naked and make her come every night. Eventually, when they got that far. He wouldn't push her on that. He wanted her to need his cock as much as he needed to lose himself inside her.

"So you'll marry me?" she pressed. "Or do you need to think about it some more?"

Neo thought of his sister and her kids again. How would he feel if some guy married her to help her protect the kids? To provide security—and health insurance—as well as do his best to be a dad they could depend on?

He'd be wary, but he'd be glad too. *If* the guy really cared about her and meant to do the best job he could.

Yeah, Neo's teammates had found women they were crazy for. They'd fallen hard and fast, but he didn't think it had to be that way to work. Marrying Kayla didn't mean he was somehow going to miss out on finding his soulmate, the one who completed him. He wasn't sure he believed in that bullshit anyway. His sister hadn't had any luck in that department, and neither had his parents.

What he had with Kayla stood as much of a chance of working as anything. They had chemistry, and he cared about her and Ana. He wanted to protect them, and he was tired of the single scene. Surely that was good enough?

He held his hand out. She took it. He didn't squeeze, didn't shake it up and down. Just held her there, his hand engulfing her much smaller one.

He liked touching her. Liked the zip of attraction that hummed through his veins. The current of possessiveness. He took a deep breath. Studied her hazel gaze.

"Yes," he said solemnly. "I'll marry you."

Chapter Four

Relief flooded her. Kayla closed her eyes and bowed her head as the weight of dread lifted from her shoulders. Zach was going to marry her. It was a huge thing, and she knew she could never thank him enough. With him on her side, whoever'd threatened her wasn't going to win. He would make sure of it.

"Thank you, Zach. Thank you so much."

His expression was fierce. "I've got your back, Kayla. It's not what I expected would happen when I opened the door, but you can count on me. I won't let anyone take Ana away from you, and I won't let them hurt you either."

He made her tingle inside, and he hadn't done a thing but vow to protect her. "I know," she said, her heart hammering. He was so damned gorgeous. Her body was already starting to melt, to prepare for something more. Her pussy grew hot and achy with anticipation. Remembering his touch. Craving it.

She told herself to slow down before she turned this into something it wasn't. They were only going to pretend to be in love. That didn't mean they were. Or ever would be. She'd never been lucky in love. She was good at attracting men, especially the wrong kind of men, but she wasn't good at being the kind of person they loved.

James hadn't loved her, though she'd thought he did for a while. He'd been different from the guys who normally hit on her. He hadn't been filled with himself, talking for the good of his own ego. He'd been interested in her. Who she was, what drove her. She knew now that it had all been an elaborate game that men like him played. His job had been finding vulnerable young women to lure into sex trafficking, and the surest way to do that was make them feel heard and valued.

Zach was still sitting close, still studying her. His scrutiny made her self-conscious.

"I don't know what's going on in that pretty mind of yours," Zach said softly. "I've seen six different emotions cross your face in the span of moments. You're scared. I get that. But is it of the guy who threatened you? Or are you scared of me?"

"I'm not scared of you," she blurted, embarrassed that he'd seen so much of her chaotic thoughts. "I'm grateful."

"I would never force you to do anything you don't want to do, Kayla. I hope you know that. We'll get married to protect you and Ana, and we'll take the rest a day at a time."

"I know you wouldn't."

This man had never been anything but wonderful to her. Even on the single night they'd shared, he'd been concerned with her enjoyment, her pleasure. Yes, it had been wild and dirty and fun, but she'd never had a moment of fear or doubt. He'd pushed her to her limits and she'd loved every exciting moment of it. Then she'd run out of his house like there'd been a serial killer with an axe behind her the next morning.

She thought he might ask her about that night, but he didn't. She was relieved because she didn't know what to say in response. How did you tell the man who'd had his tongue all over your body and his cock and fingers deep inside you that you'd run away because you were afraid you'd taken things too far? Or, worse, that you suspected he'd fucked you out of pity?

"How soon do you want to get married?" he asked, all business.

Kayla worked to pull her emotions back from the brink. She had to. She'd gotten what she came for and now they had to make a plan. "As soon as we can? I don't need a ceremony with friends and family. I don't care about white dresses or any of that. It'd be ridiculous anyway since I have a baby."

He frowned. "Anybody who thinks you can't wear white is an asshole. It's not about purity anymore. It's tradition. If you want a white dress, I'll kick anyone's ass who says you shouldn't wear one."

A warm feeling spread through her. "It's okay. I really don't. But thank you."

He picked up his phone and typed something. "Says here you can marry in as quickly as forty-eight hours in Maryland. We have to file for the marriage license first, though. It requires you and me and our identification at the courthouse. We'll have to wait until Monday. We can marry anytime after Wednesday, but we'll have to find someone to marry us. If we want to marry at the courthouse, we have to make an appointment after we have the license. That could take another couple of days."

"I can get the morning off on Monday."

"Next question. How do you want to do this? Get married at the courthouse or plan something our friends can attend? We only need an ordained minister and a location if we don't want to marry at the courthouse."

"I'd rather do the courthouse. I don't want to take away from Bailey's wedding by planning my own."

He studied her. "If you were getting married for the usual reason, what kind of ceremony would you want?"

She didn't have to think about it. "When I was a little girl, I wanted the white dress with a long train, lots of attendants, and a giant church wedding. Like a princess. But I was a kid with an active imagination back then." And such a shitty home life that she'd needed things to dream about. She sighed. "Now, quite honestly, I like simplicity. I imagine a garden wedding with a view like Cash and Ella have in the background. A simple ceremony with a friend doing the officiating after they've gotten ordained online. I'd wear a flowing cotton dress, maybe white, maybe yellow."

"No wedding dress?"

She shrugged. "They're expensive, and you wear them once. Probably not."

He nodded. "Okay. And what does the groom wear?"

"Easy. If he's you he wears his Navy dress uniform. If he's not in the military, he wears a nice suit." Though now that she was talking about getting married for real, she could only picture Zach in the role of groom.

"Dress uniform, huh? With Navy SEAL trident and everything. Got it."

"In an ideal world. But Zach, don't worry about it. All we need to do is get married. It doesn't matter how." A thought occurred to her then. "What about your sister? Or your parents? Will they be upset if they aren't invited?"

She didn't know anything about Zach's parents, but she knew he had a younger sister named Lesley who'd had a shitty husband that'd left her and their three kids for another woman. She also knew that Zach adored and admired Lesley very much.

"My sister couldn't get away even if we did invite

her. She works two jobs." He frowned. "My parents have been divorced for years. My mom's a classic narcissist who'd make it all about her, and my dad has a new wife who'd also have to be invited. She and my mom hate each other. They used to be best friends."

"Oh boy."

"It's a mess and I don't like either one of my parents enough to have them here. So no, we're not inviting them, even if we were planning a wedding for six months from now. They'll get over it. I'll call Lesley. She'll be sorry she missed it, but she'll understand."

She hated hearing about his parents, but she understood too. Her parents were both dead now, but even if they'd been alive she wouldn't want them at her wedding. They'd been two drug-addled disasters who should have never had children. Bailey had been the one to raise Kayla, the one who showed Kayla the meaning of hard work and dedication. Bailey had done everything for Kayla, and Kayla had fucked it all up by getting involved with James Dunn and the Kings of Doom. She was still paying for that mistake, but she was determined that her daughter wasn't going to.

"I'm sorry, Zach. I know what it's like to have a messy family. Or did."

"I know, beautiful. I didn't forget."

She'd thought he might've since they hadn't talked about it in a long time. Clearly, she'd been wrong. She

53

dropped her gaze to her lap, uncertain what to say next.

He tipped her chin up with his fingers. "Whether or not we invite anyone to the ceremony, we probably ought to start working on the part where we convince them we're in love."

Her belly flipped. "What do you suggest?"

"You go home and I'll come over. Camel and Bailey will see my car."

Kayla swallowed. She hadn't expected to launch into this so soon. No, strike that. She hadn't known what to expect because deep down she didn't think he would agree to her proposal. Not really.

But he had. Because he was the kind of man who wasn't going to let anyone threaten her baby.

"They have Ana, so I'll leave her with them. I don't know what they'll think, but they won't knock on the door." She got to her feet. "I'd better head that way then."

"Hang on while I lock up. I'll follow you."

Once Zach had turned off the television and grabbed his keys, they left the house. He walked her to her car and held the door for her. It wasn't a fancy car, but she'd bought it with her own money after she'd started working and saved up enough to put a down payment on it. Alexei had gone to the used car dealer with her and made sure she didn't get fleeced. She was proud of the car because it represented hard work, even if it was old enough that it didn't have bluetooth. Thankfully, Alexei had installed an after-market bluetooth device for her that meant she could use her phone handsfree.

Zach leaned down as she started the car. "Don't worry, Kayla, we'll make this work. We'll get Bailey through her wedding, if that's what you want. But then she needs to know the truth."

She looked up at him, her heart flooding with gratitude. "Thank you. She deserves her happiness, and I want her to have the perfect wedding before subjecting her to my drama."

"It's not your fault, beautiful."

"It feels like it is," she said, her throat tight.

He skimmed his fingers over her cheek and her skin tingled in response. "There are a lot of assholes in this world. You had the misfortune to get involved with a group of them. Doesn't make what they do your fault. They'd be assholes regardless." He straightened. "I'll be right behind you, Kayla. All the way."

———

NEO FOLLOWED Kayla back to her place, thinking about what it was he'd agreed to. *Marriage.*

And not just marriage, but instant fatherhood. He knew how *not* to be a father, thanks to personal experience, but he wasn't sure that meant he'd get it right. He hoped he did. He'd try like hell to get it right, that's for sure. Ana deserved that. Every kid did.

He thought of what Kayla had said about her

caller threatening Ana, and a hot darkness filled him the same way it had when she'd first said it. He would kill anyone who tried to harm that little girl. Rip their fucking heart out and stomp on it without a shred of regret.

He didn't know what his teammates would think when they found out about his marriage, but he couldn't say no to Kayla. Not when she'd stopped pretending it was all about his benefits and told him what was really happening. About the threats.

He had the ability to protect her and Ana, and he was going to do it. It's what any of his teammates would do. Hell, Cash "Money" McQuaid had married his wife to protect her—and look at them now. Married, happy, living the dream. Didn't hurt that Ella was a real life princess with a fortune, but Neo was certain that Money didn't care if she was rich or poor. When he'd married her, she had been poor. It was only later they'd learned she was the true heir to the throne of Capriolo.

Neo wasn't marrying Kayla for money or a throne. He was marrying her because she needed his protection.

And yeah, it didn't hurt that he still wanted her two months after their hot night together. That he still dreamed about her beneath him, panting for more. Begging him to make her come. He dreamed about her tight pussy, so fucking wet for him, and the smell of her skin, the taste and texture of her nipples, the way she shook apart when she finally tumbled over the edge. The way his name sounded on her lips.

He hadn't been with anyone since that night with her. He'd been lonely every night since. If he was hung up on anyone, it was her. Not that he intended to admit it to her since she clearly hadn't had the same reaction that he'd had.

The lights were on in the living room and kitchen of Camel's house when they pulled in. Kayla's suite was an addition, attached to the main house by a long hallway. She had a separate door, thankfully. He'd hate to have to walk through the house on the way to Kayla's apartment.

There was going to be a lot of explaining to do at some point, but first things first. Right now he needed to establish a presence in Kayla's life. A definite presence, not the back and forth they'd done out of sight of prying eyes. Maybe he should have made her talk to him after that night together, but when he'd woken up alone, he'd figured she'd said it all by leaving. If she didn't want to explain what that had been about, he wasn't asking.

Kayla was waiting for him when he parked behind her in the long driveway. She stood on the sidewalk that led to her door, her purse on her shoulder, her hands clasped around the strap like it was a lifeline. Not for the first time, he thought about how small she was, how delicate. And he wished he'd been the one to encounter James Dunn at the Kings of Doom compound several months ago instead of Camel.

Camel hadn't killed Dunn, but he'd wanted to. Neo had wanted to as well. The bastard had imprisoned Kayla long before he'd kidnapped Bailey. He'd tried to sell Ana to an adoption agency. And he'd probably been planning to put Kayla into the trade as a sex worker since that's what the Kings did. Dunn deserved to die, but it hadn't been in the cards that day.

Kayla smiled at Neo's approach. It was a nervous smile. He wasn't sure why she was nervous, though maybe it was the thought of the task before them and convincing her sister she was in love. He wished she'd just tell Bailey the truth, but he understood why she wanted to wait.

"I called Bailey on the way and asked if she could keep Ana for the night. She said she could," Kayla told him.

"Did she ask questions?"

"No, she knows better. But I could tell she was curious." Kayla glanced at the house. Then she snorted softly. "And she's looking outside to see what's going on. I saw the curtain twitch."

Camel would know at any minute. Neo didn't think his teammate would come outside and demand to know what was going on, but it was very likely coming soon. Probably at work on Monday. It wasn't that Camel felt proprietary toward Kayla, but she was for all intents and purposes his little sister. Bailey was protective, which meant Camel would be too.

"I don't think I should stay all night," he said.

"That would be overkill, especially since we didn't spend much time together at the cookout today."

"Agreed."

"I'll stay a couple of hours. Long enough to watch a movie."

"Do you want to watch a movie?"

He shrugged. "Sure, why not?"

It'd be a lot easier than halting conversation or awkward silence for two hours. There was still a lot they needed to talk about, but he wouldn't push it. They'd put something on and see what happened.

Kayla led the way to the door. There was a light on overhead. She unlocked the door and led him inside. There was a lamp burning in the small living room. He'd only been inside a couple of times before, and not for long, but she'd added some things since then. He took it all in, noting the feminine touches. Kayla liked flowery pillows and plants. The space was small but neat. The kitchen and living room were all one space, but there was a small hallway that led to the single bedroom and bath. The kid toys were minimal, and all collected in a basket beside the television. A high chair sat at one end of a small round table where Kayla went to put her keys and purse.

"I've decorated a little since you were last here. Home sweet home."

"It's nice. You won't mind moving out?"

She looked around the room, then back to him. "I like it, but no, I won't mind. The furniture isn't mine

anyway. Just the pillows and some of the decor items."
She shrugged. "I'm used to moving around."

He knew she'd had a chaotic childhood and that
she and Bailey had moved often. Until Bailey met
Camel, she'd been living in a crappy apartment in a
not so nice part of town.

"I'll apply for base housing once we're married,"
he told her. "It won't happen right away because
there's a waiting list. We can live in my house until
one comes available, if that works for you."

He hoped it did because he didn't envision
moving in steps away from Camel and Bailey. Plus
he'd have to break his lease, which wouldn't be ideal.

"That would be great. I'll love being across the
street from Chloe."

"You two are close, huh?"

"Closer than I would have expected, but we hit it
off when I went to work at the salon."

She didn't say anything more but he figured part
of the reason they were close was the shared experience of having had men who'd tried to hurt them in
their lives.

"Do you want something to drink?" she asked. "I
don't have any beer, but I have some white wine."

"Thanks, but no. I'm fine."

"The remote is in that basket on the table. I'm
going to change if you'd like to find something."

He went over and sat on the small couch, found
the remote, and powered up the television. She had
Amazon, Netflix, and Hulu. It was nearly fifteen

minutes before she returned. He was beginning to wonder if she'd bailed on him, but she walked into the room wearing a pair of black yoga pants and a loose knit top. Her hair was piled on top of her head in a messy bun. She went over to the kitchen and got a glass of wine then came over and sat at the opposite end of the couch. She put a bottle of water on the coffee table and slid it toward him.

"Just in case."

"Thanks." He nodded at the screen. "What do you want to watch?"

"Oh, I don't care. Anything."

He grinned. "Looks like you watch a lot of home decorating shows."

She flashed him a smile. "I love how pretty everything is in the end. They take an old rundown house and before you know it, boom, gorgeous new space. Kinda reminds me that you can makeover the ugly parts of your life at any time if you're determined enough and work hard enough."

He liked that thought. "You want to watch one now?"

Because he'd watch whatever made her happy.

"That's okay. Let's find something we both like."

In the end, they settled on Tom Clancy's *Jack Ryan*. Neo watched it with increasing amusement as the main character navigated the Special Ops world. It wasn't that the show was bad or that the actor wasn't good. He was good, and Neo enjoyed that part. But some of the stuff that went on....

Neo shook his head. Those guys were practicing some very bad operational security at different points of the show.

"Is that what you do?" Kayla asked at one point when the hero had single-handedly taken down a terrorist.

"Not entirely, but it can get dicey sometimes. I have a team, though. We don't typically go it alone."

She was looking at him with wide eyes. "That's good. But how do you do it?"

"Depends on the situation."

She shook her head. "No. How do you face that kind of thing and not get scared? I'd be paralyzed with fear."

"It's not that we aren't sensible enough to fear for our lives," he said, thinking how best to phrase it. "But we don't stop to think about it. Our training kicks in and we do what we've practiced thousands of times before."

She toyed with the edge of her knit top and didn't look at him. "I could almost wish you were an accountant or something."

"If I were an accountant, I'd be pretty useless against the Kings of Doom MC."

She looked at him, her eyes shining. "I suppose so."

"And that's not what you want, right?"
"No."

He reached for her hand, wrapped it in his. She

didn't try to pull away. "Maybe we should turn it off, huh?"

"Okay."

He exited the show and set the channel to one of her decorating shows. "We've still got some things to decide, beautiful," he said as somebody on the television swung a sledge hammer at a wall.

"I know." She sighed. "I just—I don't know what else to say yet. It's happening fast, which is what I wanted. But there's still so much to think about. We can apply for a license Monday, and we can get married as soon as we have it, so this week. And now I've got to convince Bailey I'm madly in love and this is the right thing to do."

"Or you could tell her we're doing it for your protection. It wouldn't be the first time someone on the team got married to protect his wife. Camel will understand that logic, believe me. And he'll convince her."

She shook her head. "No, I can't. It's four weeks to her wedding. I won't spoil her plans or her big day."

"Okay, beautiful. We'll do it your way. I won't lie to my team, though. If they need to know the truth, I have to tell them."

"I know." She kept toying with the shirt and he let go of her hand and stood.

She tipped her head back to gaze up at him, a question in her eyes.

"It's been two hours. I should probably get going."

He held out a hand. She took it and he lifted her to her feet. "Walk me to the door."

The apartment was small so it was only a couple of steps away. He slipped an arm around her waist and tugged her in close. She came freely, putting her hands on his chest and resting them there. She was small, but she fitted against him in all the right places. It'd been a long time since he'd held her, and he'd missed it.

"Are you going to kiss me goodnight?" she asked.

"Do you want me to?"

"I think it'd be nice."

He arched an eyebrow. "Nice? The last time we kissed, things got a little out of control. It was a lot more than *nice.*"

Her skin colored and she dropped her gaze. He tipped her chin up with this fingers, forcing her to look at him. "Now's not the time, but I think we're going to have to talk about that too. Don't you?"

She nodded.

"Goodnight, Kayla," he murmured.

Her eyes closed before he dropped his head toward hers. He studied her for a second. She was more innocent than she should be considering what she'd been through, but he knew she was damaged as well. That she trusted him enough to close her eyes and wait for his kiss moved him more than he could say.

Why had she run out on him after their night

together? He intended to find out now that he planned to marry her.

He kissed her softly, a press of his lips to hers, and then lifted his mouth away. She opened her eyes, gazing up at him with a question in them. He kissed her forehead and let her go.

"Thanks for a nice evening."

"Will you text me when you get home?"

"Sure. Night, Kayla."

"Night, Zach."

Neo got in the car, started the engine, and put it in reverse. When he backed onto the street and shifted into drive, a figure appeared in front of him, cross-armed, spread-legged, and glaring.

"Fuck," he groaned. Just what he needed right now.

Neo rolled down the window as the figure stalked forward.

"Hey, Camel. What's up?"

Chapter Five

THERE WAS A KNOCK ON THE DOOR THAT CONNECTED the in-law apartment to the hall leading to Bailey and Camel's. Kayla sighed as she went over and opened it up. Bailey stood there with a concerned look on her face. She was holding a baby monitor, but Kayla was certain the look had nothing to do with Ana and everything to do with Kayla's visitor.

"Hey, Bale. Do you want me to come get Ana?"

Bailey still frowned. "No, she's completely passed out. No need to wake her."

"Do you want some wine?" Kayla asked as she stepped back to let Bailey in. Bailey didn't drink often, but Kayla asked anyway.

"No, I'm good." Bailey walked inside, taking in the couch, Kayla's glass, Zach's empty water bottle, before she turned to face Kayla again. "Was that Zach here with you?"

Kayla folded her arms. "You know it was."

She thought she still heard the rumble of Zach's car outside. She went over to peer out the window. Sure enough, his car was idling beside the curb and he was standing next to it, talking to someone.

Not someone. *Alexei.*

She dropped the curtain and turned, anger flaring deep. "Y'all know it's none of your business, right?"

Bailey's eyebrows climbed her forehead. Kayla cursed inwardly as she watched the play of emotions on her sister's face—disbelief, defensiveness, protectiveness, and anger—before Bailey got control of herself.

For heaven's sake, why had she gone all defensive like that? She wanted Bailey to be happy, not upset.

Stress, that's what it was.

"We're concerned about you. That's all," Bailey said more than a touch defensively.

Kayla waved a hand. "I know. I'm sorry. It's been a long day and I'm tired."

Bailey looked wary. "Is everything okay? You and Zach seemed to be interested in each other once before, but then nothing happened. I worry about you."

Kayla impulsively gave her sister a hug. Bailey smelled like vanilla and chocolate chip cookies. She'd been baking again, practicing her newfound cooking skills. When they'd been kids, the only thing Bailey knew how to cook was macaroni and cheese, and ramen. That was more than Kayla had known. They'd subsisted on those things quite often.

"I know, sweetie. I'm fine. Zach and I are seeing each other. I'm fine and I'm happy."

Bailey hugged her back. "Okay. I just want you to be careful, that's all. Zach is a good guy, but he leads a dangerous life."

As if she didn't know that.

"So does Alexei, honey."

"Well, yes. And that scares the shit out of me. If you don't have to go through that, then don't."

Too late.

"There's more to both of them than danger."

"I know."

Kayla sighed. "Do you want to text Alexei and tell him to let Zach go home?"

She hoped Zach and Alexei weren't having a deep heart to heart about her situation, but there was no way of knowing that. She could only pray that Alexei would see her side of things if so.

Bailey's cheeks were a touch pink as she took her phone from her pocket. She typed out a message and hit send. "Done."

"Thank you."

"Do you want to talk about anything?" Bailey asked.

Kayla's heart thumped. "Such as?"

"You and Zach. I've seen you looking at each other lately. Though not at the same time. It's almost like something's been going on, but you aren't speaking to each other about it. I guess that changed tonight and you started talking again."

Embarrassment heated her cheeks. Of course Bailey had noticed. Her sister was sharp.

"Nothing to talk about, Bale. Zach and I are dating, and that's all I want to say right now."

Bailey blinked. Kayla could see her take in that information and process it. "Okay."

Kayla went to grab her wine glass and Zach's empty water bottle. "Sure you don't want some wine?"

"Maybe a tiny bit."

Kayla refilled her glass and got one for Bailey. There was a knock on the outside door.

"Better let Alexei in," Kayla said.

Bailey opened the door. Alexei strolled in, looking big and bad and handsome as hell. Kayla had been interested in him once upon a time, back when she'd been waitressing at Buddy's Bar & Grill and telling everyone her name was Harley. She gave herself a mental eye roll. Why had she done those things?

Alexei smiled. Kayla smiled back. She loved Alexei like a brother. Her one-time attraction to him had been based on how nice he was to her, not on any real chemistry. Thinking about it now, she was almost embarrassed by her youthful hero worship. Worse, she would always be somewhat mortified that she'd accused him of being Ana's father when there was no way he could have been. He didn't hold it against her, and for that she was thankful.

"Did you and Zach have a nice talk?" she asked.

"Yeah, fine. Why?"

Bailey took a sip of wine. "She's onto us, babe."

Alexei sighed. "What gave it away?"

"Uh, the fact Bale showed up without you and wanted to know if Zach had been here. Oh, and his car was still idling outside. I looked out the window. I hope you were nice, big brother."

He grinned. "Of course I was nice. Neo's my bud."

"So long as he doesn't think about getting busy with your almost sis-in-law?"

"I didn't put it that way."

Kayla eyed them both. "I love the two of you. You know that. But I get to decide what's best for me, not y'all. And right now that's Zach. Okay?"

"Copy that," Alexei said.

"Got it," Bailey added.

"Alexei, you want a beer?"

"Sure."

Kayla took one from the fridge and handed it to him. "Now tell me what you said to Zach so I know how much apologizing I have to do."

Alexei lifted the bottle and swallowed. Then he shrugged. "Not much. I told him he'd better not get involved with you if all he wanted was a good time, that you'd been through enough shit, and you have a baby to take care of. If he's not interested in her too, then he needs to hit the road."

Kayla nearly choked on a swallow of wine. "Wow. That's kinda a mouthful, Alexei. It's hardly *not much.*"

Alexei shrugged again. "I've known Neo for a long time, which means I've seen a lot of the women he's dated." He frowned, considering. "Okay, maybe *date* is an inaccurate term. *Slept with* is more accurate. Probably."

Bailey went over and looped her arm through his. "Okay, pumpkin. I think that's enough. She gets it."

Pumpkin? Lord. Kayla shook off a sudden desire to giggle. Alexei was big and bad and hardly a man you'd call pumpkin. Unless you were her sister. Maybe she needed to lay off the wine for the rest of the night. She set the glass down and tried not to dwell on the number of women Zach had *slept with.*

"Now look here, I already told Bailey and I'm telling you too. I'm a grown woman. I have a baby who is my number one priority. No man is getting between me and Ana ever again. Zach knows that. He also knows that I can and will make my own decisions, and he knows what my priorities are. He knows what he's getting into. We both do."

Bailey and Alexei exchanged another one of their secretive glances. "Okay," Bailey said. "You've made your point."

"Yeah, I got it too. He says he's serious about you and I respect that. But understand, Kayla," Alexei continued, "if Neo ever does anything to hurt you, I will be obligated to rip his nuts off and feed them to him. He knows it, too."

"Good to know," Kayla said. "But that's not going to happen."

They finished their drinks, and then Kayla went over to their guest room to check on Ana. She was sound asleep as Kayla bent over the crib, her little bow mouth and long eyelashes so pretty in repose. She had pink cheeks and creamy skin, and her dark hair was growing longer. Soon, Ana would be walking and talking, and Kayla's heart pinched tight at the thought she'd missed even the tiniest bit of Ana's life when she'd left her with Bailey and Alexei shortly after her birth.

"Do you want to leave her here? Or take her back to your place?" Bailey had followed her into the room.

Kayla smiled down at her baby even though Ana wasn't awake. "I want to take her, but I don't want to wake her up either. Maybe just give me the monitor and I'll come get her if she fusses."

Bailey had put Ana down in the portable crib that she and Alexei kept for just such a purpose. Kayla thought about how she was going to have to break it to her sister that she was moving out, and felt a pang of regret.

It's necessary.

Bailey handed over the monitor. "She's growing so fast," Bailey said with a sigh.

"Tell me about it." Kayla straightened. "Thanks, Bale. For everything. You're the best sister a girl could have."

Bailey leaned against her and they put their heads

together. "Thank you, Kay-Kay. That's sweet of you to say."

"I mean it. I want you to be happy, and I don't want you worrying about me."

"I'll always worry about you. It's what I do."

Kayla squeezed her sister's arm. "I know. But you don't have to. We aren't scared kids anymore and I got this."

Bailey smiled. "I know you do. It's serious, huh?"

Kayla felt suddenly shy. The conversation was so normal, but she was aware she was engaging in a tiny bit of deception. *Justifiable.*

"Yes, it is."

"Well then. Okay. I'm happy for you."

"And slightly worried," Kayla added as they walked out of the room and stood in the hallway.

"You know me well. I don't want you hurt, Kay-Kay."

"I don't want that either. But if I don't take the chance, how will I know?"

"That's true."

They said goodnight and Kayla traipsed back to her in-law suite. She left the inner door open to the house so the monitor would pick up Ana if she cried, and went to get ready for bed. When she lay down, she had a text from Zach.

I'm home.

Kayla frowned as she texted him back. *I'm sorry A was waiting for you.*

Zach: *Wasn't a problem. He knows I'm serious about you.*

Kayla's belly fluttered. *Is that all he knows?*

Zach: *For now.*

She let out a breath. *I feel like I'm causing trouble for you. I'm sorry.*

Zach: *I thought about the consequences before I agreed to marry you. Camel was always going to be protective. I'm glad. But we're brothers. I said I'm serious and that's enough. I'll pick you and Ana up tomorrow and take you to lunch if that works.*

Kayla: *Sounds good. 11:00?*

Zach: *I'll be there.*

NEO ARRIVED PROMPTLY at eleven a.m. Kayla was waiting outside, dressed in a long flowery skirt that went to her ankles, and a sleeveless blue top that tied at the waist. She was wearing sandals, and her blond hair was loose. It hung almost to her ass, and he swallowed at the sight. He loved a woman with long hair.

She had Ana on her hip, a diaper bag slung over her shoulder, and a car seat at her feet. She also had one of those small folding strollers. She was beautiful and his heart thumped once in response. He parked in the drive and got out. Camel's truck was gone so he assumed Bailey and his teammate weren't home.

Kayla smiled at him, and his chest tightened. Damn she was sweet. And she was all his. He couldn't wait to taste that sweetness again. When the time was right, of course.

"Good morning, beautiful," he said as he brushed his lips against hers. "You look amazing today."

Her color was high as he straightened. "Thank you."

Neo dropped his gaze to Ana. She was a rosy cheeked baby, and she was currently grinning up at him with the cutest little grin. A grin remarkably like her mother's. He knew she had traits that belonged to James Dunn, but he couldn't see them. All he saw was Kayla.

"Hey there, cutie pie. You ready to go for a ride?"

He tickled her belly lightly and she grabbed his finger. Then she tried to put it in her mouth.

"No, baby girl," he said, pulling his finger gently away. "No icky fingers in your mouth."

Ana squealed happily and pumped her little arms up and down. Kayla laughed as she handed her a plastic key ring with huge keys. Ana immediately stuck one in her mouth.

Neo got Ana's car seat anchored into the back with Kayla's supervision. It occurred to him as he contorted himself that a Camaro wasn't exactly a family friendly vehicle. Getting that car seat in and out was going to be a pain in the ass. Maybe an SUV was a better option. He said as much to Kayla after she buckled Ana in and she stilled. Her eyes widened as she met his gaze.

"I don't want you to have to give up your car,

Zach. Mine works fine with the car seat. We could take it in the future."

He shook his head. "I don't mind. I was starting to think about trading this thing in anyway."

On a new model Corvette, but he wasn't telling her that. He expected to feel a prick of disappointment at the idea he wasn't getting that C-8 body style after all, but he didn't. The idea of a big SUV wasn't such a bad one. He liked sitting up high. He'd had a truck before the Camaro, so going back to something big wasn't going to be a problem.

"I guess I didn't think about all the ways you'd have to change your life when I asked you to marry me. I should have."

He held the door for her while she got into the passenger seat. "I thought about it. And I said yes."

Her eyes shimmered as she gazed up at him. "Only after I told you about the guy who called me. You wouldn't have said yes if not for that."

"And you wouldn't have asked. Baby, we've moved beyond the question of *if* and we're on the *when*. Tomorrow we're getting a license. Later this week we're getting married."

She nibbled that plump lower lip he wanted to suck. "I know. But I didn't expect you to sell your car."

He bent and kissed her lush mouth. It was a quick kiss, but it shut her up. "Give me a chance to get in the car and take us to lunch, okay?"

She nodded and he closed her door, then went

around and got into the driver's seat. The car started to life with a rumble. He glanced in the rearview, but Ana didn't seem upset by the sound. She was still gumming the keys.

"Where are we going?" Kayla asked as he put the car in reverse.

"I was thinking about a café with an outdoor seating area not too far from here. The patio is shaded and cool."

"Sounds good."

They reached the restaurant and got a table on the patio. He'd timed it to arrive just before the church crowd so they didn't have any trouble getting seated. Another half hour and the place would be jammed.

Kayla put Ana in the high chair and gave her a handful of Cheerios. The waitress came and they ordered—a burger for Neo and pasta for Kayla. Once the waitress returned with their drinks and glided away again, Neo reached for Kayla's hand, threading his fingers through hers. She didn't resist, but she looked at him with a question in her gaze.

"We've got to start somewhere," he told her. "If we don't seem natural with each other, we won't sell this to your sister."

"You're right. It's just that I've spent the past two months being embarrassed around you, and now we're acting like it never happened."

His senses prickled. Was she ready to talk about that night? "Why were you embarrassed?"

She shrugged and looked away. "That night... I didn't give you a chance to say no."

And there it was. Finally. She wasn't talking about last night when she'd asked him to marry her. She was talking about the night they'd spent together. He knew he needed to tread carefully now that the subject had come up.

"Do you honestly think I couldn't have said no if I really wanted to?"

She wouldn't look at him. "You were always so nice to me, and then I had to go and make it into something it wasn't supposed to be. Afterward, you were stand-offish with me. I figured you had to be pissed as hell."

Neo sat back in his chair. He felt like someone had smacked him over the head with a two-by-four. She'd thought he was ignoring *her?*

"You ran out on me, Kayla. Not the other way around. When I woke up, you were gone. You didn't leave a note, didn't text me, didn't call. Nothing. We had a fantastic night together and you ran away the next morning. I figured you'd tell me what was wrong but you never did. Yeah, I did get pissed. But not because we had sex. I got pissed because you pretended like it never happened."

Her face turned pink. "I didn't know what to do. You'd never even kissed me before that night—and then when you did, I practically forced myself on you."

Neo could only gape at her. "Wait—is that why

you avoided me? You thought you forced yourself on me?"

It was laughable, but she didn't look anything other than serious. Her gaze dropped to the table and he knew she really believed it. After everything he'd done to her that night? *What the fuck?*

"You were trying to be a good friend, and I crossed a line. I didn't mean to, but I was lonely and you were always so nice to me. And yes, I had a crush on you. When you kissed me, I lost my head—" She broke off, shook her head. "Anyway, I'm sorry I did that. I didn't know what to say after it happened, and you never said anything either. I assumed you wanted to forget about it."

She astounded him. All this time he'd thought she'd been the one who wanted to forget it happened. He leaned toward her. Put a finger beneath her chin and forced her to look at him. Her skin was still flushed pretty pink. He had a strong urge to kiss her, but he didn't. If he did, he might not stop.

"I wasn't pissed at first, Kayla. I was confused. You left without a word, and I figured you had a good reason. So I didn't push you, even when you never said anything about that night. But I did get angry— at you for leaving, at me for letting that night happen in the first place. I thought I'd pushed you too far, asked too much of you in bed. Hell, I even convinced myself you needed a different kind of man in your life. A doctor or a lawyer or something. A plain vanilla kind of guy with a good job and all the stability you could hope for."

She wrapped her fingers around his wrist and squeezed. "I don't want a doctor or a lawyer. I never did. I want you, Zach. You're exactly the man I need."

Chapter Six

Kayla's heart thudded at what she'd said. *I want you.* Those words were filled with so much meaning. Too much meaning. More than she wanted to admit to herself right now. Or to him. Especially to him.

She started to pull her hand back. Zach stopped her with a hand over hers. His skin was warm, reassuring. His palm was callused in places, smooth in others. The hand of a warrior. The hand of a man who could protect her.

The hand of a man she wanted with her whole heart.

A frisson of joy and pain rolled through her at that thought. What if he didn't want her the same way? What if he never did? Real marriage or not, he'd never mentioned love. Not once.

She thought of what Chloe had said. He'd denied it, but that didn't mean there wasn't someone in his past he'd never gotten over. Someone he couldn't have for some reason.

"I want you to understand something," he said, and her belly tightened. "I wanted you badly that night—but I wasn't going to make the first move beyond that kiss. I didn't want you to think I expected anything from you when we were hanging out as friends. When we kissed and you wanted more—well, hell, it was a fantasy come true for me. You're hot, Kayla, and I wanted you. Then I woke up and you were gone. I thought you regretted it and wanted to forget all about it, especially when you seemed to be pretending it hadn't happened. Do you understand why I believed that?"

She did. The knowledge of what he must have thought after she'd fled that morning made her ache with regret. She'd waited for him to text her, but he never did. She hadn't texted him either. If she could go back and do things differently, she would. "Yes," she whispered. "I understand."

The waitress arrived to top off the drinks they'd barely touched and then flitted away again. Zach sat back in his chair and Kayla turned her attention to Ana, who'd scattered Cheerios everywhere. But Ana was happy and steadily gnawing the little treats, so Kayla didn't have to do anything for her.

"She's a happy baby, isn't she?" Zach asked.

Kayla could genuinely smile at the question. "Yes. She doesn't fuss over much. She sleeps through the night most of the time and she never gives me trouble. I'm a lucky mama."

"She looks a lot like you."

"Except for her dark hair. That's all James." Kayla hated saying his name. She hated that she shared a child with the man, but she wouldn't trade her time with him if it meant she'd have never had her baby. Ana was worth the pain that being with James had caused. "I hate that her father is a criminal. Someday I'll have to tell her the truth. She deserves to know."

Zach nodded. "She does, but that day is pretty far in the future, don't you think?"

"Yes." Kayla took a sip of her iced tea, feeling more hopeful as the prospect of a future with Zach stretched before her. But how much of a future? That was the part she didn't know. The part that troubled her.

"I see the gears turning in your head, Kayla."

She looked at him in surprise, then laughed softly. "I guess they are. I was just thinking about the future. Wondering if you might regret getting married."

"Regret taking care of you and Ana when you need me? Not likely."

She didn't say what she was really thinking. That he would regret *her*. Saddling himself to her. That she was manipulating him into something the same way she'd manipulated Bailey and Alexei into caring for Ana when she'd gone into hiding several months ago.

"You can't really know that."

His eyes flashed hot with anger. It surprised her

and she sat back, blinking at him. He didn't tamp it down though. He held her gaze and spoke very deliberately.

"You need to stop trying to make me into someone who's going to let you down. I know you've had a lot of that in your life, but it stops now. I said I was here for you and I am. You can't push me away, Kayla. You should realize by now that a SEAL lives and dies by his honor. And even if I wasn't a SEAL, I'd still keep my word. I said I'm going to marry you and protect you both, and I am. We've got just as much of a shot at making a go of this as any of my teammates and their wives and fiancées."

Her heart throbbed. As much of a chance as Bailey and Alexei? Chloe and Ryan? The others? She didn't know. She'd seen them all together and they were clearly in love.

He leaned forward as if he knew what she was thinking. "Yeah, I know they're all madly in love with each other—but love isn't all it takes to make a successful marriage. We don't have the love part, but nothing says we won't get there. But if it's going to happen, you've got to stop feeling guilty and thinking you have the power to force me into doing what I don't want to do. You don't. I'm committed to marrying you. Stop trying to second guess everything I say and do."

Her heart was pounding. Those were passionate, heated words. Not words of love, but words of honor.

She wanted the love, desperately, but she'd take the honor.

"Okay."

"Do you mean it?"

She pulled in a breath scented with the odors of delicious food and fresh air. It was sunny out, but shady under the trees, and life at this very moment was good. She needed to be in the moment.

But she couldn't shake a lifetime of conditioning.

"I'm trying. Very hard. Growing up, the only person I could trust was Bailey. Everyone I've ever put any faith in, other than her, has let me down. And I'm not saying you're going to do it too. I know you're honorable. It's me and my stupid baggage, that's all."

He leaned over and pressed his lips to her cheek. "That's an honest answer, beautiful. I can live with that. Don't ever feel like you have to gloss over what you're feeling or what you need to say. Just tell me. We'll figure it out. Now how about we eat lunch and enjoy ourselves this afternoon? No pressure about anything else. Sound good?"

Her heart felt lighter than it had in a long time. And her skin tingled where his breath had tickled it. Memories of the night they'd shared flooded back. His breath on her skin, his mouth doing things that ought to be illegal...

Kayla shivered. "It sounds really good."

Except she didn't mean lunch.

THEY SPENT the afternoon at the park, pushing Ana around and talking about the logistics of getting married and telling everyone. The day was fine, warm and breezy, and Kayla looked beautiful in the long skirt that fluttered around her ankles. Neo kept dropping his gaze there, feeling like a guy from the 1800s who got excited by the barest flash of skin. It was ridiculous, but he enjoyed it.

Kayla had finally given up and twisted her long hair into a knot at the nape of her neck when it kept blowing around her face. She wasn't the most talkative person, but he managed to get her talking about work at one point. She loved working with Chloe and the other ladies at the salon. She thought she might like to go to beauty school someday, but she didn't know if she'd have the time until Ana was older.

Neo listened more than he spoke because he wanted to hear what she had to say. Kayla was younger than him by a few years. She'd turned twenty-three recently, and he was almost twenty-eight. He forgot how young she was most of the time because she seemed mature beyond her years. He knew she'd had a rough childhood, but he didn't know all of it. He suspected she had more to say about that when she knew him better. He hoped so anyway.

By the time they got back to the car, Ana was asleep in her stroller.

"Let me," Neo said when Kayla bent down to unbuckle the baby and lift her into the car seat.

Kayla tugged her lower lip between her teeth as he carefully lifted Ana. He knew Kayla feared he'd wake Ana, but he successfully got her into the car seat and buckled in without incident. Kayla double-checked the straps. He wasn't offended by it. When she was satisfied, she straightened and smiled at him. It was a soft smile.

"Thank you," she said.

"You're welcome."

Seized by an impulse he didn't feel like denying, he tugged her against him and dropped his mouth to hers. She didn't resist. She clutched his arms in her small hands, tipped her head back, and opened her lips.

Neo hadn't intended the kiss to be anything more than a quick, chaste one. But that opening...

He groaned as he slipped his tongue into her mouth, his body aching immediately as he remembered what it'd been like to be inside her, the silky walls of her pussy gloving him tight. He didn't know why she twisted him up inside the way she did, but he wasn't planning to fight it. Not anymore. What was the point? He was marrying her and he meant to share a bed with her whenever she was ready.

She tasted warm and sweet, like the strawberries on the cheesecake they'd split. Her hands slid up his arms to wrap around his neck, trailing fire in their wake. Her body was pliant against his. Melting. As if she too remembered how they'd fit so well together.

He'd tried not to think about that night too often,

but he couldn't stop when it was late and he was alone. He'd jerked off more times than he cared to admit to the memory of her wet heat surrounding him, her tits bouncing as she rode him with her head thrown back and her fingers curled into his pecs.

Yeah, Kayla Jones's hot, luscious body was the feature film in his spank bank these days.

Their tongues moved together, tasting and stroking, until his dick started to throb and he had to remind himself where they were. When he broke the kiss, Kayla's eyes were glazed as she looked up at him. He saw the moment they cleared, the moment she realized what they'd been doing. Her cheeks flushed pink and her mouth dropped open before snapping shut again.

"Oh dear. Sorry," she said.

He didn't let her go. He'd meant to, but then she'd apologized and he wasn't letting that shit fly. "Why are you sorry?"

"I, um…." She dropped her gaze.

He tipped her chin up, made her look at him. "I kissed you first. And I'm not sorry. Wait, no I *am* sorry. Sorry we aren't alone and there isn't a bed nearby, because I'd really like to kiss the rest of you, Kayla. Everywhere."

Her breath scissored in. "Oh."

He stepped back to give her room and held the door while she got into the car. He bent down to meet her gaze.

"I don't want to intimidate you, beautiful. But I

want you to know how much I want you in my bed again. I don't want you ever again thinking you somehow forced me to sleep with you, or that I don't want it to happen. Got it?"

She nodded. Then she grinned suddenly. "It sounds ridiculous when you put it that way. How could I have ever forced you into sex?"

He laughed. "Exactly."

Chapter Seven

Neo waited at the entrance to the courthouse
for Kayla. He'd offered to pick her up, but she'd
wanted to meet him so Bailey wouldn't ask questions.

Yesterday afternoon, Camel and Bailey had been
home by the time he and Kayla got back. They'd
been planting flowers, and Neo offered to help Camel
with the mulching. It'd turned into a pleasant afternoon as Bailey directed them where to put the bags of
mulch and gave them fresh mint iced tea that she'd
brewed. They'd worked up a sweat, which meant
more tea, and by the time they'd finished placing
everything where she wanted it, Bailey suggested subs
for dinner.

They'd all agreed, and Bailey drove off with
Kayla to pick up dinner while Ana stayed with the
men. Once the women returned, they ate outside on
the patio and had nice time together.

Bailey seemed to accept their relationship at face

value, which was good, but Kayla had yet to realize that her sister was going to need a whole lot more convincing once they moved to the actual wedding phase of the courtship. He knew it was coming even if she didn't, but he wasn't pointing it out yet. She'd figure it out.

This morning, Neo had managed to get a couple of hours off to take care of personal business. The military wasn't the kind of organization where you called in sick or didn't show up to work without an excuse, but HOT was a little different because everyone was elite. Since they were elite they were treated like it. Which meant he could ask for time to run an errand and nobody questioned it since they weren't currently in lockdown for a mission.

At nine-thirty, Kayla strode up the sidewalk, looking pretty in coral capri pants and a white cotton top with little coral flowers on it. She wore white Keds and her hair was loose. She smiled when she saw him.

"Hey, Zach," she said as she approached.

"Hey, beautiful. Where's Ana?"

"Bailey doesn't have class today, so she kept her for me."

She came into his arms easily and he kissed her. They didn't linger, much as he wanted to. One simple kiss and his body started to rev up. Would he always feel this insane heat with her? He hoped so.

He looped an arm around her and they walked toward the entrance. "You ready for this, babe?"

"Yes. You?"

"Yep."

She stopped him before they went inside. Her expression clouded with worry. "Are you sure you're ready?"

He hated that she always expected the bottom to drop out. "Yes, Kayla. I'm ready to get a marriage license. And I'm ready to marry you."

He'd done a little covert inquiring this morning and learned that James Dunn was still in prison, so he hadn't been the one to call her. But somebody had threatened her. Somebody had been watching her at the salon. He was going to have to do something about that, but he'd discuss it with her after they completed the first task of the day.

She sucked in a breath. Then a smile broke out on her face, transforming her features. He loved it when she smiled. She looked carefree then, even if she was anything but.

"Okay, so we're getting married. Wow."

"Yeah, wow." He pulled the door open for her. "Let's get this party started."

It took less than half an hour to get inside, get to the license office, apply, and head back outside again. Neo walked Kayla to her car.

"I'll follow you to the salon, babe."

She blinked. "You don't have to do that."

"Yeah, I do."

They stood in the parking lot beside her car and he could see the moment the fear returned to her eyes. He hated that, but she needed to be aware of her surroundings. He skimmed his fingers over her check.

"You can't go anywhere alone anymore, you understand? Don't go get lunch for the ladies either. You arrive when they do and leave when they do. You don't go to the store alone, or the gas station. You act like the Kings of Doom are out there watching."

She swallowed. "Yes, of course."

"If you get another call, or see anyone hanging outside the salon who shouldn't be there, you call me right away."

"I will."

"Give me your phone, Kayla."

She pulled it from her purse and handed it to him after she put in the code to unlock it. She had an older iPhone with the button and he opened her contacts. He found his name and added a number. "I'm giving you the unsecure line to work. If you need me and I'm not answering my cell phone, you call that number and tell them it's important. Someone will find me."

She took the phone back and looked at what he'd typed. "Okay."

"It goes without saying, baby—if the threat is immediate, use the silent alarm or call the cops. Call me after if you can."

Her eyes were big as she nodded. He hugged her to him and she wrapped her arms around him and squeezed. He kissed the top of her head.

"It's okay," he told her. "We're just being cautious.

Doesn't mean anything's gonna happen. They'd be stupid as fuck to try it in the daylight on that street with all the security cameras."

He hoped like hell that was the case anyway. He couldn't be there 24/7 and he couldn't send HOT assets to guard her either. He also couldn't expect her to hole up at home and never go anywhere. Not until they had a specific and credible threat against her.

She shuddered. "They might be that stupid."

"If they were, I doubt they'd have called to warn you first."

"That's true." She sighed and stepped back. "There can't be many of them left anymore. Whoever it is, they'll be careful to protect what's left of the club. They also want me to suffer, because that's how they operate. I betrayed them, which calls for revenge— but not before they terrify me first."

He opened her car door for her. "Get in and follow me over to my car so I can follow you to the salon."

She sank onto the seat, buckled her seatbelt, and started the car.

He was still holding the door. "I'll see you after work," he told her. "How's pizza for dinner?"

"Sounds great."

"I'll bring one over around six. Does that work?"

"Yes."

"Any preferences?"

"My favorite is cheese."

His eyebrows rose. "Just cheese? Nothing else?"

"Yep, just cheese."

Neo made a show of frowning. "I dunno, Kayla. That's pretty weird. I'm not sure we're going to be compatible after all…."

She laughed, which is what he'd hoped for. "Goofball," she said. "I didn't say I wouldn't eat whatever you want, just that cheese is my favorite. Put whatever you want on it. I can pick it off if I don't like it."

He dipped down and kissed her. He was liking this courting thing. "I promise you'll like what I bring. See you tonight."

"I can't wait," she said.

"Me neither."

————

KAYLA FED ANA and changed her into her jammies by six. Ana sat on a blanket on the floor, playing with her soft cloth blocks. Kayla kept on eye on her in case she started crawling off the blanket, but she was content at the moment so Kayla got plates and napkins out, poured herself a small glass of wine, and waited for Zach to arrive.

He'd followed her to the salon today, waited for her to park in the employee lot behind the building, then waited for her to walk inside. Once she was in, she turned and waved at him. He didn't pull away until she'd shut the door and locked it. She'd been on the lookout, but she didn't see anyone suspicious all day. By the time she left work at five with everyone else, her nerves had relaxed again.

Zach knocked on the door at five after six. Kayla went to open it. The sight of him started the butterflies swirling in her belly again.

He was tall, dark-haired, sharp-eyed, and looked like he could bench press a small car. Not that he was overly muscled, but he had the hard look of a man who didn't lose any of the challenges he set for himself. He was still in uniform, which told her he'd gone to pick up pizza and come straight over instead of going home first.

He grinned at her. "You look pretty, Kayla."

She fought off a blush. She'd changed into a soft jersey shirt dress when she'd gotten home because Chloe'd had a perm customer today and Kayla didn't want any of those smells around Ana. She hadn't smelled the chemicals on herself, but she wasn't taking any chances.

"Thank you."

Zach held up two pizza boxes. "I came prepared."

"You can put them on the table," she said, stepping back so he could enter. A quick glance outside after he walked in told her that Bailey and Alexei were home, and there were no cars she didn't recognize parked on the street. She'd never really gotten out of the habit of checking her surroundings, but these days she was even more alert. She had to be.

Kayla shut the door and went over to the table where Zach had put the pizzas. "How much do you think we're going to eat?" she asked as he flipped open the boxes.

"I don't know about you, but I can eat a lot of pizza after a day's training."

Her heart squeezed when she realized he'd brought a cheese pizza and a pizza loaded with meat.

"The cheese is for me," he said with a straight face. "I figured you'd like a bunch of meat on yours. Barbarian."

Kayla blinked, and then she laughed when it hit her that he was teasing her. "That's right, mister. I love a pizza loaded with saturated fats. My favorite thing in the world. Mmm, more meat for me!"

"Knew it."

"Seriously though, you didn't have to get a cheese pizza just for me."

He shrugged as he picked up two of the cheese slices and set them on her plate. "You're my girl now, Kayla. I'm going to take care of you to the best of my ability. You want cheese, you get cheese."

She sat down and lifted a slice. "Thank you, Zach. That's sweet of you to say."

He put three big slices of loaded pizza on his plate and flipped the covers closed. "Wasn't trying to be sweet. It's an easy thing to do, so I did it."

James had done nice things for her at the beginning, but they hadn't been the kind of things where he paid attention to what she wanted. He went for the grand gesture, like flowers and chocolates and little things like bead bracelets, and then he told her what he thought she wanted to hear. All a part of softening her up for easier exploitation. He'd never done anything like brought her a cheese pizza because he knew it was what she preferred.

The pizza was a small gesture, and yet it said something about the kind of man Zach was. He *listened.*

Ana turned to look at them both. Then she threw her block and started crawling toward the table. Kayla was still struggling to wipe her hands free of pizza grease when Zach reached down with his free hand and scooped Ana onto his lap.

Ana reared back to stare up at him as he grinned at her. "Hey, cutie," he said. "Do you like pizza?"

Kayla's heart lodged in her throat as her baby watched the big man holding her. "She could probably eat a little bite of cheese. I think the crust is too chewy though."

Zach set his pizza down and took a small bit of cheese off the top. He blew on it and offered it to Ana. She grabbed it and shoved it into her mouth. Then she squealed and pumped her arms.

Zach laughed. "I think she likes it."

"I can take her if you want to eat without a baby on your lap."

Zach's green eyes met hers. "Why don't you eat your dinner? I'll hold her. She's no problem."

"Okay," she said quietly. She picked up her pizza and took another bite. Zach ate with one hand, folding slices in half like a sandwich, which left him with a free hand for Ana. He gave her another small bit of cheese and she squealed again.

Kayla laughed because it was such a sweet sound. Zach laughed too.

"This kid has great taste. Mmm, pizza," he said to Ana.

She put her hand on his mouth.

"Pizza," he said again.

"Za!" she yelled.

They spent the next twenty minutes at the table, eating and laughing with Ana, talking about the day and how work had gone for each of them. It was pleasant. Normal. Kayla felt like a part of her observed from afar, always analyzing, always wondering if things were about to fall apart. She'd spent so much time watching her world implode as a kid that she just didn't trust it. She didn't know how Bailey did it. How did her sister have such a normal existence with Alexei? How did she not fear it was all going to come unglued tomorrow?

Because it had, so many times before, and they'd been left to pick up the pieces.

Except this time. So far. Bailey had been with Alexei for seven months now, and she'd never been happier. She didn't have that haunted look anymore. She didn't look like a woman trying to survive and making contingency plans if the first plan didn't work out.

For months, Kayla had ridden that same wave, happily going to work, living in the in-law suite, and making a home for her and Ana. She'd been uneasy at first, but as time went on she relaxed and began to believe she was finally in a good place, that life was going to get better and the bad times were over. James and the Kings of Doom were gone from her life and she'd stopped looking over her shoulder for them to pop up again.

It had all been going so well until she'd gotten that phone call. Now, she was fearful again. Making plans upon plans in her head. Trying to focus on the initial plan and not trusting her judgement there either.

"Hey," Zach said.

Kayla focused on him. "Yes?"

He looked a little puzzled. "You seemed a million miles away."

She noticed that he'd finished his pizza. She had too. She stood to gather the plates. He gently wrapped his fingers around her wrist and she stopped. Swallowed.

"What is it?" he asked.

Ana stared up at Kayla with wide-eyed innocence, a smear of tomato sauce on her cheek. Kayla's heart flooded with love. "It's nothing. I just… I was thinking about how nice the past few months have been."

"And?"

He'd said he wanted the truth, so why not tell him? "And I was thinking that I shouldn't have let myself believe in it too much."

"Because someone called you and scared you."

She nodded.

"I'm going to find whoever did that, Kayla. I'm going to find them and make them pay for putting that look in your eyes."

He would do it, she knew that—but how many times would he have to?

"What about the next guy? Or the next? What if they keep coming after me? If the Kings know it was me who told Alexei how to find them when they took Bailey, they'll never stop. They're out there. Maybe only one or two of them at a time, but they're still there—and they're never going to let me go."

"They don't have a choice, beautiful. You wanted protection, you got it. If they keep coming, I'll keep fighting."

Chapter Eight

Neo hated that she was so upset. He could see the fear in her eyes, the doubt. They'd been having such a good time together, but he'd known when she'd started to distance herself emotionally. He'd seen the vacant look as she got lost in her head, as her brain churned out doomsday scenarios for herself and baby Ana.

He understood where it came from. Kayla had PTSD, whether she knew it or not. He was trained to recognize the signs. She'd been traumatized as a child and traumatized as a young woman, and they both worked against her when she started to feel happy and secure. The fear reared its ugly head whenever she got too comfortable.

It was his singular goal in life to make her feel safe. Two days ago, he wouldn't have thought that, but now? Now he meant to give her the best life he could. He never did anything half-assed. He went all in, and he was all in now. He cared about Kayla and Ana and he meant to protect them.

One way or the other, he would fix this problem for her. He'd find those motherfuckers and put the fear of the United States Navy SEALs in them. He might not have official sanction to do it, but his team would help. Wouldn't be the first time they'd gone after some asshat for threatening one of their women.

Ana started to squirm. Neo let go of Kayla's wrist and picked up his napkin to wipe Ana's cheeks and hands before he set her down again. She immediately started to crawl back to her blanket and the blocks she had there. Kayla busied herself with cleaning up. Neo got up to help. She still hadn't said anything in response to his vow to keep fighting.

He turned to lean against the counter while she set the plates and silverware in the sink. "Why don't you get some things together and spend the night with me?"

Kayla jerked, her eyes wide as she fixed them on him, and he realized how that sounded.

"I didn't mean like that," he told her. "Though I wouldn't say no if you felt the urge to jump me."

He tried to make it sound funny, but she merely swallowed.

"I'm kidding, baby. Just trying to make you smile. Bring Ana and stay in Dirty's old bedroom. I'll be downstairs. You won't have to worry about those assholes knowing where to find you at my place."

She pulled in a breath. He thought she might

come up with a reason why she couldn't—or shouldn't—go with him, but she didn't. Instead, she nodded.

"You're right. I'll pack a bag and get some of Ana's things."

"Tell me what you need help with."

"Can you wash the dishes?"

"I can do that. How about we take the leftovers with us?"

"Good idea."

"I'll get everything together while you pack. Want me to grab some wine? I've only got beer at home."

"Please," she said.

"Done."

Neo started the water running while Kayla swooped Ana up and took her to the bedroom. He washed and dried and put everything away, then consolidated the leftover pizza in one box before taking the other box out to the trash and stuffing it in the can. When he went back inside, Kayla emerged from the bedroom with Ana on her hip.

"Can you take her while I get our stuff?" she asked.

"Sure." Neo held out his hands and Ana came willingly. She grabbed onto his collar and then bent to put it in her mouth. He didn't stop her. She smelled like baby powder, sweet and clean. It reminded him of holding his nephew the first time he'd gone back home after Lesley'd had him. Neo hadn't known dick about babies, but Lesley didn't let that stop her from handing her son to him. She'd taught him a lot about babies in the stretches of time when he went back to visit.

He wasn't scared of them or afraid they'd cry. If it happened, he'd do what his sister did. Check diapers, offer food, hold them or put them down if they didn't want to be held. That kind of thing.

Ana didn't do any of that, though. She just gummed his collar and made little noises from time to time.

Kayla returned with a tote bag and Ana's diaper bag, which she sat on the couch. "I need to get the portable crib."

"I can get it for you."

"It's okay. It's folded up. It's a playpen and crib in one. Very convenient."

She returned carrying the crib and Neo gave her the baby. "I'll take everything to my car."

"Okay, but I need to drive my car so I can get to work in the morning."

He wanted to drive them to his place, but he decided it wasn't a big deal. It was simple enough to let her follow him home tonight. She was going to have to bring her car when she moved in anyway, and that would be this week sometime if everything proceeded according to plan.

"All right. I'll still put everything in my car. You can follow me."

Kayla grabbed her purse and keys and locked up while Neo packed his car with their things. He set the pizza on the backseat and started the engine. Then he went over to where Kayla was putting Ana into her car seat. Kayla finished buckling the baby in, then looked at him questioningly.

He opened her car door and waited.

"You came over here to open the door for me?" she asked.

"That's right. Did you think I only opened the door if you rode with me?"

"Um, I guess I didn't think about it."

"Get used to it, because that's the kind of guy I am. I open car doors. Unless you strenuously object because it's against your personal code or something."

He'd been raised to be a fucking gentleman, but that wasn't the only reason he did it. He did it because Kayla didn't expect it, and because he wanted her to know she worth these continual shows of respect.

She smiled. "Not against my code. I think it's sweet."

"Good, because I like doing it."

She sank into her seat and clipped the belt into place. Neo shut the door, then bent and put his face on a level with hers. "I won't lose you, so don't worry that you need to speed to keep up with me. If a light turns and I'm through it, I'll pull over to wait for you. Take your time and drive safe."

"I know how to get to your place, Zach."

"Yeah, I know. But I still won't leave you behind. Buddy system, Kayla."

"Another one of those things you do?" she asked.

"That's right. It's part of the full service package."

"I'm liking the full service package."

He gave her a quick kiss, then straightened and winked. "Just wait until you try some of the other services I offer."

KAYLA'S PHONE rang before she'd driven a mile. It was Bailey. Kayla answered using the bluetooth hands-free device that Alexei had installed for her.

"Hey, Bailey," she said brightly. "What's up?"

"It's after seven. I was wondering if everything's okay."

Kayla's heart thumped. "Why wouldn't it be?"

"You don't usually take Ana out this late."

"No, I don't." She gripped the steering wheel. "I'm going over to Zach's place. I won't be back tonight."

"Okay." Bailey sighed. "We could have kept Ana for you, honey."

"It's okay. Zach wants to spend time with both of us. That's a good thing."

"Yes. Of course."

Kayla stared at Zach's taillights. "You're worried," she said. It wasn't a question.

"I don't want you getting hurt. That's all. I like Zach, I really do. It's just that y'all haven't been together, and now you suddenly are. It's a little surprising."

"I know. But trust me when I say there's a lot more going on than you realize." That was certainly true. "Zach and I are together, Bale. He's a good man, and I love him."

There. She'd said it. Her heart hammered and little beads of sweat popped up on her skin. She'd never spoken those words about Zach before, but they felt like spilling the deepest secret of her heart. Did she love him? Or did she just lust after him?

"Wow. Okay. I had no idea."

Guilt pricked her. "I know."

"Just be careful, Kay-Kay."

"I'm doing my best. But when you fell for Alexei, were you careful? Or did he make you feel so crazy good inside, so safe, that you just leapt and hoped he'd catch you?"

Bailey didn't say anything at first. Then she sighed. "Definitely the second thing. I jumped off a cliff without a parachute and prayed there was a cushioned landing somewhere below me."

Kayla laughed. "And there was. Alexei caught you and he didn't let go."

"Well, I wouldn't say it was *that* simple, but yeah, nobody splatted on the ground in the end. It worked out."

"So let me see if this works out for me. If it doesn't, then I'll have learned yet another lesson on the reliability of men."

"Nothing I can say to that, honey—except I pray he doesn't disappoint you."

"I know. I pray for the same thing—and that I don't disappoint him, because it's a two-way street. But look on the bright side, Bale—he's not a criminal and he won't keep me prisoner."

"Nope, that's true. You've chosen a good man."

"I think so."

"Call me if you need anything. I love you, Kay-Kay."

"I love you too, big sis. Now stop worrying about everything and go kiss your man."

Kayla let out a breath when the call ended. That had certainly gone better than it could have. Kayla knew that Bailey's concern came from a place of love, so she couldn't be mad at her sister for speaking her mind. Bailey always and forever had Kayla's best interests at heart. Same as Kayla did for her.

"Za!" Ana exclaimed from the backseat, and Kayla laughed in spite of herself.

"That's right, sweetie. Pizza!" It wasn't quite Ana's first word, but it wouldn't surprise Kayla if that's what it ended up being. She'd been teaching Ana to say mama, but so far her baby hadn't done it. She'd said *mmmmmmmm* and *aaaaaaa*, but she'd yet to put it all together.

Fifteen minutes later, Kayla parked beneath the carport beside Zach's Camaro and let out the breath it felt like she'd been holding all the way over. When Zach had asked her to spend the night, she'd frozen for a second. At first she'd thought he wanted the kind of night they'd had before. Her body had started to react to that idea, but he'd quickly squashed it with his assertion that wasn't what he'd meant. Confusion had gone a little haywire inside her until her brain caught up.

He'd made so much sense though, and she'd had to admit that she'd feel safer in his house with him than she would in the in-law apartment. Not because Alexei couldn't protect her, but he didn't know he had to. Or not more than he usually did, anyway.

"I could just tell Bale and Alexei, couldn't I, pumpkin?" she asked Ana in the rearview.

Ana kicked her legs and nodded her head in agreement.

"I could, but they're so happy right now. And they wouldn't be if I told them, would they? Auntie Bailey's schooling would suffer because she'd want to stay home with us. Then she'd want to postpone the wedding. She and Uncle Alexei wouldn't spend as much time together because they'd be worried about us—and what if Uncle Alexei decided the only way to secure your safety was to marry me himself? I can't do that to them. Much better to marry Zach. Not to mention, Mommy really, *really* likes Zach, even if she can't say that aloud to him yet. Zach makes Mommy's wires sizzle and melt, baby girl."

Big time.

"Za!"

Zach's door opened and he got out of his car, a big, competent mountain of a man who made her tingle inside even when he wasn't touching her. Kayla shivered.

It was dark out now, but the porch lights were on. Across the street, Kayla could see Chloe's car in her drive and Ryan's truck parked beside it. Chloe had been in danger not that long ago, and Ryan had taken care of her. He'd stopped her ex before he could hurt Chloe any further.

If Kayla were honest with herself, that's where she'd first gotten the idea. Sitting at Chloe's house on Saturday, eating fried chicken and watching the SEALs and their ladies, she'd been seized with a powerful envy. More than that, she'd realized that she could get that kind of protection for her baby.

Even if she couldn't get the love, she could secure Ana's safety and well-being, and get them both a lethal and effective protector who would stop James— or whoever was threatening her—from finding them and hurting them ever again. That was worth more than love to her.

Zach stood and started pulling her things from his car. Kayla shut off the engine and went around to get Ana. Crickets sang in the night, and somewhere in the distance frogs chorused.

"Is there a pond nearby?" she asked.

Zach paused to look at her. The heat of his gaze made her ache in places she desperately wanted him to touch again.

Easy, girl. Slow down.

"Yeah, there's a neighborhood pond a couple of

blocks over. Good fishing there. You didn't notice the frogs the other night?"

She shook her head. "Honestly, I was so keyed up about talking to you that I didn't."

"Don't worry, you won't notice it when you're trying to sleep. The house is insulated pretty well. If you try to sleep with an open window, you'll hear it."

"I won't open my window. No worries there."

He paused to listen. "I grew up with that sound. We lived in the country, and I spent many a night going to sleep with the sound of frogs in my ear. And other things."

"Other things?"

"Coyotes. Owls. Cows too. It was the country."

Kayla studied him. "I don't think I knew that about you. You told me you were from Missouri, but not the country."

"Well, honey, a lot of Missouri *is* the country."

"I've never been there."

She'd been dragged all over Tennessee, Alabama, and Kentucky as a kid, and she'd moved to Maryland with Bailey, but that was the extent of her travels.

"I'm sure we'll get there at some point," he said as she followed him over to the side door. The same side door she'd fled from a little over two months ago when she'd stayed the night with him. The *only* other time she'd spent the night in his house.

He unlocked the door and flipped on the interior light. Kayla followed him inside. There was a big landing and stairs that went up or down. Up was the kitchen and main living area, along with the master and another bedroom. Downstairs was a large living area with two bedrooms and a wet bar. There was one bathroom downstairs and one up.

Zach led her upstairs to the master where there was a queen-sized bed and a dresser. He set up the crib while Kayla looked around the room.

"How did you and Ryan decide who got upstairs and who got down when you rented this place?"

He finished expanding the portable crib and straightened. "We flipped a coin. I lost."

"He moved out a couple of months ago and you're still downstairs."

Zach shrugged. "It's just a room. Besides, I'd have to move all my shit—sorry, stuff," he corrected, glancing at Ana.

Kayla laughed. "I don't think she's going to repeat it yet, but the time is probably coming."

"I'll clean up my language, promise."

"I know. Trust me, I'm still working on mine. There are times when the only correct word is a vulgar one."

He grinned. "So true." He hooked a thumb over his shoulder. "I left the wine and pizza in the car. Better get it."

"Za!" Ana yelled, and they both laughed.

Zach went outside to retrieve the pizza and wine. Kayla walked into the kitchen with Ana and looked out the window at the street. She heard the car door slam, heard the beeping of the locks, and then the door closed and Zach bounded up the steps. He put the pizza in the fridge and grabbed a beer.

"Want a glass of wine?" he asked.

"Yes, please."

He retrieved a glass from the cabinet and poured wine before putting the bottle in the fridge.

"I need to put Ana down for the night," she said. "It won't take long, but I'd like to stay nearby in case she wakes up."

"We can watch TV up here. Dirty took the one from his bedroom but left the one in the living room."

"It'll take me a few minutes."

"Take your time. No rush, Kayla."

Kayla took Ana back to the bedroom and changed her diaper. Then she put Ana into the crib. Ana kicked her legs but her eyes were drooping. Kayla put a hand on Ana's tummy and rubbed softly while she sang a lullaby. She felt rather than heard Zach's presence. He was behind her, and then he peered over her shoulder to look down at Ana.

"Can I watch?" he asked, his breath soft in her ear.

Kayla tried not to shiver. It didn't work. Every nerve in her body prickled at his nearness.

"Yes," she whispered. Then she kept singing until Ana's eyes stayed closed. She glanced up at Zach, who wore a serious expression as he gazed down at her baby. He'd changed out of his uniform and into a white T-shirt and faded jeans. In uniform or out, he made her belly clench with longing.

Kayla took his hand and led him from the room. She pulled the door mostly closed, leaving a crack so she could hear any noise, and went over to the couch to sink down into the cushions and take a drink of her wine. She needed it to calm her jitters.

"She's not fussy at all, is she?" Zach asked as he sat on the opposite end of the couch.

Kayla shook her head. "No. She's always been really good. I know I got lucky. Everyone says if your first baby is easy, your second won't be." She realized what she'd said and hurried to correct herself. "I mean if you have a second one. Not that I think you and I will want to.... Uh."

She took another swallow of wine while Zach grinned at her.

"It's okay, beautiful. I know what you meant." He shrugged. "Who knows? Maybe we'll give Ana a brother or sister someday. And if not, that's okay too."

Kayla's throat tightened. "You're sweet, Zach. God knows you didn't have to agree to any of this, but you did and now you're trying to make the situation feel normal for me. I really appreciate it."

He looked thoughtful. "When SEALs go on missions, we don't spend any time thinking about what might have been or how we might have responded to a situation. We do what we were trained to do. And we don't question ourselves once we're operating. Second-guessing our actions could result in death. Once we commit, we follow through. Do you understand?"

"I think so."

"It's more than that, though. Yeah, I committed. But I didn't have to, Kayla. I did it because I wanted to. Because I can imagine waking up every day in a house with you and Ana in it—and liking that feeling a lot."

Her heart thrummed and her vision blurred. Dammit, she wasn't going to cry. He hadn't said he loved her or anything that monumental. But still. What he'd said was so damned lovely, and her heart ached with it.

He held out his hand. He didn't say anything, just held it there.

And she knew it was her choice. It would always be her choice.

She put her fingers in his palm, skimmed them upward, and curled her hand around his.

Chapter Nine

KAYLA'S HAND IN HIS WAS SMALL AND SOFT. NEO waited—and she moved into his side, settled there. He curved his arm around her. He thought about kissing her, but decided that was too much for him to handle just now. She put her head on his shoulder and he knew it was the right decision. He felt like he'd gotten a baby bird to land in his palm.

Without another word, Neo picked up the remote and powered on the television. He flipped to HGTV, because he knew she liked that channel, and settled in to watch a couple in Mississippi restore old houses.

"I love this show," Kayla said after they'd been watching for a few minutes. "Thank you for turning it on."

He made a mental note that it was Monday and she loved to watch *Home Town*.

"I'll be honest and say I didn't know that, but I do now."

She leaned back to look up at him. "What's your favorite show, Zach?"

He frowned. "I don't know that I have a favorite. I like car auctions. Car repair shows. Tattoo reality shows."

She laughed softly. "Manly stuff."

"Well, yeah."

"No *SEAL Team* or *N.C.I.S.?*"

"Nope. I have to live with the reality of that life so I'd rather not watch the Hollywood version on TV."

"We watched *Jack Ryan* together."

He nodded. "We did. It was interesting."

"I thought you liked it. You said you did."

He ran his hand down her side, over her hip. He liked feeling her curled against him. It was nice. Was this how Dirty felt every night when he cuddled up with Chloe? It wasn't a bad way to feel.

"I did like it. Mostly I liked watching it with you."

"If you want to watch something else right now, I understand."

"You said you love this show. Why would I turn it?"

Her lashes dipped to cover her eyes for a moment. "You don't have to watch it to make me happy."

"And if I say I do? You gonna argue with me?"

She frowned. "But why, Zach? If anyone should be bending over backwards to please someone, it should be me. You're marrying me because I asked you to protect me and Ana. The least I can do is try not to disrupt your life more than I already have."

She astounded him. Saddened him. What had her life been like that that she was always willing to tamp down her wants and needs in order to please others? It made him sad to think it.

"Listen to me, beautiful. You aren't disrupting my life, and you don't need to bend over backwards to please me. That's now how this works. When I had a roommate, we had to be considerate of each other when it came to things like stomping around at all hours, smelling up the kitchen, hogging the washer and dryer, or blocking the driveway. Now I get to do what I like whenever I like—and I'm still thinking about not waking Dirty or making sure the washer and dryer are clear so he can use them. Maybe if I lived alone for another six months, I'd get into the habit of only thinking about myself. But that's not how I am. Being part of a couple means compromise. You get your way sometimes, and I get my way sometimes. That's how it's supposed to be."

"I've never been in a relationship where that was true before."

He brushed her hair back from her cheek. "You are now, so better get used to it. Monday night, you get to watch HGTV. Tuesday night, we'll find a car show. Wednesday we can stream more episodes of Jack."

She smiled. "Is that the schedule then?"

He shrugged. "It's up for discussion. *Everything* is up for discussion, baby." He twirled a lock of her hair around his finger. "Speaking of discussing things, we still making an appointment at the courthouse once we get the license?"

"I think it's the best plan."

"I've gotta assume you intend to have Bailey and Alexei at the ceremony."

"I think they'd be hurt if we didn't invite them."

"I think you're right. You still planning on keeping the truth about why the rush from Bailey until her wedding?"

"If possible." She sighed and looked up at him. "I told her tonight that we were in love. She didn't freak out. That's a good sign."

"Was this in person or on the phone?"

She frowned. "The phone. Are you suggesting she was freaking out and pretending not to?"

He laughed. "I don't know your sister as well as you do. You tell me."

Her face twisted adorably. "Maybe. I hope not, but maybe." She groaned as she dropped her head against his chest again. "Oh god, she's never going to believe we're crazy in love. I mean she'll understand me wanting you. She won't understand you wanting me. It makes no sense."

Neo put his fingers under her chin and made her look at him. Her hazel eyes were golden green and she barely wore any makeup. Not the polished beauty of Chloe or Avery. Better. So much better.

He liked how pretty she was, how unaware of it she was. She was the girl you took home to Mom—if your mom wasn't a selfish bitch who preferred polish over substance. Not that Chloe or Avery had no substance. He knew for sure Chloe did. He suspected Avery did too.

It was just that his mother would be more interested in how a woman looked and comported herself, not in who she was down in her soul.

Kayla was one of the good ones.

"What the hell do you mean it doesn't make sense? You're gorgeous, Kayla. Any man would want you."

She laughed softly. "Oh Zach, you *are* sweet. But it's not really true. I'm nobody special."

He frowned. "Yeah, you are. Never think you aren't."

She stared at him. He knew he looked fierce, but he wanted her to believe it.

She made a soft sound in her throat. And then she stretched up and pressed her lips to his.

———

KAYLA'S HEART THROBBED. Her body trembled. He said she was special. He said it like he meant it, and she believed him. Maybe because she wanted to, but it was oh so sweet to hear.

She pressed her lips to Zach's and heat unfurled inside her belly, melting into her body, her bones. Zach cupped her face tenderly as he kissed her back.

He tasted like beer, his tongue lightly teasing, and she pressed into him a little harder, seeking more.

More heat. More Zach.

He didn't give it to her. He held her where she was, kissing her softly, lightly. It wasn't the desperate kiss of two months ago, the kiss that had rocked them both and sent them over the edge of sanity, ripping at clothing, touching, tasting, teasing. Joining their bodies in a sensual dance that wrecked them both.

She wanted more of *that*, but Zach wasn't giving it to her. He didn't seem in any hurry to do so.

She pulled back. "What's wrong?"

He traced a thumb along her lower lip and her body trembled. "Nothing's wrong, Kayla. I didn't say you were special so you'd have sex with me tonight. I said it because it's true."

She dropped her gaze to the neck of his T-shirt. "I think maybe you don't know me as well as you should. I've done some shitty things."

"Tell me about them."

Her belly flipped. "It's a long list. You'd get sick of it before the end."

He dragged her onto his lap, turning her so she sat across him with her legs on the couch and her bottom on his lap. He cradled her against him, and she felt safe for the first time in so long she couldn't remember. Which was silly because all he was doing was holding her. That didn't make her safe.

"Tell me what you want to tell me, then. I won't judge you."

Fear fluttered to life deep inside. "You might."

"Honey, let me explain something to you. No matter what you've done, it's probably not worse than what I've had to do in the line of duty. I'm not ashamed of any of it, believe me. But you've seen the shows on TV. You know what kind of things I do, even if the Hollywood version isn't the real story. Unless you've done stuff like that, then don't fear telling me anything."

Kayla sucked in a breath. Then she put her head against his shoulder, taking comfort in the solidity of his presence. "I never killed anyone, if that's what you mean. But I turned a blind eye to things when I should have known better. The Kings—God, they don't deserve to be called kings of anything." She gritted her teeth. "They were traffickers. Sex and drugs. They lured girls in. Runaways, rebels, addicts. They lured me in."

She hated admitting that, but it was true. James had lured her as surely as if he'd hooked a fish.

"It's not your fault."

"I'm trying to remember that. But I feel so stupid. James paid attention to me when nobody else would. He was nice, attentive. He didn't grab my ass or catcall me."

"You worked at Buddy's Bar for a while."

Her heart thumped. "I did. Do you remember me?"

"I remember you had shorter hair then. And you called yourself Harley."

123

She was surprised he remembered her. Most of the guys hadn't. Even Alexei hadn't until Bailey had shown him a picture. A blush crawled up her neck as she thought of who she'd been then. How clueless and naïve.

"I rarely waited on you guys. The waitresses with seniority wanted the SEALs, but a couple of times I helped out. Alexei was nice to me. You already know that I lied and said Ana was his when she wasn't. I did it because he helped me once when a customer stiffed me on a bill. I needed to pull a name out of thin air to give to Bailey when I ran away again, and his was the one I thought of."

"I know, honey. I don't think either of them blame you for it."

"No, I don't think they do either. But I still feel badly about it. It was stupid and selfish of me."

"Selfish? You were trying to protect Ana and doing the best you could. That's not selfish."

"I could have told someone what was happening. I probably should have."

"Maybe so. But you made the choice you made. Maybe it wasn't the best choice, but leaving Ana with Bailey is what got her and Camel together. If you hadn't done that, they might not have met. All you can do is learn from mistakes and try to make better choices in the future. That's all any of us can do."

"I've tried to learn from my mistakes. And I realize that refusing to tell Bailey what's going on might fall under the category of *didn't learn a thing*, but instead of leaving her to deal with a tough situation like last time, I'm trying to deal with it and fix it without it affecting her this time."

"Yeah, I get that."

Kayla leaned back and blew out a breath. "Last time, Bailey got hurt because of me. I can't let that happen again. And I won't let Ana get hurt either. I'd walk into the Kings' clubhouse naked if it meant they'd leave my baby and my sister alone."

Zach's grip on her tightened a fraction. "I'd rather you didn't."

She met his light green gaze. So gorgeous, this man. It felt good to have him on her side.

"I don't intend to. But I won't let my actions cause trouble and pain for those I love again. Not if I can help it."

"You can't blame yourself for what Dunn did to your sister. If he'd gotten you and Ana, he'd have sold her. And you probably wouldn't have escaped again."

Kayla shuddered. She knew what would have happened to her. It wouldn't have been pretty.

"No, I'd either be addicted to drugs and pimped out to as many men as I could handle in a day, or I'd be dead. That's what they did to girls. And I deliberately didn't examine it too deeply so I wouldn't know."

Zach sighed and pressed his lips to her forehead. "Kayla, honey. You were—*are*—young. And you were scared. You were also pregnant. You had a baby to worry about, and a man who was telling you every-thing was fine, am I right?"

"Yes," she whispered. "It was a motorcycle club. A family, he said. There were old ladies and club whores, and the whores wanted to be old ladies. I was an old lady and I was lucky. That's what James said. He said the club whores weren't as good as the old ladies. They were paid for sex, and some of them were addicts looking for their fix. I was supposed to be above all that. I was his property, cherished, marked so the others would know they shouldn't fuck with me."

"The tattoo on your back."

"You mean the tramp stamp. I hate it. I'm going to get rid of it someday."

Of course he'd seen her tattoo. She'd known he had when they had sex that night, but they'd never talked about it. Hell, they'd never talked about much of anything after that night.

Her fault because she'd run away.

Again.

No more. She was tired of running.

"You can do that anytime. I'll help you get it done."

Her heart flipped. "It's expensive. And it's not your problem. It's mine."

"Baby, when are you gonna understand? We're getting married. That makes it my problem. If you hate it, we'll get it removed. Or covered. Whatever you prefer. One of the guys at work is married to a tattoo artist. Her name's Eva, and she used to ink for a motorcycle club. She could probably cover it if you wanted to go that route."

"Really? Wow."

The stamp wasn't too big, thankfully. It was a skull and crossbones in gray and white with the letters K.O.D. inked above the design. She'd felt so wicked getting it, and then she'd grown to hate it. She'd never thought of covering it up before. She'd always wanted it gone, but maybe a redesign was something to consider.

"Yeah. I've seen her work. It's good. I've been planning to get something new myself, but haven't gotten around to it yet. We could go see her together if you want. It's one option. Doesn't hurt to see what she says."

"That would be great."

He ran a palm up her arm, down again. "Any other shitty things you did that you want to tell me?"

"You don't think that's shitty enough? Lying about who Ana's father was, leaving her with my sister without telling her where I was going, suspecting the Kings of Doom were far worse than they seemed and blissfully ignoring the evidence? Oh, and I lied about my identity and I dropped off the face of the earth and didn't contact Bailey for months while she was worried sick about me. She didn't even know I'd had a baby until I showed up on her doorstep and dropped her niece in her lap."

Kayla's throat ached and her eyes stung. Zach

stroked her hair, cradled her tenderly, and the tears built inside until she had to gulp them down or never stop crying.

"You were a twenty-one year old girl who listened to a man's lies. You did the best you could while pregnant and cut off from your family. You made mistakes, but you didn't give up. And you fought for your baby when you realized what Dunn intended. You aren't a terrible person, Kayla. You're brave. I think you did a fucking amazing job of getting out of that situation. I've watched you with Ana, and I think you're a great mom. You're fierce and determined, and you'd sacrifice yourself in a second if you thought it would save her."

Kayla sucked in a breath and squeezed her eyes shut. What the hell was he doing to her? He made her tremble inside, and he made her look at things in a different light. *Was* she brave? She didn't feel brave when she'd banged on his door a few nights ago and begged him to marry her and keep her and Ana safe. She'd felt like a lost little girl searching for someone to hand all her burdens to. Giving up responsibility as usual.

"You don't know what you're saying," she whispered.

"Yeah, I do. Stop beating yourself up, Kayla. Give yourself credit for being the fierce mama bear you are."

The ache in her heart was intense, but it wasn't a

terrible ache. It was an ache that spoke of strong emotion and gratitude. For this man.

Zach Anderson said things to her that no one else had said. It was like he saw deep inside her and pulled out the shiny parts. The golden, happy parts. She adored him for it even while she wasn't entirely sure she believed him. Maybe he was the kind of guy who saw the good in everyone, or maybe he knew exactly what he was doing and said what she needed to hear when she needed to hear it, whether or not it was true.

Like James had, though he'd never actually seen this deeply into her.

Zach isn't like that. You know he's not.

"I'm trying," she managed while her brain whirled with confusing thoughts.

"I know you are."

There was a wail from the bedroom that had Kayla bolting upright. Zach got up too. "She rarely wakes once she's down, but sometimes she does. I need to check on her."

"I'll come with you, if that's all right."

She didn't hesitate. "Of course."

Kayla pushed the bedroom door open. Ana was sitting up in her crib, crying. Kayla went over to check her.

"Wet diaper," she said. "An easy fix."

Her heart pounded as she retrieved the changing pad and a fresh diaper from the bag. She couldn't get over Zach telling her she was brave and fierce, not the cowardly liar she'd always thought she was. It was monumental to her. Bailey had said similar things to her, but Bailey was her sister. Bailey was supposed to see the best parts of her.

Nobody else had to.

"Let me help," Zach said, taking the changing pad and placing it on the bed for her.

"Thank you."

Kayla put Ana on the pad and changed her. Zach took the dirty diaper and left the room. She didn't know where he was taking it but she finished with Ana and rocked her a bit before putting her in the crib again. When she turned around, Zach was in the doorway.

"Do you need anything?"

"No. Thank you for taking care of the diaper."

"No problem. I took it outside and threw it in the trash."

They looked at each other for a long moment. Kayla's heart throbbed with emotion but she didn't know what to say.

"I think I'm headed to bed," Zach finally said. "I've got to be at work at six."

Disappointment flared deep inside. She didn't know what she'd expected him to say, but she hadn't expected him to leave her just yet. "Okay. What time should I be ready to leave in the morning?"

"You don't have to get up when I do. I'll leave a key on the kitchen table. It's yours."

"Thank you, Zach. For everything."

"You're welcome, Kayla."

"I had fun tonight."

"So did I."

"Goodnight," she said quietly.

He shut the door and left her alone. It was a long time before she slept.

Chapter Ten

It was before eight when Kayla went into the kitchen to find coffee and a note from Zach on the counter.

I made coffee for you. Eat whatever you like. There's cereal or bagels and cream cheese. The dairy is all good. I sniffed it. Here's the key. Have a good day, beautiful. I'll call you later. Z

Kayla laughed. He'd sniffed the dairy. Such a man thing to do. She went over and grabbed a bagel from the bag he'd left on the counter and popped it into the toaster. Ana was in her playpen in the living room where Kayla had turned on a morning show so she could listen to the news while she fixed breakfast. She poured a cup of coffee, then found a small pan, added water, and turned on the gas so she could make oatmeal for Ana.

Kayla felt pretty good, all things considered. She'd

finally fallen asleep around midnight, and she'd slept better than she had in a few days now. Maybe being in Zach's house let her relax enough to finally sleep without fear. The fear was still there, humming along at a low frequency now that she was awake and Zach was gone.

The bagel popped up and she grabbed the cream cheese from the fridge. There wasn't much in the fridge, which told her that Zach ate out a lot, but he had a few staples like cream cheese and milk and cream for coffee. There was butter and cheese, and some apples too. A couple of eggs.

Kayla fixed the bagel and took a bite. The water wasn't ready yet so she stood and waited while the television blared in the background and Ana chirped from time to time as she reacted to the show's hosts or played with her toys.

A knock on the door made Kayla jerk. Coffee spilled over the side of the mug and dripped onto the counter. Kayla grabbed a paper towel to swish it up while telling herself to be calm. Just *be* calm. It could be anything.

It wasn't very likely that the asshole who'd stalked her on the street in front of the salon would find her here instead of at Bailey's place.

She went over to the front door and peered out the peephole, telling herself she didn't have to answer it if she didn't want to.

But it was Chloe. Relief flooded Kayla as she opened the door. "Hey, Chloe."

Chloe squealed. "I knew that was your car! You and Zach finally figuring it out?"

Kayla blinked as she stood back to let Chloe in. The other woman was wearing a long skirt, glittery sandals, and a lacy top. She always looked so pretty and put together.

And happy. Kayla envied her that.

"Yes, I think we are," she said.

"Hot damn. Ryan about had a cow this morning. He said it's about darn time. I told him not to count his chickens yet."

Kayla laughed. She loved that Chloe spoke country. It was almost like being back in Tennessee where she'd been born.

"Never count the chickens before they hatch. But we'll see."

"Oh my goodness, is that my little Ana-banana?" Chloe said as she spotted Ana in her playpen. Ana chortled with glee as Chloe went over and picked her up. Chloe turned to study Kayla. "You *both* spent the night. Wow."

Kayla felt her face heating. "Nothing happened. I slept in Ryan's old room."

"Well, pooh. But baby steps, right?"

"Right."

"Oh honey," Chloe said, "I know you've been hung up on him for a while. I think he's hung up on you too. I mean I never wanted to say anything, because it wasn't my business, but the way you look at each other." She shook her head and bounced Ana on her hip. "*Sizzling,* little princess. That's what it was. Sizzling, and almost... mournful."

"Mournful?" Kayla asked, surprised at the word choice. And the insight.

"Well, yeah. Like you wanted each other so bad but there was a giant barbed-wire fence between you, and you couldn't figure out how to scale it."

"Wow. That obvious, huh?" At least on her part. She didn't know about Zach. Surely he hadn't been pining for her the way she had him.

"Yep."

"So when you said Zach was hung up on someone the other day at the salon... you meant *me?*"

Chloe gave her a *duh* look. "Well of course you. Who else?"

Heat flooded her. "I don't know. I just thought...."

"Honey, I didn't want to say it to JoJo and Avery if you weren't going to claim the man, but believe me, I'm pretty sure he's yours."

Kayla's heart thumped. She certainly wished it was true even if she wasn't entirely certain. I mean yes, he was marrying her to protect her and Ana. And when he touched her, she melted for him. But that didn't mean he was *hers.*

Did it?

"You want coffee?" she asked, tamping down the chaotic thoughts before they drove her crazy. "I was just fixing Ana's breakfast."

"Sure thing, sugar. I had a cup with Ryan, but I could use another."

They went into the kitchen and Chloe sat at the little table with Ana in her lap. Ana promptly reached for the placemat that was there, but Chloe headed her off by pushing it away. Kayla poured coffee and brought it to Chloe along with the cream and sugar.

Kayla went back to fixing the oatmeal packet she'd brought for Ana and took another bite of her bagel. Then she wiped her mouth and gulped the bite down. "I'm sorry. Did you want a bagel?"

"No thanks, honey. I ate with Ryan."

Kayla tested the oatmeal. It was done, so she put it in a bowl and took it to the table. "I can take her."

"I don't mind feeding her. Unless you prefer to."

Kayla smiled as she sat. She loved these friends of hers who adored Ana. She'd never had friends like Chloe and Avery before. And definitely none like JoJo. "No, that's fine. You go ahead."

Chloe dipped the spoon in the oatmeal while Kayla fastened Ana's bib around her neck and sat down again. Chloe blew on the oatmeal to cool it, then started to make train noises. "Here comes the choo-choo, Ana-banana."

Ana opened obediently.

"Do you want one?" Kayla asked.

Chloe looked up. "A baby?"

"Yes."

"Someday. I'm not ready yet though. I want to spend time with Ryan first, make sure we're really ready before we go there. We've only been together a little over two months, and we're still planning a wedding."

Kayla thought of Zach and all they'd been talking about. "Have you ever thought about just getting married at the courthouse and to heck with the big wedding?"

Chloe blinked. "Truthfully? Yes. But Ryan wants me to have the white dress and the special day. And I want it too, but sometimes I think it would be easier to just get married."

"But then you run the risk of disappointing friends and family."

"True. Though you can always have a reception later, right?"

Kayla nodded.

"Still, I'm Southern. I've always wanted the white wedding with all the traditions. And there's no hurry, so that's what we're going to do."

"No, there's no hurry for any of it. Not even babies," Kayla said. "But to tell you the truth, I don't think you're ever ready for a baby. Not until it happens, and then it's sink or swim."

"Probably true. I guess you can think yourself to death on babies."

"You can." Kayla sighed. "I didn't plan to have Ana, but it happened. I'm not sorry, but I won't say it's been easy either."

"You don't have to explain. In fact, I should apologize."

Kayla blinked. "What for?"

"For saying I wasn't ready and needed to think. I mean it kind of implies that I think having a baby right away is somehow bad or something. Like I'm judging you for having this little one."

"I didn't take it that way at all. Honestly. It's good to think about a baby. They aren't dolls, and they have needs. I didn't get the chance to think about it, but that's my fault."

"And the father's," Chloe added.

"Well, yes." Kayla bit into the bagel. Chewed. Chloe continued to feed Ana, and Kayla made a decision. She couldn't talk to Bailey about this, but maybe she could talk to Chloe. She knew Chloe had gone through something, but not exactly *what*. "He's in prison. You probably know that."

Chloe looked up. "I'd heard."

"He's a pimp and a dealer. Probably a murderer too."

"Oh honey. I understand. I really do. My ex was… well, he was abusive, and though he skated the line of criminal activity, he crossed it in the end. He's dead now, and I'm not sorry at all. I'm glad. May the good Lord forgive me," she added.

"I wish James was dead," Kayla said vehemently. "He tried to sell Ana to a black market adoption agency."

Chloe's mouth dropped open. "Oh my God! That's evil!"

"Yes," Kayla said bitterly. "It is. He never wanted her, but he saw an opportunity to make money off her. There are rich people who will pay a lot for a no questions asked adoption."

"That's just... I can't imagine what kind of person would want to sell their own child. I'm so sorry."

Kayla sucked in a breath to calm her roiling emotions. "Thank you. I'm sorry I hit you with that out of nowhere. I kinda thought you might know. The team knows a lot of it."

"Ryan tells me a lot of things, but he's also an honorable guy. He wouldn't tell me things about you that he wasn't allowed to talk about. I mean I knew Ana's daddy was in prison, and I knew he was in a motorcycle gang. I didn't know about the pimping or dealing—or that he tried to sell his own child. I just can't imagine how difficult that must have been for you."

"It was horrible. I ran away, then I dumped Ana on Bailey, telling her that Alexei was Ana's father. I knew she'd go after him, and I thought that would somehow keep her and Ana safe because he's a SEAL. I went into hiding, thinking if James couldn't find me, he'd give up."

"But he didn't?"

"No, he didn't. He kidnapped Bailey and threatened her. Alexei and his team rescued her. That's how James ended up in jail. The entire motorcycle club was swept up and scattered. Many of them went to jail." Kayla bit her lip. "That's why I was scared the other day at the salon. I'm pretty certain the guy who harassed me on the street was one of them."

"Oh, honey," Chloe said. "I'm so sorry. Do you think they're still looking for you?"

Kayla considered what to say. "It's possible. I think it will always be possible. That's why I can't stop looking over my shoulder."

"I completely understand. It was the same way for me when I left Alabama. Travis was a militia leader, and he was determined to get me back and make me pay."

"What happened to him?" She knew he was dead, but she didn't really know how it'd happened.

Chloe concentrated on feeding Ana. Then she looked up, her eyes flashing. "Ryan shot him. He had to do it—but I wish like hell it was me who'd done it."

She should be shocked, but she wasn't. "I understand that. I really do."

Chloe looked stricken then. "Honey, please don't tell anyone I said that. About Ryan, I mean. I'm sure that's supposed to be a secret or something."

"I won't, Chloe. I promise."

Chloe set the spoon down and wiped Ana's mouth with the bib. She reached over and squeezed Kayla's hand. "Thank you. Anytime you need to talk about what happened to you, or how you feel about your ex, you can always talk to me. I understand how you feel and where you're coming from."

Kayla squeezed back. "I know you do. Thank you." She finished the bagel and got up to get the coffee pot. "I really like working with you and Avery and JoJo. It means a lot to me that y'all took me in," she said as she refilled their cups.

"I'm glad you're there. I love Avery and JoJo a lot. But you and me—well, we've made some bad choices in men and we've managed to survive. Not the usual bad choice like a guy who cheats or freeloads, but a really bad choice. The kind that could kill you. You don't ever forget what that's like. But when you find the guy who'll slay those demons for you, you gotta surrender your heart and know he'll take care of it."

"It's not easy though, is it?" Kayla asked.

Chloe smiled wistfully. "No, it's not. But it'll happen. I know it will because it did for me."

"I'm so happy it did. You and Ryan are perfect together."

"Maybe you and Zach are too. I hope so."

"Honestly, I hope you're right. Time will tell."

———

WHEN NEO GOT HOME from work, it was quiet in the house. Too quiet. He'd liked having Kayla and Ana there. He knew he hadn't really experienced any full-tilt baby fits, but having Ana in the house had seemed right somehow. She was cuter than heck, and her little laugh was infectious. Hell, the way she screamed "Za!" in response to the word pizza cracked him up—and made him feel fiercely protective of her.

Just like he felt fiercely protective of Kayla. He'd been attracted to her from the beginning, and he'd lusted after her plenty. But he hadn't really known her. Still didn't, but she was opening up more than she had in the past and it really showed him who she was inside.

Kayla was a lost little girl in some ways. He knew some of her childhood because he'd heard it from her and from Camel when he talked about Bailey. Bailey was four years older and she'd done a lot to shield Kayla when they were children, but they'd still suffered from having drug addicted parents who cared about their next fix more than they cared about their children.

They'd moved around a lot. When Bailey was sixteen, she'd had to take care of her and Kayla both because her parents were either dead or useless by then. Neo couldn't imagine the strain on Bailey, or the fear it caused both her and Kayla.

Add in a psychotic boyfriend who got Kayla pregnant and kept her prisoner with lies, then his threats to Ana, and what'd happened when he went looking for Kayla but got Bailey instead, and it was no wonder Kayla didn't trust people.

Neo wanted to make her feel safe. He wanted it now more than ever. He wanted Kayla to smile, and he wanted her to take care of Ana without the fear in her eyes that he saw there sometimes.

And yeah, he *wanted* her. But that would wait until the time was right.

He went upstairs right away instead of going to his room, and he walked through the kitchen and living room, then into the master, looking for signs that Kayla and Ana had been there. Other than a wet towel on the rack in the bathroom, everything looked like it had before she'd arrived. Kayla had made the bed, tidied up the kitchen—including the coffee pot—and removed all traces that she and Ana had ever been there.

Neo stood in the middle of the master bedroom, staring at the bed and the spot where he'd set up Ana's crib, and felt strangely empty inside. He walked across the hall to the other upstairs bedroom. It was small, but it would be a perfect room for Ana. It had a twin bed, a night table, and a dresser, but he imagined a white crib, sunny colors, and a rocking chair by the window. He could see it all, almost as if Kayla's decorating shows had taken root in his brain.

For half a second, he considered going for paint and surprising Kayla with a room makeover, but then he realized she wouldn't like that. Oh, she wouldn't say she didn't, but she watched all those shows and she surely had ideas of her own. He thought pink walls would be cute for a little girl, but it was entirely possible that Kayla would hate it.

He took out his phone and sent a text. *I want to take you somewhere tonight. Could you get Bailey to watch Ana?*

Her reply came back quickly.

Kayla: *I can ask. What time?*

He looked at his watch. *6:30?*

Kayla: *I'll let you know in a few minutes. Do I have to dress up?*

143

Neo: *No. Wear something you don't mind getting dirty.*
Kayla: *??*
Neo: *Trust me.*
Kayla: *Okay.*

He stared at that one word for a long moment. She'd responded without hesitation. It made him happy that she had. She might not know it yet, but she could trust him with more than her safety.

She could trust him with her heart.

Chapter Eleven

KAYLA THREW ON A PAIR OF TORN JEANS, A CLINGY tank top, and a pair of flip flops. She pinned her hair up in a messy topknot and waited for Zach to arrive. Bailey had given her clothes a disbelieving once over when she'd dropped Ana off.

"Where is he taking you? A barn?"

Kayla laughed. "I don't know. He said to wear something I didn't mind getting dirty."

Bailey held Ana and shrugged. "Okay. Well, have fun. We'll be here staying clean, won't we Ana-banana-boo?"

When Zach arrived, Kayla didn't wait for him to open the car door before she jumped inside. He frowned at her.

"I was coming around to open the door."

"I know. It didn't make sense to let you do it though. Where are we going?"

"It's a surprise. And you have to kiss me."

Kayla's heart thumped. Was she the one he'd been hung up on? She didn't know if Chloe was right, but she sure liked the idea. She leaned forward and pressed her lips to his. He caught her before she could pull away and dipped his tongue into her mouth. Kayla shuddered with pleasure at the stroke of his tongue against hers. Too soon, he was straightening and giving her an appraising look.

"Have you eaten yet?"

"I had an energy bar."

"How about a hamburger? I could use a burger."

Kayla laughed. "You're a junk food junkie, aren't you?"

"Yeah, but only good junk food. Like I prefer the Mom & Pop burger joint to the fast food chain. Didn't you notice the pizza wasn't from a chain last night?"

"I did. It was really good, too."

"Damn right it was. Okay, so how about dinner and then I take you for the surprise?"

"Do I get a hint? Are we going mud wrestling or something?"

He waggled his eyebrows as he backed the car out of the drive. "That sounds fun, honey, but we'll have to save that for next time."

"So no hint?"

"No hint. You're too smart."

She didn't feel smart, but she glowed with the compliment anyway. Zach took her to a local diner where they ordered hamburgers and french fries, and they sat at a corner table and talked about the things they'd done that day. Kayla had shampooed a variety of clients, washed and dried towels and smocks, swept the salon, and had her nails done when JoJo wanted to practice her skills with gel nails after she was done with hair for the day. Zach listened as if it was the most interesting stuff he'd ever heard, but then Kayla stuttered to a halt after she realized she'd been talking for fifteen minutes straight and he hadn't gotten a word in.

"I'm sorry," she said. "I've been hogging the conversation."

He grinned. "I don't think I've ever heard you say so many words all at once, beautiful. But I like it."

Her ears grew hot. "You're just saying that."

"No, I'm really not. I like listening to you tell me about your day."

Kayla dragged a french fry through ketchup. "Well, I've got nothing left now. Tell me about yours."

"Hmm, I shot a thousand rounds of ammo today—"

"A thousand rounds?" she exclaimed. "Did that take all day?"

He laughed. "Not at all. Trust me, babe, a thousand rounds goes fast. It was range practice followed by a live fire exercise where we had to rescue some hostages and take back a naval ship from pirates."

Kayla could feel her jaw dropping. "You let me talk for fifteen minutes about shampooing hair and sweeping floors like it was the most exciting thing in the world, and you did *that?*"

"Baby, it's your day. I'm interested in it. And yeah, it sounds normal and sane. I like it. What I do isn't sane."

She thought about that show they'd watched together. *Jack Ryan.* It was Hollywood and over the top, but people really did that kind of stuff. Zach did that kind of stuff. Maybe not in exactly that way, but he was a real life badass hero who did things for the right reasons, not a criminal who thought he was tough because he rode a Harley, trafficked women, sold drugs, and carried a gun while he did all of it.

God she'd been naïve when she'd fallen for the bad boy who paid attention to her instead of staying strong and realizing she was being manipulated. She would never let that happen again. Not with anyone.

"Maybe not," she told him. "But it's necessary. Thank you for doing it. The world is a better place because of you and Alexei. All of you."

"The world is a better place when people cooperate and help each other out. We're there to balance out those who would use their power over others to do harm. Terrorists, rogue states, drug cartels, dictators —those people don't care about anyone but themselves. We put a stop to it when we can."

"I think it's wonderful, Zach. I really do. There will always be people who do bad things. They don't need to get away with it."

"Unfortunately, some people always get away with shit. But those who can be stopped need to be stopped. That's my mission." He tossed down his

napkin and gave her a look. "You finished? Because
we've got a lot to do tonight."

She pushed away the last of the fries. "Yep, I'm
done. I could keep shoveling in fries but truthfully I'm
stuffed already."

"Then let's go."

He stood and took her hand to help her up, then
led her to the register and paid the bill. She tried to
offer him money, but he refused. They walked out to
his car hand in hand. He opened her door for her and
she got in while he waited. She smiled up at him as he
closed the door, her pulse thumping because he'd
been touching her. How did he do that? How did he
make her temperature rise just by holding her hand?

He started the car and pulled out of the parking
lot. When he turned into Home Depot, she scrunched
up her face in puzzlement. Zach laughed at her
expression. "Trust me," he said.

She did. So much. They went inside the store and
Zach led her to the paint aisle. He held out his hands
with a flourish. "Ta da!"

Kayla looked at the paint chips, then at him. "I
don't get it."

He reached for a strip that had six different colors
of pink on it. "I was thinking one of these would work
for Ana's room. It's the one across the hall from the
master. Did you look at the room?"

Kayla's throat tightened. Her heart skipped a
beat. "You brought me to Home Depot to pick out
paint for a baby room?"

"Yeah." He frowned. "Is that okay? You seem a little upset."

Kayla swallowed. She could barely find the words. "I'm not upset, Zach. I'm… I'm…" She closed her eyes and pinched the bridge of her nose. Strong arms went around her body and pulled her against a solid form. She clutched his shirt and breathed deeply through her nose, trying not to cry. She hated crying. It was weak to cry and she never did it if she could help it.

And yet she couldn't stop the trickle of tears that leaked down her cheeks.

"Hey, hey, hey," Zach said, his breath hot against her ear as he held her tightly. "I'm sorry. I should have told you what I was thinking. I don't want to make you cry, Kayla."

"It's just so… *nice!*" She sniffled. "I love that you thought about Ana. It means so much to me."

"I almost screwed it all up," he told her, still holding her tight. "I thought about painting the room as a surprise but then I realized I might pick Pepto Bismol pink or something and you'd hate it."

Kayla laughed a watery laugh. "It's so sweet of you. Really." She sucked in her tears and pushed back so she could look up into his face. "You're such a great guy and I couldn't be happier that you thought I'd want to help. Even if you'd painted the room Pepto pink, I'd have been happy that you thought of doing it for her."

"Anything for you and Ana. I mean that."

She pulled in a breath. "I know you do."

"So you think we can pick out some paint or what? I thought maybe you'd want a white crib, too. Does she have a wooden crib?"

Kayla's heart hurt, but in a good way. "No, she doesn't. I use the Pack'n Play. It's a crib and a playpen, and it's what I could afford."

She didn't tell him that Bailey and Alexei had wanted to buy Ana a crib but she hadn't accepted. She'd told them the portable crib was fine, and maybe by the time Ana was ready, she could afford a bed for her. Maybe she should have accepted the crib, but it was a few months ago and she'd felt so guilty for taking their help already.

"Maybe we could get one of those cribs that can be converted into a toddler bed when it's time. What do you think?"

"I think that would be great. But I can't let you buy it."

"Why not? If we're getting married, then Ana is my responsibility too. Besides, they don't cost that much. My sister buys shit online all the time and she's gotten all her cribs there. They convert to toddler beds, and then to kid beds. I know she doesn't spend a lot of money on them because she doesn't have it."

Kayla couldn't breathe. It hit her, standing in the aisle of the freaking Home Depot of all places, that she loved this man. There was no other word for it. She loved him. He was honorable and decent and even though they'd barely been speaking just a few days ago, he'd stepped up to help her when she'd asked him to. And he was thinking of her baby like Ana was his own. Thinking about a pink room and a sweet little crib that converted to a bed.

He really cared. At least about Ana, that was clear. And he cared about her, though she couldn't say he loved her or anything. But he cared enough to agree to marry her and protect her. It was more than she'd thought possible just a few days ago.

"We'll look online then. Maybe there's something," she said, suddenly shy with all she was feeling.

"I'll ask Lesley where she gets her stuff. It's got the word *fair* in it or something."

Kayla laughed. "Wayfair?"

"Sounds about right. So which color, Kayla? It doesn't have to be pink. It can be whatever you want."

Kayla fingered the paint chips, looking at all the pink colors available. "Wait—what about your landlord? Won't he mind?"

"Not so long as we paint it back again when we move out."

"It's a lot of work if we're moving out, don't you think?" She desperately wanted to do it, but it didn't make a ton of sense if they were going to apply for base housing.

"It can take time to get base housing. Months. Pick whatever you want and we'll make her room beautiful for her. If we move on base, we'll paint it back. But we'll still have the furniture, and that'll fit wherever we go."

Kayla's heart beat with wild joy. She had a moment where she thought she needed to Google colors for baby rooms, but then she'd been looking at Pinterest for months and she knew what she wanted to do. "Would you mind if we chose a cream instead? And then a pale pink for the accent wall?"

"Honey, pick what you want. If you want black paint and green trim, I'll do it."

Kayla couldn't help but giggle. "Ewww, no way." She slid her hand over to the whites and went through them until she found the shade of cream she liked. Then she went back to the pink chips and found a pink color that was a little darker and more velvety. "These two. With white trim."

"You up for starting tonight?"

Happiness blossomed inside her like a flower opening for the first time. It was such a small thing in a way, and such a huge thing in all the ways that mattered. Zach wanted to paint Ana's bedroom and make it perfect for her. And he wanted to start tonight.

Love, fierce and bright and strong, was a living thing in her heart. She loved Ana more than anything else in this world. She loved her sister. And she loved this man. It both terrified her and thrilled her.

"Yes," she said. "I'd love to start tonight."

———

IT TOOK ABOUT two hours to move the furniture

and then tape and paint the first coat on the walls, but when it was done, Kayla beamed. "It's going to be perfect for a little girl. Just perfect. I can already see it done and decorated in my mind."

Neo leaned against the door jamb and watched Kayla turn around in the room. She was happy, and that made him happy. She smiled like her heart wasn't heavy with fear, and he wanted to make her smile like that all the time.

He also wanted to strip off her faded jeans and tank top and lick her all over. His dick thought that sounded like a plan and started to grow in his pants. He cleared his mind of those images and focused on the idea of Ana sleeping in this room every night instead. His body responded by returning to normal.

He knew it wasn't going to last long with Kayla around. She was sexy as fuck and he wanted her. Badly. But he wasn't going to push her because she'd probably give in out of gratitude for what they'd done tonight.

He didn't want her gratitude. He wanted her desire. He'd had it once and he knew it was a beautiful thing to behold. Even if she'd run away the next morning and made him crazy for two whole months wondering what the fuck had gone wrong.

"Shouldn't take us long to finish painting tomorrow night," he told her.

"I can't wait."

"Baby, tomorrow's Wednesday. We should have the license. Then we can make the appointment to get married. Everything I've read about the wait says it'll be Friday. When do you plan to tell Bailey we're getting married?"

She sighed, her expression falling a little. "Friday morning?" She laughed and shook her head. "That won't work, will it?"

"I don't think so."

Kayla's shoulders slumped. "She's going to ask what the rush is."

"Yeah, probably. But you have an answer for that. We're crazy for each other, we've been secretly seeing each other for a while, and we don't want to wait. That's the plan we made, right?"

"Yes. It sounded more reasonable a few days ago when I said it." She laughed and shook her head. "She's going to be sooo suspicious."

He could have told her that, but she'd been determined. Now he was, too.

He stalked over to where she stood and put his hands on her slim hips. Pulled her into him and lowered his forehead to hers. "It will work, Kayla. We're going to make it work. I care about you and Ana. I don't have to pretend. I can pull off the crazy part."

She was quiet. Then she raised her lashes, and he was pierced by the look in those pretty eyes. "I can pull it off, too. It's not going to be difficult. You wanted to give Ana her own sweet little space. I'll never forget how you made me feel when you took me to the paint aisle."

He grinned. "Romantic guy, aren't I?"

"A girl couldn't ask for more romance than what you gave me tonight, Zach. I can't tell you how important this was to me."

"I'm glad you had fun. I did too."

"I can't wait to fix it up for her. Ana should have her own room. I always wanted my own room as a little girl, but I never had it."

He rubbed his hands up and down her arms. "Because you shared with Bailey."

"No," she said softly. And then she said, "Sometimes. But a lot of the time we didn't even have a room, Zach. We slept on the couch, each of us at one end, when we were smaller. Then we took turns on the couch and one of us took the floor when we were bigger. Sometimes we huddled together in the closet and slept on the floor if Mama and Daddy were bad off…"

His throat tightened. His parents were self-centered dicks, but that was nothing compared to hers. He'd never had to worry about where his next meal was coming from when he was a kid, or if he had a bed to sleep in. He and Lesley had bedrooms of their own. They had toys.

They didn't have people who'd put their emotional needs first, but he'd survived. They both had, though it'd been harder for Lesley. He still felt guilty over leaving home to join the military when she was still in high school. But what could he have done to fix their self-absorbed parents and their toxic relationship long enough for Lesley to graduate and escape?

"I'm sorry, beautiful," he said, his forehead still pressed to Kayla's. "That sucks. I can't fix it for you, but I can make sure you and Ana have all you need now."

She ran her hands up his arms, looped them around his neck. "I know you will. I'm sorry for the way this happened, but I'm not really sorry it happened. I hope that makes sense. I couldn't find a better man to be a father to my child than you."

Her words kind of shocked him. He hadn't thought of himself as a father but of course that's what he was going to be. All in, balls to bones.

"It means a lot that you trust me to take care of you and Ana."

"I do, Zach."

He sighed. "I hate to say this, but it's getting late. I should take you home."

She hugged him tight, surprising him. He hugged her back, loving the feel of her lithe body in his arms. Remembering what it'd been like to hold her when they were both naked, bodies moving together in sync as he drove deep inside her.

"I wish I didn't have to go. I wish this room was done and Ana was already in it."

He wanted that too. So much it surprised him. "Move in with me. Tomorrow. You and Ana and me. We'll finish the room for her, but she can stay in the master with you until it's done. We don't have to wait until we have a ceremony to move you and Ana over here."

She pushed back to look up at him. "Really? You would do that?"

"Yeah, really. Let me start keeping you and Ana safe now."

Kayla's forehead scrunched. Then she beamed at him, and he felt like someone had socked him in the gut. *So beautiful.*

His.

"Okay, we'll do it."

Chapter Twelve

KAYLA COULDN'T STOP THINKING ABOUT ZACH AND painting Ana's room together last night. He'd taken her home around ten. Ana had been asleep in the in-law apartment and Bailey had been at the small table with her laptop, doing homework.

Kayla hadn't said anything about moving in with Zach yet, but she would this afternoon when she went home. It wasn't going to be easy, and yet she wasn't going to have any trouble convincing Bailey she was head over heels in love with him.

Oh, she was still coming to terms with it. Still figuring out the depth and breadth of all she was feeling. But she didn't doubt it was love. She loved him because he was good and honest and, most of all, he'd thought about Ana first. A pink room for her baby girl.

She'd dreamed of a pink room when she was little. And a princess bed. She'd wanted one of those most of all. She'd also wanted her own bookcase filled with precious books that she could read over and over. She'd loved the school library and she'd spent as much time as she could there. But she'd never had a book of her own until she was an adult and bought one for herself. It had felt like the greatest indulgence to spend money on a book.

She hadn't read a book in ages now, and she missed it. Maybe it was time to start again.

"Hey, girl. Where are you off to in your head?"

Kayla jerked at the sound of Chloe's voice. "Oh, hi, Chloe. I didn't hear you come in."

"You've been standing there with that towel in your hand for a full minute," Chloe said. "Is everything okay?"

Kayla looked at the towel in her hand. She'd been folding towels fresh from the dryer. She hurriedly finished the one she was holding and put it on the stack.

"Everything's fine. Sorry, I was just thinking about something."

Chloe raised an eyebrow. "Zach?"

Kayla couldn't help but nod. "Yes."

Chloe grinned. "You have no idea how much I want this to work out. Zach is the second SEAL I ever met, and he's always been terrific to me. Plus he compliments my cooking, so I'm predisposed to love him for that alone."

"Zach is a great guy." Kayla hesitated for a second, and then she decided she really needed someone to confide in. "Can I tell you something, Chloe? I haven't even told Bailey yet, and I need to. But maybe if I practice on you…"

Chloe looked intrigued. And eager. "Of course you can, honey! Spill."

Kayla took a deep breath. "Ana and I are moving in with Zach."

Chloe's jaw dropped. Then she closed the distance between them and wrapped Kayla in a big hug. "Oh that's so exciting. I'm happy for you both."

"I don't think Zach has told anyone yet, so please don't mention it to Ryan. I probably should have asked if that was a problem before I told you."

"I won't and it's not a problem. I mean I really, *really* want to. But it's not my secret to tell and it's not the kind of secret that I shouldn't keep from the man I love. It's kinda like a surprise birthday party. When it's time, he'll know."

"Thank you." Relief flooded her, both at Chloe's promise not to tell and at the fact she'd finally been able to share it with someone. Not that she'd told Chloe everything.

"Why haven't you told your sister, honey? Are you worried she won't approve?"

Kayla pursed her lips. "Bailey practically raised me and she's very protective. She'll probably think it's too fast and I'll get hurt. And maybe I will, but I've never felt this way for another man, not even Ana's father. I want to be with Zach," she finished in a rush.

Chloe's smile was huge. "Oh, I'm so happy you

two are in love. It's amazing news. I mean it seems like it's coming out of the blue, because you appeared to be avoiding each other ever since I've known you, but clearly there was a lot more going on beneath the surface than anybody knew."

"There was," Kayla said truthfully, though she didn't correct Chloe about who was in love with whom. "We had some things to sort out. But last night he took me to the paint aisle in Home Depot and told me to pick out a color for Ana's room. Then we went back to his place and painted the first coat."

"Gracious, that's so romantic! And I'm absolutely thrilled you'll be across the street. We can ride to work together sometimes, and I'll watch Ana for you if you need me to."

"Thank you, Chloe. That means a lot."

Chloe smiled reassuringly. "I can't claim to know your sister's mind, but I think she'll be touched that Zach thought of Ana like that."

"I hope so. She's probably going to be a little unhappy about the rest of it, though. I've been afraid to tell her."

"I understand, but you're going to have to, right? You can't move out in the middle of the night. She's going to notice you're not there."

"I know. I need to gather my courage and just tell her."

And then invite her to a civil ceremony at the courthouse. Lordy.

The bell over the salon door chimed and then JoJo

poked her head into the break room. "Man alert, ladies! There's a Mr. Sexy Pants out here asking for Kayla. Lucky girl."

Kayla's pulse revved as heat prickled along the back of her neck. Zach had called her that morning and offered to go pick up the marriage license by himself. She'd agreed because she didn't want to ask for more time off, and it didn't take two of them to get it. She hadn't realized he was coming by, though.

Chloe arched an eyebrow. "Taking you to lunch today?"

"I guess so."

Kayla walked into the salon and stopped dead in her tracks. The man standing near the register wasn't Zach. He was good-looking, but not in the way Zach was. He was tall like Zach, broad, but not as muscled. He had an earring and tattoos and he wore a cut. When Kayla looked beyond him, she could see a Harley parked in front of the shop. She took a step backward, but he looked her way at that moment and their eyes met.

She didn't know him, but she knew what he was. Fear was an endless pit in her stomach.

The smile that crossed his features wasn't friendly. "Hello, Kayla. I've been looking for you."

———

NEO'S PHONE rang as he was leaving the courthouse. He'd picked up the license and made an appointment for Friday to get married. Now he needed to tell her. Lucky for him, she was already calling.

"Hey, beautiful," he said as he trotted down the steps and strode for his Camaro. "I was planning to call you in a few minutes."

"Zach." He could hear the strain in her voice and he stopped, instantly going into alert mode, that tickle on the back of his neck unmistakable.

"Kayla, what's wrong?"

"There was a man. He's one of the Kings. Th-they're rebuilding the club. He wants money, Zach."

Blinding fury rushed through him. "Where are you? Did he hurt you?"

"At the salon. He was here, but he left. He didn't hurt me. But he—he says he wants what I owe."

Neo saw red. "How much?"

"Seventy-five thousand. That's what he said Ana's adoption was worth. If I don't pay it, they'll take her."

"No they fucking won't," he growled. "Do you hear me, Kayla? No they fucking won't."

She made a noise and he realized it was a sob. The anger inside him turned incendiary. He'd kill for her. He'd use all his considerable skills to keep her from a moment's fear over her baby. He wasn't letting *anyone* take Ana away from Kayla. Or from him.

"I'm coming to get you."

She sniffed. "No, you don't have to. I have to finish work. It's only three more hours and I need to be busy. I just… I wanted to tell you. He's not coming back today."

"Did he say when he expects the money?"

"He gave me a week. And he told me if I ran, they'd go after Bailey."

He could hear the tears in her voice. Tears for Ana and Bailey. He wanted to pummel something. Preferably a biker.

"I'll pick you up after work and we'll go get your things together."

"My car—"

"I'll follow you. But don't leave until I get there."

"Okay."

"I won't let anything happen to you, Kayla. You and Ana are mine, do you understand?"

"Yes. And thank you."

"You don't have to thank me. I said I'd protect you, and I will."

She sniffled and it damn near broke his heart.

"Is he the same one who called you before?"

"I think so."

"Where's Ana today?"

"Bailey kept her." She gasped as her thoughts tumbled forward. "Oh god, I need to call and make sure they're okay—"

"Kayla," he said as sternly as he could, and she subsided. "If he'd intended to go after Ana, he wouldn't have come to you first. It's a threat, but he hopes the threat motivates you to produce the money.

It's easier than stealing the child. Fewer complications."

He could hear her pull in a breath. "You're right. But if I can't come up with the money, they'll take her."

"I won't let them, baby."

"I don't have that kind of money, Zach. I've never seen that much money in my life."

"I know. Even if you did have it, it's not theirs to take. You don't owe them anything, Kayla."

"I'd still give it to them if I thought they'd go away."

"They never would, honey. That's the whole point. If they can bleed you for any amount of money, they won't stop until they've gotten everything you have."

"All I have is Ana and Bailey. I won't lose either of them."

His gut churned with hot anger. "You've got more than that, baby. You've got me."

———

KAYLA WAS mess of nerves for the rest of the day. Every time the chime over the door rang, she jumped. Chloe, JoJo, and Avery watched her with worried expressions. They hadn't heard what the man had said to her, but they'd figured it wasn't anything she wanted to hear.

She'd turned to flee into the stock room when he'd

said her name, but he'd told her to stop right where she was. And she did because he'd had such authority in his voice. He'd reminded her of James and the time she'd spent with the Kings of Doom. She'd known the man was in a club based on the Harley and the leather cut he'd worn, but she hadn't realized which club because she couldn't see the patch on the back of the cut.

But when he'd told her they needed to talk about her debt, she'd known. He wasn't from a rival club and he hadn't come for a friendly chat. He was Kings of Doom, and he'd come for her.

She'd approached him warily, certain he wouldn't grab her with witnesses who could identify him, but scared nonetheless. That's when he'd told her, in low tones meant only for her, what he expected from her.

Seventy-five grand in one week, or he'd take Ana. Running wasn't an option either. Not unless she ran with Bailey and Ana both, but she pushed that thought away as quickly as it formed. She was *not* ruining her sister's life and happiness by even suggesting it.

She vaguely remembered the man from the Kings. He wasn't someone she'd have thought would take over, but considering they'd been decimated after the SEAL raid on their compound, he was probably the most senior member left. And he was determined to reclaim the club glory and their territory.

She'd been trying to remember his name. It finally came to her when she was shampooing Mrs. Talbot.

His name was Dal Gentry and he'd been a lieutenant during her time with the Kings. James had outranked him, which was why she hadn't seen a lot of him.

Still, he was the boss now and he knew what he wanted.

"Sweetie, are you okay?" Chloe asked at one point.

"I'm fine. Why do you ask?" She tried to inflect her voice with mild surprise, but it came out sounding so falsely chipper it was painful.

Chloe saw through the act and frowned. "You were scared of that man. Who was he?"

"Nobody," Kayla said, her natural instinct to keep everything close to her chest coming into play.

Chloe didn't push her. "Okay, hon. But if you need to talk, I'm here."

Kayla reached out and squeezed her hand. "I know. Thank you, but I'm fine. He's a friend of my ex. He wanted me to visit James in prison. I refused," she lied.

The frown lines on Chloe's face didn't dissipate. "I wouldn't visit him either if I were you." She hesitated. "You know you can count on me, right? I'll help however I can."

"I know you will, but there's nothing to worry about. He only wanted to intimidate me a little bit, make sure I didn't have anything more to say about the club to law enforcement. Since I already told them everything I know, I could honestly assure him I didn't."

Chloe studied her for a long moment. "I know that type of man, Kayla. My ex's militia was filled with men just like that. They don't let go easily or willingly. I don't think you've seen the last of him."

Kayla's heart thumped. "I don't think so either, but he'll get the hint eventually."

The hint? What a joke. Dal Gentry was determined to make her pay and he wasn't going to take no for an answer.

When Zach came to get her, she nearly melted with relief. It was five-thirty and the salon was closed. Everyone was still there, cleaning up, when he arrived. Avery let him in the front door and Kayla's throat closed up at the sight of him in his camouflage uniform with the SEAL trident over his pocket. She didn't even think before she flung herself in his arms and held on tight.

He squeezed her to him and dropped his mouth to her ear. "It's okay, honey. You're safe. So's Ana. I'm sorry, but I had to tell Camel so he could take care of his woman."

Kayla pushed back to look up at him. Apprehension skated down her spine. "Bailey knows?"

"Not yet. I got Camel to promise not to tell her."

"Oh thank god."

Zach gripped her arms and looked at her, his expression serious. "Only until you have a chance to do it, Kayla. He'll tell her tonight if you don't."

Kayla's belly was a ball of nerves. "I didn't want this crap to touch her," she gritted out. "I just wanted her to have her perfect wedding and be happy without me fucking it all up."

"You aren't fucking anything up, Kayla. Bailey loves you and she deserves to know what you're up against."

He sounded stern, and she knew he meant it. "I know," she whispered, even though it tore her up to think about telling Bailey what was going on.

"You can do this, Kayla. You'll be fine."

She managed a smile. "I know. I just hate how this is going to affect her."

"I know, baby, but you have to tell her. She can handle it."

Kayla nodded, knowing he was right but hating it anyway. When she managed to push herself away from him, she realized that three pairs of eyes were staring at them. Chloe was smiling like the cat that ate the canary. Avery looked intrigued. And JoJo waggled her eyebrows and hooted beneath her breath as Kayla went past her to retrieve her purse from the back.

Kayla blushed. "Stop it, Jo."

JoJo fell in beside her. "Honey, I'd have climbed that last bad boy like a tree—but this one, shit. This one I'd tie to the bed and not let up again. Please tell me that's your plan."

For the first time all afternoon, Kayla laughed. "I don't know my plans yet," she said truthfully. "But I'm definitely not letting him go."

"Atta girl," JoJo said.

Chapter Thirteen

"WAIT JUST A MINUTE," BAILEY SAID, HER EYES flashing between the two of them. "Some asshole from the fucking Kings of Doom motorcycle club threatened you today and now you're moving in with Zach?"

Beside him, Kayla stood stiff and still. She had his hand in a death grip though. From all appearances, she was scared of her sister. But he knew that wasn't really the problem. She was scared *for* Bailey. Scared that Bailey would somehow sacrifice her own happiness and her dreams yet again in an effort to protect Kayla.

Kayla had a huge heart and she loved her sister very much. And she felt like Bailey had done enough over the years. He understood where she was coming from. If he could prevent Lesley from sacrificing her dreams or her happiness for him, he'd do it in a minute. Not that they'd ever faced that choice, but if so, he'd be as fierce as Kayla in trying to stop it.

"Yes, Bale. That's exactly right. I'm moving in with Zach because I want to be with him—and he wants to be with me. The Kings are secondary, but you don't need to worry about them. Zach will protect me."

Camel stood beside his girl, calm on the outside but no doubt boiling on the inside. Boiling because his girl was upset, not because he was. Neo was pretty damned sure that Camel trusted him to protect Kayla. They'd had the same defensive training, with the exception of Camel being the team sniper. His shots over long distances were more accurate, but Neo didn't have any trouble hitting targets. Or winning in close combat situations.

Bailey's eyes fixed on his. "Will you, Zach?"

"I think you know I will."

Bailey frowned. Hard. "I really like you a lot, Zach. I know what you are and what you're capable of. But this whole thing seems sudden. Like you two are trying to pull one over on us."

"What possible incentive do I have to ask your sister to move in with me unless I care about her?"

Bailey didn't have an answer.

"It's not sudden, Bale," Kayla said softly. "Zach and I have had a complicated relationship over the past few months. We've been off and on, for reasons that I'm not explaining to you, but we're on again.

And this is what we're going to do. I don't need your approval."

"Babe," Camel said softly. Bailey looked up at him. "The Kings have found her again. If I were running this op, I'd move her to a new location until we could hunt them down and put an end to the threat."

She didn't say anything for a long moment. Then she sighed. "I know."

Neo could hear the defeat in her voice.

"But how are you going to end the threat?" she continued. "Those assholes are supposed to be in prison, not out starting their club again."

Camel shot Neo a look. They both knew that sometimes the bad guys didn't stay down. Sometimes they crawled out from under their rocks again. And sometimes you had to wait for them to make another mistake before you put them down once more.

"We took down as many of them as we could," Camel said. "We dismantled their operation and freed the women they were holding. This guy is starting from next to nothing, but there are a few of them left and they've been trying to rebuild their network. He wants money so he can do that. We're not going to let it happen."

"I feel safe with Zach," Kayla said. "Alexei has you to take care of. He doesn't need to spend all his time looking out for me and Ana too."

Bailey's brows drew together. Then she threw her hands up and her head back. "Okay, okay. It's three against one. I get it." She went over and wrapped her arms around Kayla. Kayla hugged her in return. "You're the only sister I have, Kay-Kay. I already thought I lost you once and I don't ever want to go through that again. You're too important to me. You and Ana and Alexei are the only family I have."

"I know, Bale. I'll be fine with Zach. He's the right man for me. I love him and I want you to be happy for me."

Neo's gut clenched at hearing her say she loved him. She was saying it for Bailey's sake, but he wished it were true. What would it be like to have the kind of love in his life that Camel clearly had? And then there was Dirty, living across the street and head over heels with Chloe. Not to mention the rest of Neo's teammates. It was only him and Shade left in the bachelor category.

And he wasn't going to be a bachelor much longer, though Kayla hadn't mentioned that part to her sister. Neo had left it up to her. She'd clearly decided that springing two things—a threat from criminals and moving out—was enough of a blow for her sister in one night.

"I *am* happy for you. Both of you," Bailey said, stepping back and giving him a look that contained both a question and a threat. "Take care of my baby sister and my precious niece, Zach. I need them."

"I need them too, Bailey. Both of them." He put his arm around Kayla and pulled her close. She clung to his side as if it was the most natural thing in the world to be there. She made him feel fiercely protective. He'd do anything for her and Ana.

"I know it's sudden," Kayla said, "but after the visit from Dal today, I think it's wise to go now. I don't know that he knows where to find me other than the salon, but I'm not taking any chances."

"You can't keep going to work," Bailey said. "It's too dangerous."

"I have to for now. It's my job, and I won't leave the girls in a bind."

Neo gave Kayla's shoulder a squeeze, signaling her not to keep protesting. "We'll figure something out, Bailey. I won't let her put herself in danger."

"We're going to track down this Dal Gentry," Camel said. "Find out where the club is hanging these days and precisely what the state of it is."

They'd already talked to their team commander about it. Dane "Viking" Erikson was taking it up the chain to see what they could do.

Hell, if he had to, Neo would pay Ian Black a visit. He knew where to find the man's HQ building and he wasn't too proud to ask for help. He'd probably find his ass in a sling with Viper and Ghost, aka General Mendez and Colonel Bishop, if he did that—but when he said he'd do anything to protect Kayla and Ana, he meant it.

"I guess I can't argue with that," Bailey said, still frowning. And then her frown faded as if she'd made a decision to put it behind her. "Hey, do y'all want some dinner before we start loading up your car? I made meatloaf and mashed potatoes with gravy, green beans, and rolls. Oh, and Chloe gave me her strawberry pretzel salad recipe, so I made that too."

Neo's belly growled like Pavlov's dog hearing a bell. "You made Chloe's dessert recipe?"

Bailey grinned. "Sure did. And I'll be honest and tell you she gave me the meatloaf recipe too, so it's not the dry brick I usually end up with. My cooking skills are improving beyond breakfast these days."

"Baby, you always make a fine breakfast," Camel said. "Those pancakes of yours. Mmm."

Neo wasn't sure, but he thought Bailey might have blushed.

She gave Camel a little smack on the arm. "You're too sweet to me. But I swear y'all will love tonight's meal. Promise. So will you eat with us?"

Neo wanted to stay for dinner for the strawberry thing alone. But he waited for Kayla to decide. She was the one whose opinion mattered. If she wanted to leave, they would.

She glanced up at him. "I'm willing if you are."

"Oh yeah," he replied before she changed her mind. "It sounds delicious to me."

"Okay then, we'll stay. I'll help set the table," she said to Bailey.

She and Bailey headed for the kitchen, though she stopped to scoop Ana from her playpen before disappearing through the door. Once the clatter of plates and silverware sounded, Camel turned to him.

"Come on, dude, what's *really* going on with you two?"

———

KAYLA WAS SPENT, but too keyed up to fall asleep right away. After she put Ana down for the night in the master bedroom, she emerged to find Zach waiting with a glass of white wine.

"Thank you," she said as he handed it to her. "How did you know I wanted wine?"

He lifted an eyebrow. "After the day you've had?"

She sighed. "True."

He put an arm around her and hugged her to his side. "Proud of you, babe. You did good telling Bailey about Dal Gentry, and about moving in with me."

Kayla took a sip of wine. "But I didn't tell her we're getting married."

"Yeah, I noticed that."

She glanced up at him. "You're not mad?"

"Why would I be mad? I think you had enough to tell your sister tonight."

"Me too. Hey, I want to see the room."

He grinned. "Thought you might."

He pushed open the door to the bedroom across the hall from hers and stepped back so she could enter first.

"Oh, I love it." The creamy white paint was even richer now that it had dried, and the pink on the feature wall was so light and airy and perfect. "I can't wait to finish it. But it looks really good for only one coat," she added.

"I painted a second coat," Zach said. "I woke early this morning and I had time, so I rolled it on. It's ready."

Her heart filled with love as she walked over and examined the feature wall. "It's perfect, Zach."

"Yeah, I kinda like it too. All you gotta do is take the painter's tape off the trim. I left that on in case we needed another coat, but I don't think we do."

"No, I don't think so either."

She carefully picked at one corner of the painter's tape and pulled it off. Zach started pulling off the others. When they were done, they stood in the middle of the room and looked around at their handywork.

"Love it," she said. "I can't wait to decorate it for Ana."

She'd set her wine on the window sill when she was pulling tape and now she turned and flung her arms around Zach. "Thank you, Zach. Thank you so much for making my dream for Ana's room come true."

He caught her and held her to him. His body was big, hard, and she felt a little thrill deep inside as she pressed up against him. Her nipples tightened. She ached for a repeat of their single night together, but her emotions were high and it might not be the best time. No telling what she'd say to him in the heat of the moment.

"You're welcome, beautiful. But we aren't done yet. We need to shop for that crib, and for the accessories and shit you'll want."

"I know, but I'm just so happy about it. I mean I showed up at your house with a half-baked plan only a few days ago, and you've been nothing but terrific since. I have to admit I didn't expect it would be like this, even after you agreed to help me."

His hands roamed over her back and down to her hips where he gripped her and pulled her lightly against him. "I don't do anything half-assed," he said. "Once I'm in, I'm in."

Kayla couldn't help but laugh. She was so incredibly happy at this moment, even with the stresses of the day. "Is that innuendo? Because it sounds like it could be."

He grinned and pressed closer. She caught her breath at the evidence of his growing arousal. Her body responded with a surge of liquid heat, making her wet and oh so ready for him.

"If you're asking if I want to be inside you, yeah, I really do. But I'm not planning to pursue it tonight. You've had a shitty day and you're tired. I'm not taking advantage of that."

She threaded her fingers into his hair. It was short, military-style, but she'd seen him with it shaggier too. She liked both ways. "Maybe I want you to take advantage of me. Did you ever think of that?"

So much for her heightened emotions and her fear of what she might say in the heat of the moment. The thought of having him inside her was fast chasing out other considerations.

"Honey, I've wished for it harder than you know. But I want it to be right, not rushed." He kissed her, a chaste peck on the lips that had her aching for more.

Kayla couldn't stop the jaw-cracking yawn that hit her at that moment. Zach gave her an *I told you so* look. Then he reached past her to where her wine was sitting on the sill and handed it to her. She took a sip and turned around slowly to take in the walls again.

"Come on, beautiful. You look like you're about to fall down," Zach said. "Let's sit on the couch for a few minutes."

She followed him to the living room and sank onto the couch beside him. It wasn't a great piece of furniture, but it was comfortable enough. "Is this yours or did it come with the house?"

"It's the landlord's. Most of the furniture is, with the exception of the stuff in my bedroom. And the bed in the master. That was Dirty's but he left it when he moved in with Chloe."

Kayla yawned again, feeling drowsy and secure as she snuggled in beside Zach. "It's a comfortable bed. And a lonely one…" She jerked as the words left her lips. Had she really just said them aloud?

"I know, honey. I'm lonely too."

A hot feeling rushed over her. She didn't want to be alone. Not tonight. Not when she would probably wake up a million times in fear that someone was coming into the room to steal Ana away. "Then sleep with me, Zach. Just sleep. I'll keep all my clothes on and everything—"

God, what was she saying? Begging him to sleep with her? Sounding desperate and pitiful at the same time?

But she'd said it and it was out there now, hovering between them.

He sighed and skimmed his fingers down her cheek. "I don't know if that's a good idea."

Heat flooded her cheeks. "It's okay. I understand." She sipped her wine to cover her disappointment.

He put his fingers beneath her chin and turned her to face him. "Is it important to you?"

She started to tell him no, it was fine, forget it. Instead, she nodded.

He dropped his chin. Sighed. "Okay, honey. I'll sleep beside you tonight."

Chapter Fourteen

NEO HAD TO ASK HIMSELF IF HE'D SUFFERED A moment of temporary insanity when he'd agreed to sleep with Kayla all night. Especially once they were in bed and lying quietly in the dark. He could hear her breathing and he knew she wasn't asleep. He lay on his back, staring up at the ceiling, and his dick was harder than stone.

Her small hand groped for his, and he closed his fingers around hers.

"It wasn't fair to ask you to sleep here," she said softly. "I'll understand if you want to go."

"I said I'd stay. I just need a moment to get things under control."

A moment? Hell, what he needed was to bury himself inside her and take them both over the edge into that wild heat they'd explored before. Barring that, he needed a few minutes alone in the shower so he could jerk off and release some of the pressure.

He wasn't getting either of those things, though.

Kayla turned onto her side and put a hand on his chest. She didn't move it and she didn't snuggle up to him.

Thank God for small favors.

"I'm sorry, Zach. I seem to cause you nothing but trouble."

He put his hand over hers and held it. He liked touching her, even such a simple touch as this. "I'll live, Kayla."

She didn't say anything in response. Soon after, he heard her breaths lengthen and he knew she'd fallen asleep. Considering how exhausted she'd seemed earlier, he wasn't surprised. He thought about slipping away now that she'd passed out, but even though he convinced himself he was going to do it, he never moved. He listened to her breathe, listened for Ana's breathing, and felt himself relax. It took a while, because his body had a primal need to mate with hers, but it wasn't the first time he'd been horny with no relief and it likely wouldn't be the last. That was life.

Camel had asked him earlier what was really going on between him and Kayla. He'd told his teammate the truth: he didn't really know, but it was intense and emotional and he'd put his life on the line to keep her and Ana safe. Camel had frowned for a second, but then he'd nodded and said, "Okay, brother."

Neo didn't remember falling asleep, but when he

snapped awake sometime later, it was still dark. Kayla was beside him, softly snoring. She'd curled up to him, and he'd turned onto his side to bring her closer. They were tangled together like the roots of a tree.

A sound came from Ana's crib, and he jolted into greater awareness, listening hard. Sure enough, she was starting to fuss. It was a small sound, but he suspected it would grow louder quickly if not attended to. He disentangled himself from Kayla without waking her and padded to the crib. Ana's eyes were wide open and she was snuffling.

He picked her up and checked her diaper. Wet.

"Za," she said sleepily.

Neo turned to look at the bed. Kayla hadn't stirred. "Shh, Ana," he whispered. "I think I can do this. You'll help me, right?"

"Za."

Zach reached for the diaper bag and walked out of the bedroom. He found the changing pad and placed it on the couch, then put Ana down and went to work getting her a fresh diaper. He wasn't a pro or anything, but he'd changed his nephews a few times when he'd been visiting his sister and could tell she really needed the help.

It took him a couple of tries, but he found everything in the bag. When he got the diaper changed, he took Ana to her new room and walked around with her, talking and bouncing her softly, until her eyelids drooped and her little head lay on his shoulder.

A wave of tenderness flooded him as he carried

her back to bed. She wasn't his child, but it didn't matter. She was going to be his in all the ways that counted. He'd be there for her as she grew up. He didn't really know what the future held, or what marriage to Kayla was going to be like, but he knew he wasn't ever abandoning the baby girl in his arms.

Once he had her down again, he went into the bathroom to wash up. A glance at his phone on the nightstand told him it was nearly five, so he left the room again and went to make coffee before putting on his workout gear. He'd have a cup and then he needed to head in and hit the gym before starting the day at HOT HQ.

When he got back up to the kitchen, he grabbed the notepad sitting on the counter and started to write Kayla a note. He wrote about the coffee and the food —he'd stocked up and had a few more things now— and then he continued to write, telling her the things he thought she needed to hear before she started her day.

He hadn't intended to do it, but one of the things he'd always regretted about leaving home when Lesley was still in school was that he hadn't been able to be there every morning and counteract his parents' bull-shit. He hadn't been there to tell her she was pretty and strong and smart—and worth so much more than she gave herself credit for. He'd let her confidence be chipped away by their perfectionist mother, and he still regretted it.

After he finished writing the note to Kayla, he

took it to the bedroom and left it on the nightstand, on top of her phone. He wanted it to be the first thing she read when she woke. She lay on her side, her golden hair spread over her pillow, her lashes resting on her cheeks, her mouth slightly open. Ana was asleep too, her little chin quivering as she dreamed about something he'd never know.

Neo tiptoed over to the door and stood there for a long minute, looking at the two women who'd turned his life upside down in the space of days.

It wasn't what he'd expected to happen. But maybe it was exactly what he'd needed....

———

KAYLA WOKE SHORTLY AFTER SEVEN. She lay in bed for a second, listening to the sounds of birds and dogs, and the occasional car passing by, before she pushed up on her elbow to look at Ana. Her baby was still asleep. She turned to the side of the bed where Zach had been, amazed that he'd gotten out of the room without either her or Ana hearing him. She ran her palm over the spot in the sheets where he'd lain, and sighed.

When she flipped over to get her phone, she found a piece of paper folded in half. She sat up against the headboard and unfolded it.

Morning, beautiful. Coffee's made. I bought more groceries so eat what you like. I changed Ana during the night. I think I did it right. You'd better check. I showed her the new room too. I think she'll love it. Today is the first day you'll wake up inside a house you're living in with me, so I want it to be a good one. You're a beautiful, smart, wonderful woman and a great mom to your daughter. Don't spend too much time thinking about the past. Think about the future and all you're going to do. I'll be here for you. Z

Kayla's heart squeezed with so much love it was painful. *Careful, Kay-Kay. You're gonna get hurt. You always do.*

"No," Kayla whispered fiercely. "Not this time."

Zach was a good man, and he wasn't going to hurt her. He might not love her yet, but he would.

Don't count on it...

"Stop it," Kayla muttered to herself before she reread the note again. Writing a note like this one wasn't the sort of thing a man did when he didn't care. Sure, she might have begged him to marry her, and he might have agreed because she was in trouble, but they *could* build something good out of the situation. He'd surprised her with paint for Ana's room, for heaven's sake.

Kayla forced down the negative thoughts that came from a lifetime of having her hopes squashed and got out of bed. After a quick shower, she emerged to find Ana crawling around in the crib. Kayla lifted her baby out and took her to the kitchen where she poured a cup of coffee. Then she went and turned on the television, found *The Today Show*, and retrieved the

Pack'n Play so Ana could play inside it while she fixed breakfast.

She was just about done with breakfast when she got a text from Chloe. *You dressed? Coming over if so.*

Kayla texted back. *Yes. I'll open the door for you.*

Kayla was waiting when Chloe came up the steps. She looked gorgeous in a maxi-dress and sandals and she beamed when Kayla pulled the door open.

"Hey, girlie! I was thinking we could ride to work together today."

"Sure. I can drive if you like," she said, closing the door and locking it.

Chloe frowned a little. "Well, I was hoping you'd ride with me."

Kayla blinked. It took her a minute before suspicion dawned. "Did Zach ask you to drive me to work?"

"Ryan called and suggested it would be a good idea, yes. Also, Ella McQuaid can watch Ana today. We can take her over there on the way."

Kayla's heart thumped. She knew Ella and liked her just fine, but taking Ana over to her instead of to the salon brought the reality of what Kayla was facing crashing down on her like a bucket of ice water. It wasn't that she didn't take Dal Gentry seriously. She did. But with him out of sight, and with a man like Zach in her life, she'd let herself temporarily be lulled by the thought that having Zach around was all it would take for Dal to go away.

It wouldn't. He wanted 75k and he'd given her a week to get it. He wasn't disappearing.

It would take much more than simply having Zach around, at least until Dal and the remaining members of the club could either be scattered again or taken into custody. The thought was almost enough to make her sink to her knees and weep.

"Hey," Chloe said, coming over and putting a reassuring arm around her. "It's going to be okay. Zach and Ryan and the rest of the guys will make sure you and Ana are safe. They'll make everything better. I swear."

Kayla pulled in a breath. "I hope so."

"They will," Chloe said, giving her a little shake. "I know from experience."

"Be honest—did you believe it before it happened, or were you still scared?"

"Oh honey," Chloe said on a sigh. "I was terrified. When Travis kidnapped me, I just knew he'd won. But then I realized Ryan would find me. I had such faith that he would. And he did. But sure, I was scared stiff. I spent a lot of time before Travis showed up again worrying about what would happen if he did. I can't lie about that."

Kayla wrapped her arms around herself. "That's what I do too. I was worried James would get out of prison or something. I never thought of somebody else coming after me, but it happened."

"I knew that man was bad news yesterday. I'm so sorry you had to go through that. Ryan told me what he wants. I'm furious for you. Just furious. I hope he drives his motorcycle off a cliff or something."

Kayla couldn't help but snort a laugh. There wasn't much humor in it though.

"That would be awesome. I don't think it'll happen, much as I wish it would. I didn't know Dal very well when I was with James, but I heard some of the women talk about him. He liked to hit girls. He also liked choking them during sex. They said he killed one of the girls he was pimping, but I don't know if it's true." Kayla shivered and Chloe hugged her harder. "I'm sorry I didn't tell you the truth about him, but I didn't want to involve any of you."

"Oh honey, it's okay. I'm sorry you went through that. Boy, you and I sure picked a couple of losers before we found the winners we have, didn't we?"

"Definitely." Kayla bit her lip. "Do you ever worry it won't last, Chloe?"

Chloe frowned. "You mean with Ryan? No," she said, shaking her head. "I don't think like that at all. I just know he's the one for me—and I'm the one for him. I have no doubts. I've never felt this way before. Neither has he. I believe him when he says that."

Kayla nodded. She'd never felt this way before either—but so far, Zach wasn't on the same page as her. Maybe he never would be. Maybe she was hoping for more than she deserved.

"Do you doubt your feelings for Zach?"

"No, not at all. But Chloe…" She blew out a

breath and said what she wouldn't dare say to her sister. "He's not in love with me."

Chloe smiled softly. "Oh honey, I wouldn't be so sure about that. I saw him with you yesterday. And he took you to Home Depot for paint for that baby girl, right? He might not know he loves you yet. But he does. Mark my words, he does."

Chapter Fifteen

Neo sat at his desk, searching through files on his computer, when Camel's voice came from behind him.

"You find anything on those bastards?"

Neo nearly went through the ceiling, but he managed not to show his reaction. Or at least he hoped he managed it. Camel's stealth game was strong. He thought the dude did it on purpose sometimes, just hoping to make one of them scream in terror. Camel would never sneak if they were armed, but inside HQ was safe enough. Nobody was going to shoot him. And nobody'd get the drop on him either.

"Nothing we don't already know. The Feds seized the land the compound was on and sold it. The big players are still in jail, though it looks like James Dunn's got a new lawyer who's trying to get his conviction thrown out on a technicality."

That had been an unpleasant surprise, but so far nothing had come of it.

"Shit," Camel said as he grabbed a chair and dragged it over to sit beside Neo so he could see the screen. "No way I want to tell Bailey that Dunn might get out."

He wasn't telling Kayla either. Not until he had to. She had enough to worry about without worrying over Dunn too. "I wonder if Ian Black knows?" Neo mused.

"Yeah, I wonder too." Camel scrubbed a hand over his face. "Christ, Bailey and Kayla deserve better than that."

"They do."

"Ella has Ana, right?"

"Yep. And Kayla rode to work with Chloe. The women won't let her out of the salon on her own, and they know to call if Gentry shows up again. Or anyone suspicious."

"I don't like that Ana's involved. Complicates everything."

"Yeah. She can't keep staying with Ella, and we can't farm her out to different babysitters either."

"Bailey can keep her on the days she doesn't have class, but I think Ana going to work with Kayla has to end for a while."

"Agreed." He thought about it for a minute. Kayla might be angry with him for this, but he'd sworn to protect her—so that's what he was going to do. "Ana would be safer in daycare on base," Neo said. "And Kayla would be safer in base housing."

Camel's brows lifted. "There's only one way I know to get that done, Neo. Are you suggesting that you and Kayla need to get married?"

"That's what I'm saying."

Camel pushed a hand over his head and blew out a breath. "Okay, I did not see that one coming. Should I have seen it?"

"Dunno. You're the sniper. You know all about sneaking up on things, so you tell me."

Camel shook his head back and forth slowly. "You didn't say you loved her last night. You said it was intense and emotional. And while Bailey may worry about Kayla like she's twelve instead of twenty-three, I think she's an adult and if she wants to shack up with you, then it's not up to me to stop her. But marriage? That's pretty intense, dude."

"I know it is. But you can't deny that her becoming my dependent would open up a lot of opportunities for her and Ana both. She struggles to pay for Ana's doctor visits. Wouldn't be a problem once we marry. Ana would be covered and we could get her into daycare. Their lives would both be more stable in a family unit."

"I'm not disliking this option, just so you know. But I can't guarantee that Bailey will like it. She likes you, but she loves her sister. And the two of them have been through so much together. She wants the best for Kayla, and she wants her to be happy."

"I'll make her happy. But getting married is the right way to protect them both, and you know it. The sooner, the better."

"What does Kayla think? Or haven't you told her all this yet?"

"She knows and she agrees."

"Gotta admit that I'm surprised you thought of it. I mean marriage. That's a serious step."

There was no reason to tell Camel how it'd really happened. "I know. But it feels right."

"So you love her?"

He hesitated. He didn't know how to label what he felt for Kayla yet. It was more than friendship. More than lust. But how did you know when it was love? "Honestly, I don't know what to call it. But Kayla and Ana are important to me. I want their happiness, and I want them safe from bastards like Dal Gentry and James Dunn."

Camel nodded. "Okay. Good enough for me. Maybe not quite good enough for Bailey, but I'll bring her around. When are you doing this?"

"Tomorrow. Eleven-fifteen at the courthouse. Kayla will have a dependent ID before the day's out."

Camel's eyes narrowed. "How long have you two been planning this?"

"We applied for the license on Monday."

Camel whistled. "Maybe we'd better not tell Bailey that. And hope she doesn't Google how to get married in Maryland." He shook his head. "I could wish that Kayla had come to me after she got the threat last week, but I honestly couldn't come up with a better strategy than this. Bailey might not be thrilled, but it's a solid plan."

"Will you and Bailey come tomorrow? I know Kayla wants her sister there, even if she hasn't told her what's happening yet."

"Yeah, we'll be there. I'll make sure she realizes this is the best solution."

"What's the best solution?" Adam "Blade" Garrison asked.

Camel jerked his chin toward Neo. "Neo here's getting married to Bailey's little sister."

Blade's expression said it all. "No shit? Congrats, dude. When's the big day?"

"Uh, tomorrow."

"Tomorrow? Whoa. Why wasn't I invited?"

"Invited to what?" Dirty asked as he strolled over to see what they were discussing.

Neo sighed. Then he stood up and called out, "Attention, SEALs."

All eyes focused on him.

"I'm marrying Kayla Jones tomorrow at the courthouse at eleven-fifteen."

Everybody started talking at once. Neo whistled to quiet them down. Then he continued.

"We needed to do it quick because of the danger to her and Ana, so that's why no traditional wedding or plans for inviting everyone. Though Kayla's idea of a real wedding involves Money and Ella's view of the Chesapeake and dress uniforms, just so you know.

Maybe we'll have a ceremony later on when everything calms down, but for now we're going to the courthouse. Now you know."

Dirty clapped him on the shoulder. "Man, I knew you'd take the plunge someday. Just didn't expect you to do it before I did. Congrats."

Everyone came over to shake his hand. Money grinned. "You know you can have a ceremony at mine and Ella's place whenever you want."

"Thanks. I know Kayla will appreciate that. She really loves your view."

Money leaned toward him, voice pitched only for his ears. "I don't know what's going on with you and Kayla, if you're in love or what, but I married Ella to protect her—and look how that turned out. The big L, man." Money mimed getting stabbed in the heart. "She got me when I didn't even know I could be got. That's how it goes. I really hope that's how it goes for you too. If it hasn't already, I mean."

"Thanks, Money."

"Anytime, dude."

Alex "Ghost" Bishop, recently promoted from lieutenant colonel to full-bird, strode into the room. Everyone snapped to attention. "At ease, men. What's going on? I heard the cheering at the other end of the hall."

"Neo's getting married tomorrow, sir," Dane "Viking" Erikson said. "He just sprung it on us."

Ghost's eyebrows lifted. "Congrats, sailor," he said as he offered a hand.

Neo shook it. The colonel had a firm grip. Neo didn't know the colonel's whole story, but if it was anything like General Mendez's—also recently promoted—there were depths to the man they'd never know. Surprising depths, probably.

"Thank you, sir."

"I can only assume this decision happened fast since you haven't informed command of the impending change in your status."

"Yes, sir." He'd known he was going to have to tell them, but he hadn't gotten around to it yet. Too many other things to worry about right now.

Ghost's gaze slid over the room. "I'm also assuming something out of the ordinary is going on that's made this wedding a priority. Care to tell me what it is?"

Neo didn't really think it was a request. And he didn't have anything to hide, either. He explained, with help from Camel, about Kayla and the threat from Dal Gentry and the remnants of the motorcycle club.

Ghost was frowning when they finished. "HOT can't go after a scumbag for making a threat, but if you boys happen to make yourselves busy finding out where the Kings of Doom are trying to set up operations this time, I won't stop you. Keep me informed of any new developments."

"Sir, yes, sir," Neo replied.

"Carry on, men," Ghost said.

After he was gone, Viking grinned. "You heard

the man. Let's start tracking down Dal Gentry and find out where he's living and who's with him on this one. And let's get the security camera footage from the salon and the street outside. Maybe we can get a plate number."

Blade and Money didn't move as the others walked away. They looked at each other, then at Neo.

"You know Ella and Quinn set up a foundation to help women recover from abusive relationships, right?" Money asked.

"Yeah, I know," Neo said. Both women had inherited fortunes, though you'd never know it to hang out with them. Both were down to earth, kind, and giving.

"Either one of them would give Kayla the money to pay off Gentry," Blade added. "I think you know that too."

Neo's throat was tight. He loved these guys. "Yeah, but you know it won't be enough. You know he'd keep coming back for more. If he got the idea he could use her like an ATM, he'd do it. She'd never be free and neither would Ana. I can't let that happen."

Blade put a hand on his shoulder. "Understood. I know what Ghost said, but you know we'll do what it takes to stop those bastards from hurting Kayla and Ana. I got no problem doing some off duty asskicking."

"Me neither," Money said.

"Thanks, guys. I appreciate it more than I can say."

"You know," Blade said, turning back once he'd

taken a couple of steps, "I could get the cash from Quinn and we could put a tracking device in the bag. Might be a good way to make Gentry come out from under his rock if we don't track him down before the deadline."

Neo hadn't thought of that. Mostly because he'd never ask either of these guys—his brothers—for that kind of dough. "That could work. If we don't find him, I'd be willing to try it."

"Let me know," Blade said.

"Hey, you trained killers getting to work or what?" Dirty called out. "We've got some biker assholes to find."

"Copy that," Blade replied with a wink.

"Hold onto your shorts," Money drawled. "We got this."

Neo sucked in a breath as he watched his team-mates grab computer terminals and get to work. His eyes pricked and he blinked in surprise. What the hell was what? Tears? He shook his head to clear them. No fucking way was he crying over these guys and their help.

But, damn, *this* was what it meant to be a family. He wanted to give that feeling to Kayla. She'd spent her entire life believing that relationships weren't permanent and life was meant to be complicated and unpredictable. He didn't know what the future held for them, but he knew he was going to do everything he could to make her smile every day they were together.

She needed that in her life. And she deserved it.

———

AT ELEVEN O'CLOCK ON FRIDAY, Kayla and Zach stood in front of the courthouse and waited for Alexei and Bailey to arrive. Ana was staying with Ella McQuaid again today. Zach had wanted to bring her at first, and Kayla loved him for it, but they'd ultimately decided it would be easier to do things without her since they had to go to the base after the ceremony and fill out paperwork.

Kayla worried the inside of her lip, but Zach had a firm grip on her hand that kept her grounded. She hadn't seen Bailey since she'd called her sister last night and told her about the wedding, but Kayla couldn't forget the long silence on the other end of the phone as her sister processed everything.

"Are you sure this is the right thing, Kay-Kay?" she'd finally asked.

"Yes," she'd said with a confidence she didn't quite feel. Not because she didn't want to marry Zach —because she did—but because it wasn't a wedding that was happening for any of the usual reasons. "I love him, Bale. I want to marry him."

So much it scared her. And now they were here, about to walk inside and say vows that legally bound them together. *For better or for worse....*

"You okay?" Zach asked.

She glanced up into his handsome face and her heart squeezed. "Yes. You?"

"I'm fine. They'll be here, Kayla."

"I know. I can't help but feel like Bailey doesn't approve. I hated that we had to tell her about Dal Gentry."

But at least Bailey hadn't gone into disaster mode over it. Kayla couldn't help but think that had everything to do with Zach's involvement.

He squeezed her hand. "I know you wanted her to get through her wedding first, but it's just not possible any longer. She needed to know what the danger was."

A minute later, Alexei and Bailey came striding up the sidewalk. Bailey was wearing a cotton summer dress and looked vibrant and happy, her head thrown back to laugh at something Alexei said to her. He stopped and tugged her into his arms, kissing her thoroughly, and then dragged her toward them while she laughed some more.

Kayla felt like she'd been launched into an alternative reality as the woman approaching them smiled broadly and threw her arms around Kayla. Where was the worrier and planner she knew so well?

"Honey, you look fabulous! Did Chloe do your hair?"

"Um, yes," she said, squeezing her sister gratefully.

Kayla's hair was a mass of fat spiral curls that flowed over her shoulders. She'd chosen to wear a simple sheath dress in a creamy white color with little blue flowers sprinkled over the fabric. She even had a small bouquet clutched in one hand because Zach had brought it for her.

Bailey stepped back, still smiling. "You are so beautiful, baby girl."

"So are you, Bale," Kayla said, her throat closing up with so many emotions.

Alexei produced a tissue. Bailey dabbed at her eyes. "Sorry. My little sissy is getting married. I can't help myself."

Kayla glanced at Zach, who was exchanging knowing looks with Alexei. Kayla didn't know how Alexei had done it, but Bailey wasn't behaving quite the way Kayla had expected. She'd expected a modicum of worry at the minimum. What she got was a laughing, emotional, teary Bailey instead.

"Are you okay, Bale?"

Bailey sniffled. "Of course I am. I mean I didn't expect this on top of you moving out, and I know there are reasons and etcetera, but I'm still happy for you because I know—*I know*—that Zach will take care of you. He loves you and you love him and that's what matters. Isn't that right?"

"Of course it is," Kayla said.

Bailey looked at Zach expectantly and Kayla experienced a moment of apprehension. But Zach never hesitated.

"That's right, Bailey. Love is what matters most."

He lifted Kayla's hand and kissed the back of it,

and shivers of pleasure rippled down her spine. But doubt wasn't far behind. He didn't say he loved her, just that love was what mattered most. A subtle difference, but a huge one in terms of how it made her feel. Her heart pounded and her belly twisted, but she didn't have time to dwell on what he said or what it meant when they were about to step inside and be legally bound together.

She'd do that later. Obsessively, no doubt.

"You ready, beautiful?" he asked her, and she lifted her gaze to his, struck as always by the warmth and the utter confidence in those green depths.

"I'm ready."

Zach smiled "Me too. Let's get married."

Chapter Sixteen

———————

"I WANTED TO GET YOU A DIAMOND," NEO SAID IN Kayla's ear as they sat together in Dirty and Chloe's living room while the SEALs and their ladies gathered for an impromptu reception. "But I thought you'd want to pick it out."

Kayla glanced down at the small band on her ring finger. "Honestly, I didn't even expect this. I didn't think of rings. I don't know why."

He stroked her cheek and tucked a lock of hair behind her ear. She hadn't thought of rings because she was accustomed to living her life in disaster mode, expecting little and fearing it would all be taken away if she got too comfortable. He noticed she'd been a little wistful since the ceremony today. Or maybe he was wrong about that and she was just overwhelmed. There'd been a whirlwind of appointments on the base afterwards so they could complete the process of making her and Ana his dependents, and she was probably tired on top of everything.

"It's only silver, because I didn't know if you'd want gold or platinum for your diamond. I didn't want to commit to something you might not like."

She smiled softly. "It's perfect."

She put her fingers around the ring on his hand. He was still getting used to it, but it wasn't as weird as he'd thought it might be.

"I'm really touched you thought of it," she said. "Thank you."

"You're welcome, beautiful."

She leaned into him, and he put his arm around her. He liked that she trusted him enough to do so.

"I wish we could go home and watch television together. I didn't expect a party."

"I didn't either. But we couldn't say no after we sprung getting married on everyone."

"You're right, we couldn't. Besides, there's Chloe's cooking to consider. I know you love her food."

His stomach didn't rumble, but it perked up at the thought of food. "Yeah, she's got that Southern stuff down. It's pretty awesome."

"You know, you should have asked me if I could cook before you said yes to my proposal. You might not like the answer."

"Nah, doesn't matter to me. I can cook some stuff, nothing like Chloe can though. Besides, we can eat out or we can learn to make what we like."

She leaned back to look up at him. Around them, the room buzzed with talk and laughter. Nobody intruded on their conversation though. Bailey shot them glances from time to time, but she seemed happy enough.

"We? You mean we'll cook together?"

He shrugged. "Why not?"

"I guess I thought you might expect dinner on the table when you got home. That kind of thing."

Neo shook his head. "Kayla, baby, shouldn't we have talked about this before we got married?"

He said it with a laugh and she relaxed against him again.

"Probably," she said. "I think there are a lot of things we didn't talk about. Important things like if the toilet paper goes under or over. However will we manage?"

He snorted. "I think we'll figure it out. For the record, I don't care which way the paper goes."

She looked at him in mock horror. "Zach, for the love of God, it's *over*. Always."

He shrugged. "Fine. Over. Got it. Anything else?"

"I'll have to let you know."

He ran his fingers up her arm, enjoying the fact he got to touch her like this. Openly. Freely. No more hiding his interest or denying it.

"I wish I'd met you a long time ago," she said so quietly he almost didn't hear her. "I wish you were Ana's father."

He didn't quite know how to process the wave of emotion that assailed him then. It was sweet and profound and it touched him deeply. Fiercely.

"I am now," he said, and meant it more than he'd ever meant anything.

"Dinner's ready," Dirty called out. "Come eat!"

———

KAYLA WAS OVERWHELMED. Chloe had cooked some sort of delicious casserole with chicken and dressing and cheese that was to die for. She also made a beautiful lemon cake with a sugar glaze that followed up the meal perfectly. There was champagne and wine and coffee, and everyone ate on real china plates at Chloe's dining room table and another table she'd had Ryan set up in the living room. Kayla had no idea how she made it work, but she seated everyone and performed her hostess duties flawlessly. Chloe had the kind of grace and class that Kayla aspired to.

When Ella and Money arrived with Ana shortly after everyone was seated, Kayla got up and took her baby, fussing over her sweet little daughter who hugged her neck and babbled happily. Chloe had made a little portion of the casserole for Ana where she left out some of the chewier things. Zach had brought Ana's high chair across the street earlier, and Kayla put her in it. She was between Kayla and Bailey, and they both took turns feeding her.

There were speeches, toasts, and a lot of laughter. Kayla didn't know what to say, but Zach did. Everything he did was so natural. No one looking at them could suspect that up until a week ago they hadn't actually been speaking to one another much. He made it seem like they'd always known they were meant to be together.

She appreciated that he did that even if everyone in attendance knew about the threats she'd gotten. His team members had to know that getting married was part of the plan to protect her and Ana, but no one listening to him would ever doubt their feelings for each other.

Kayla caught herself dreaming about what life with him was going to be like before dragging herself firmly back to the present. Because she didn't really know, no matter what she longed for. She knew she loved him so much it hurt, and she knew she wanted them to be a family like he said they were.

She wanted him to be there for Ana as she grew up. Wanted him to do the things that daddies were supposed to do, like bandage their little girl's boo-boos and take them fishing and tell them bedtime stories and all the other things she'd never had. She wanted it so badly for Ana, and she wanted it with this man.

But always, *always,* she had that stupid voice in her head telling her not to get too comfortable, not to blindly count on him, not to give up her vigilance. She had to be ready to act. To take her daughter and go, if that's what was necessary.

She hated that she felt like that, but life had never shown her any different. People abandoned you, either mentally or physically, and you had to take care of yourself. She trusted Zach as much as she could, but she would also be ready for disappointment.

By the time the evening was done, Kayla found herself alone with Zach as they walked across the street. Bailey and Alexei had insisted on taking Ana for the night, to give her and Zach some time alone. She had mixed emotions about that, mostly because she didn't know how to behave with him tonight. Which was stupid because the only thing that had changed was they'd gotten married. They'd been living together for two days now, and he'd slept beside her all night long both nights even though they hadn't made love. She knew he'd do it again tonight if that's what she wanted from him.

The neighborhood was quiet, at least compared to the raucous time at their impromptu reception. She could hear the frogs croaking in the pond, and a dog barked in a yard. Someone laughed and voices floated to them on the night. Happy voices enjoying a Friday night together.

Zach held her hand. He didn't take her to the side door, however. He went up the front steps and unlocked the door. Then he turned to her.

"You know I have to do this the right way, don't you?"

Kayla tilted her head. "What are you talking about?"

Before she knew what he was doing, he scooped her up. She wrapped her arms around his neck with a little squeak. Then she laughed. "The threshold. I didn't think about it."

Zach nuzzled the sensitive skin of her throat. He had a little bit of stubble and it scraped deliciously along her nerve endings. "You forgot a few things to do with getting married, didn't you?"

He said it teasingly, and she laughed. "Rings and being carried over the threshold are only *two* things, Zach."

"Fine, two things."

He carried her inside, but he didn't set her down. He shut and locked the door, then carried her into the master bedroom and set her down carefully. Kayla gasped as she took in the room. The bed was different, and someone had lit candles and sprinkled rose petals on the sheets. The soft scent of flowers hung in the air, and a scarf draped over each lamp shade to diffuse the light.

"Is that *your* bed?" She was pretty certain it was, though she'd only been in it once and that was over two months ago.

"Yeah. Blade, Money, and Dirty swapped the beds earlier. Since Ana's room is up here, it made the most sense. I didn't tell them not to because it needed to happen at some point anyway."

That was certainly true. She hadn't expected him to stay in the basement. Hadn't wanted him to either.

Especially not after the past two nights beside him. His presence comforted her, made her feel safe.

His hands slid along her hips, brought her gently to him. He dropped his mouth to hers and kissed her lightly.

"I can think of something else that happens after you get married, Kayla. Do you know what it is?"

She nipped at his bottom lip, her heart hammering. Her body was already preparing itself, her limbs loosening, her pussy growing hot and wet. "You mean the wedding night?"

"Yeah, that's it. But I told you I wouldn't push you, and I mean that. I didn't ask Camel and Bailey to take Ana, by the way. And I didn't ask Chloe and Dirty to put rose petals on the bed or anything. I mean it's romantic and I would've if I'd thought of it. But I didn't."

She looped her arms loosely around his neck. She liked the way he held her. How big and strong he was, and how small and safe she felt in his arms. She liked how honest he was, too.

"It *is* romantic, and I like it very much."

His forehead pressed to hers as they kind of swayed together, bodies making delicate contact, excitement heightening with every brush of fabric against fabric. The swell of his growing erection excited her, created a buzzing in her veins.

"Nothing needs to change tonight, baby. We don't have to rush a thing. I want you, but I can wait until you're ready."

Her heart skipped and her belly dipped. She loved that he would wait for her. But she didn't want to wait any longer. "Kiss me, Zach. Please."

"What kind of kiss, beautiful? I need to know. If it's a sweet kiss and then we go watch a show or two, that's fine. But if you want the kind of kiss that turns into more, I need to know that too."

Kayla didn't have to think about it. They'd gotten married today, and they were alone tonight. They weren't strangers in bed, even if they'd only been together once.

She didn't know what would happen tomorrow, but tonight she wanted this. She wanted *him*.

"I expect a wedding night, Zach. The usual kind, where we have lots of sex and fall asleep together."

He let out a breath. "Damn, I didn't expect you to say that. I'm fucking over the moon that you did, but it's not what I thought you'd say."

Kayla's pulse thrummed as she slipped out of his arms and turned around, pulling her hair over her shoulder and baring the back of her dress as she watched his face. "Can you unzip me?"

"I'm dreaming," he said, his voice low and thick, and then he seemed to snap out of it, grasping her zipper and tugging it slowly down. He bent to kiss her bared shoulders, then made his way down her spine as he pulled. When he got to the bottom, right above her tailbone, he pressed a kiss into the small of her back where her tattoo was, his mouth warm and wet as he slid his tongue over her skin.

Kayla whimpered.

Zach stood and peeled the dress apart, let it slip down her body. But he didn't let it fall into a wad at her feet. Instead, he held it up as his mouth found her shoulder.

What was he waiting for? Her body was electric. She was already wet, her clit throbbing with arousal. She wanted him to go faster, and she also didn't because she wanted to enjoy every moment.

"Step out of the dress," he said in her ear. "I'll lay it over the chair so it doesn't wrinkle."

She did as he told her. He was back, behind her again, his big hands coming around her body to cup her breasts. He turned them, and she started at the sight of the two of them in the mirror that hung above the dresser. She was small and pale and Zach was big, sun-darkened, his body dwarfing hers.

Her bra was white, lacy, and his hands stood out in stark contrast against the fabric.

"You're so beautiful, Kayla."

She shuddered. "So are you."

His eyes met hers in the mirror. "I have a pretty face. You have a pretty soul."

His words pierced her. "I don't know about that," she whispered, her throat tight. Had anyone ever said such a thing to her before?

He tugged the cups of her bra down, baring her breasts. The fabric bunched beneath them, making them thrust up high. Her nipples tightened, pebbling into points that Zach pinched between his fingers.

Little lightning bolts of pleasure ricocheted through her body.

"It's the truth. You're sweet and beautiful, and you love your child with your whole heart. You had a shitty childhood, but you're determined Ana won't. You love your sister and you're determined not to disrupt her life if you can help it. Those things add up to a pretty soul in my book."

"I could say the same about you," she whispered. "I've seen you put others first. You're doing it now, with me and Ana."

He didn't answer. Instead, he dropped his mouth to her throat and she tilted her head to the side to give him better access. Her eyelids fluttered closed as he licked her skin. Her body was a wire strung almost to the breaking point. She moaned softly as his long fingers pinched and tugged her nipples, heightening their sensitivity.

He kept one hand on her breast and slid the other down her abdomen, into the top of her panties. Kayla put a hand behind her and clutched his head. Then she opened her eyes to watch in the mirror as his hand dropped lower, disappearing beneath her waistband.

When he stroked lower still, his finger brushing her sensitive clit, she gasped.

"Part your legs for me," he told her.

She did, just enough so he could slide into her wet heat, his fingers stroking and teasing relentlessly.

"You're so wet, Kayla. I want to be inside you so bad."

"Then do it. Please. I want you, Zach. I don't want to wait anymore."

Chapter Seventeen

KAYLA HAD THOUGHT HE MIGHT PUSH HER TO THE bed, strip off his clothes, and slide into her, giving her what she craved. But he didn't seem in any hurry to do so—and he didn't stop stroking her pussy as he unsnapped her bra.

"Take it off," he commanded, his voice dark and delicious.

Kayla did as he ordered, letting the bra drop to the floor. Zach pushed her panties down her hips. His fingers came back to her clit, strumming slowly, and then he inserted one finger inside her as she whimpered.

"We haven't talked about how we're doing this," he rumbled in her ear.

Kayla blinked. "How? I thought you knew how it worked, Zach."

He chuckled. "That's not what I meant. I'm

talking about safe sex. I've been tested—and I haven't been with anyone since the last time I was with you."

Her heart ached with a rush of love. *Don't read too much into that, Kay-Kay. He's a SEAL and he's busy....*

She met his eyes in the mirror. "You haven't?"

"No, I haven't."

"I haven't either. I'm still on birth control, same as before."

"We used a condom that night. I don't mind using one if it makes you more comfortable."

Kayla turned in his arms. He didn't stop her. He was still fully dressed and she tugged his shirt from his jeans so she could touch hot, bare skin.

"I don't want to use a condom unless you do. I'll understand if you're worried about my birth control failing."

"Should I be?"

"I'm not. But, honestly, no method is one-hundred percent guaranteed—except sterilization, I suppose."

"I think that's a little extreme, don't you?"

"Not if you don't want kids."

"I don't necessarily want more right now, but I wouldn't freak out either."

He had no idea how those words made her feel. The idea of a baby with Zach didn't freak her out at all. And he'd said he didn't want *more* kids right now, which meant he thought of Ana as his too. She loved that about him. He had no idea how much.

"I really don't think I'm one of those women who

fall pregnant at the drop of a hat. Ana didn't happen the first time James and I were careless."

He stroked his fingers down her sides, then cupped her breasts. "Let's not talk about your ex right now. I don't want anything ruining this experience for you."

There he went thinking about her again. Her feelings. Her pleasure. Her experience.

"He can't ruin it for me, but you're right. I don't want to talk about him either. I want to be with you."

"That's what I want too."

Zach bent and sucked her nipples. Kayla clung to him, her head thrown back, her palms pressed to his bare skin beneath his shirt. He licked and sucked and her pussy grew so wet she could feel the trickle of her juices on the insides of her legs.

He straightened and ripped his shirt off but didn't move to take off the jeans he'd changed into after they'd gotten back earlier. He'd dropped her at Chloe's door when she'd said she was fine in her dress, but he'd wanted to get out of his uniform. She'd understood even if she loved seeing him in military camouflage.

He kissed her, a hot, wet, sensual kiss that had her clinging to him once more as her legs turned into noodles.

"I want to be inside you, Kayla. But I want to lick you even more. Get on the bed, beautiful."

Kayla did as he told her, leaning back on her elbows and spreading her legs to show a little bit of slick pink skin. His gaze fixed on her sex as he flicked open the button of his jeans. Once he'd unzipped them, he pushed the fabric down his hips until his cock sprang free.

Kayla made a sound in her throat. Zach's gaze met hers. He wrapped his hand around his cock and stroked it, and heat flared in Kayla's brain. She made a move toward him, but he stopped her with a soft growl. Then he was on his knees at the side of the bed. He gripped her hips and dragged her to the edge.

"I've been waiting for this to happen again for two months," he told her as he pushed her legs open. "It was worth every second."

Her heart hammered. "You can't know that yet. We haven't done anything."

His eyes gleamed. "I know, Kayla. Believe me."

Kayla gasped and fell back against the mattress as he took a long swipe up from her slit to her clit. He gently pushed open her folds with his thumbs, then flicked his tongue against her clit again and again.

She had to moan. She couldn't stop it, even if the sound embarrassed her.

But Zach didn't seem to mind. He put a finger inside her and worked it in and out slowly, heightening the tension. Kayla's body was electric, the hum inside her growing more intense with every swipe of his tongue and press of his finger.

She knew what was going to happen, wanted it badly and yet she wanted to make herself wait too.

She didn't want to come too fast, didn't want that initial buildup to be over—but she really didn't have any control over it.

He did.

Zack sucked her clit between his lips and she exploded in a gasping, moaning mess. He kept sucking, fucking her faster with his fingers and drawing out her pleasure, until she finally pushed at his shoulders and begged him to stop.

Thankfully, he did—and she promptly burst into tears. She felt more then saw him go still.

"Sorry," she said between sobs, "I'm not sad or hurt or anything. Really."

Zach climbed into bed and drew her body against his, her back to his front, nuzzling her neck and whispering to her. "You're so beautiful, Kayla. I love making you come. I'm sorry I upset you. Tell me what I did and I won't do it again."

She still twitched with the aftershocks of her orgasm. Love, sharp and hot and intense, swelled inside her and made her ache. She wanted to tell him, and yet she couldn't make the words come. It felt too risky. Like throwing down her weapons and striding out on the field of battle without any way to protect herself from a stray arrow.

"I'm not upset, Zach."

"You're not?"

She shook her head, her tears lessening as her riotous emotions subsided. Now she really was embarrassed. Heat stained her cheeks and she wanted to crawl beneath the covers and hide. What kind of idiot had an orgasm given to her by a sexy, amazing man—a man she loved—and then started to cry?

"I'm sorry," she whispered. "It's stupid."

He turned her toward him. She resisted, but he didn't let her stop him. His green gaze radiated concern as he studied her face. He wiped her tears away.

"You can tell me, Kayla."

She sniffled again and closed her eyes for a moment. "I know." It took another second before she could speak. "I'm emotional, that's all. You're so good to me, and I know how lucky I am to be your wife. God, that's weird to say," she finished on a watery laugh. "Wife, I mean."

It was more than that, but there were things she couldn't say to him yet. It was love and happiness and hope all wound into a ball, and it was fear and doubt and worry poking at the surface and trying to find a weak spot so they could wriggle in and tarnish the brightness.

He smiled. "It's weird for me too. But we'll get used to it. So... you want to go watch something? I'll get you a glass of wine and let you choose the show. And it's not even Monday."

Kayla blinked. "You would do that? Now?"

"Yeah, I would. I'm a grown man, Kayla, not a hormonal teenager. I can delay gratification if I have to."

Kayla put her hand between them, found him hot

and hard and ready. She heard the intake of his breath, and it made her sizzle anew.

"I don't want to delay anything, Zach. I want more of you. I want *all* of you."

———

THANK GOD.

He'd have dragged his sorry ass from this bed and put his clothes back on, and he'd have sat on that couch with her and watched whatever damned thing she wanted to watch, but he wouldn't have been satisfied. He wouldn't have let her know it, of course.

When she'd started to cry, he'd had a moment of bewilderment when he hadn't known what he could have done to cause it. But then his SEAL training kicked in and told him to treat her with calm efficiency. To soothe her and get her to tell him what the problem was so he could solve it.

Solving problems was what he did, after all.

He ran his palm down her side, over her hip, and drew her leg up and over his thigh. "I'd be happy to lick this sweet pussy again," he told her, skimming his fingers over her clit so that she gasped and moaned a little. "I didn't get enough the first time."

"Oh, I want that so much. But I want you inside me even more."

"Then you'll get both, honey."

He pushed her legs open and dropped down until his face was even with her slick, hot flesh. She was so damned pretty. He loved the sight of her glistening folds, the trim blond hair of her mound, her smooth abdomen with its little bit of roundness and barely noticeable stretch marks, the way her creamy flesh rose into two pretty peaks crested by tight little nipples that he wanted to suck on some more.

When Neo touched his tongue to her pussy, her back bowed off the bed. "Yesssss," she hissed out as he found his rhythm again.

He fucked her with tongue and fingers, sucked her hard little clit, flicked and licked and even nibbled a little bit. He loved the taste of her, could eat her like this for hours. But it was over quickly as she cried out, squeezing her eyes shut, her body twitching like an electric current flowed through it.

Neo kissed his way up her body to her mouth, then thrust his tongue between her lips as he hovered over her, not quite sure how he wanted to proceed. Missionary? A little doggy style? Let her ride him while he watched her tits bounce?

What decided it for him was the way she wrapped her arms and legs around him and kissed him back with all the passion and longing he could desire. It didn't take much to settle between her legs, even less to position his cock and slide into her body.

He took his time in case he hurt her, but she was so wet that it wasn't a problem at all.

"God you feel amazing," he said when he was all the way in. The one time they'd been together, it had been with a condom. But this? Being inside her bare?

Heaven.

He couldn't remember the last time he'd gone bare. Not since he was a stupid, horny teenager who'd been lucky enough not to get his girlfriend pregnant before he'd left to join the Navy.

"So do you," she said softly.

He took her mouth in a kiss and started to move with slow thrusts, getting them both used to the sensations. Kayla ran her hands up his sides, down over his buttocks, over his biceps and shoulders, into his hair. She touched him everywhere, and he loved it.

It'd been two months since he'd had sex with her, and more than that since he'd been with anyone else. He couldn't remember the last woman he'd slept with before Kayla, but he'd never forgotten one moment of the night he'd spent with her.

It didn't take long before things got a little crazy. He slammed into Kayla again and again, and she lifted her hips to meet him every time. Neo tore his mouth from hers and grabbed her ass, lifting her into his thrusts. She groaned.

"Yessss, Zach. Like that. Oh yesssss…."

Her back arched and he dropped his head to her chest, sucking each of her tits in turn as he continued to fuck her harder. She ran her nails lightly down his back, not digging or trying to draw blood, but scraping sensuously across his skin.

"Fuck, Kayla. I want you to come again. Soon, because I don't know how much longer I can last."

Her eyes fixed on his, their pretty hazel depths

glazed with pleasure. "I'm going to come. Soon—oh!" She bit her lower lip between her teeth and arched up to him again. Her breasts bounced with every thrust, her slick heat gloved him snugly, and he'd never felt so possessive of a woman in his life.

His wife.

Wife.

Jesus, what a head trip that was. He'd married her. To protect her and Ana—and maybe even so nobody else would have the right to do this to her.

She was *his*. He was the one who got to fuck her, nobody else. As often as she'd let him. Was it crazy to marry a woman at least in part because you wanted her legs wrapped around you while you lost yourself deep inside her?

"Come for me, beautiful. Come hard. Let me feel you."

Her body vibrated around him as her orgasm hit. She stiffened and then shook all over, crying out so sweetly that he had to kiss her and taste her pleasure. Her pussy gloved him tight and he kept stroking— harder, faster, dragging out her pleasure but also finding his.

His balls tightened to the point of pain—and then his release shot through him. He poured himself into her, groaning as he tingled from balls to toes to the top of his head. Kayla's eyes were still squeezed shut as she kept coming. He ground himself against her and she whimpered before subsiding. Her eyes eventually drifted open and she smiled.

"Wow."

He laughed a little. "Yeah, wow."

His dick twitched inside her and the walls of her pussy tightened around him again and again. It was almost too much sensation, but he stayed where he was and rode it out.

"You okay?" he asked.

Her eyeliner had smudged beneath her eyes, making her look sleepy and bed-rumpled. He liked it. "Yes. You?"

"Honey, I couldn't be better if I'd won the Powerball."

Kayla snickered. "You can't be suggesting sex is better than money."

He kissed the tip of her nose. "When it's sex with you I can."

Her lashes dropped, hiding her eyes from him. When she lifted them again, her eyes were a little glassy. "You say the sweetest things to me."

"I wouldn't say it if I didn't mean it."

"I think I believe you."

"I plan to make sure you do," he said very seriously.

She smiled and stretched, wrapping her arms around him lazily. "I could get used to this. Great sex with a handsome SEAL? Yes, please."

"Good thing, because I'm more than ready to give it to you."

He kissed her, their mouths melding hotly. The kiss went on for a long time, deep, wet, thorough. He didn't know why, but he was seized with a need to make her his. To brand her and let her know that she belonged to him. And he supposed that meant he belonged to her as well.

Why not? He didn't mind the belonging. He kinda understood where his teammates were coming from now. It was comforting to have someone you cared about, who cared for you too.

And he not only had Kayla, he had Ana. He was a dad now. He was gonna be the best damned dad ever.

When he broke the kiss, they were both breathing hard. His dick had swelled again, and Kayla was moving beneath him.

"You want to come again?" he asked.

"Don't you?"

"Oh yeah."

He rolled them over until she was on top. "Ride me, beautiful. I want to watch you."

She did, and it was the sexiest thing he'd seen in ages. When it was over, when they were wrung out and satisfied, they fell asleep in a tangle of bodies. They were both up at six—late for him, actually—but before they could get out of bed to start the day, Kayla reached for his cock.

It didn't take long before Neo had her on her hands and knees, taking her from behind while he pinched her nipples and slammed into her over and over. He loved watching his dick disappear in her slick heat, loved the sounds they made together too. She came crying his name, and he lost his load soon after, his hands on her hips as he held her to him and thrust deep into her pussy.

When it was over, he carried her to the shower where they explored each other again. Leisurely this time, with no thought of coming. But of course he couldn't stop from dropping to his knees and licking her into another orgasm.

"God, Zach, I'm not going to be able to walk," she said when they got out of the shower and she had to grip the counter to steady herself.

"And that's a bad thing how?"

She shot him a saucy look. "I'm not saying it's bad, but people are going to wonder."

"Not they aren't. We're newlyweds. We're supposed to be fucking like bunnies."

She grinned stupidly. "We are, aren't we? Mission accomplished."

He laughed. "Oh, I think we can do more. But maybe coffee and breakfast first."

"To keep up our strength."

"Yeah."

She went into the closet and retrieved a maxi skirt and a tank top. They hadn't had a lot of time to bring her things over yet, but they'd gotten some of it, mostly Ana's stuff. She dressed quickly while he tugged on shorts and a T-shirt. He loved watching her, loved the graceful way she moved as she put on her clothes and then brushed her hair before she flipped it over her shoulders.

"Hey, you want to shop for Ana's room today?" he asked.

She spun to look at him. "Really? You want to do that today?"

He shrugged. "Sure. Why not? We can go hit up the baby store, or we can shop online. Up to you."

Her smile was tremulous. "I'd love to shop for her room. Thank you. I've been looking online so I know what I like, but maybe we could look in person too? Compare things?"

It was so easy to make her happy. He loved doing it. "Whatever you want, beautiful. I want you to be happy."

"I am happy, Zach. So much. You have no idea."

"I think I have some idea. But you can show me later if you really want."

Her smile was mischievous and sexy. "Oh, you can count on that. I can think of several things I still want to try with you…."

Chapter Eighteen

KAYLA FOUND HERSELF LOOKING AT HER HAND several times while they shopped. It was just a silver wedding band, but she loved the way it looked on her finger. After she looked at her hand, she looked at Zach's. He was wearing a wider band on his ring finger, and it made a hot feeling swirl in her belly each time she saw it.

They were married. She was Mrs. Anderson. One week ago exactly, she'd walked into Chloe's back yard and hadn't known how to talk to him. It wasn't until she'd screwed up her courage and went to see him later that night that things had changed.

From barely speaking to married. In one week. Had to be some kind of record, right?

"What about this one?" Zach asked, and Kayla dragged herself back to the present.

He was standing in front of a white convertible

crib with a gentle scallop shape to the front and back, with evenly spaced wooden slats that weren't too wide or too dangerous. Eventually, the sides of the crib would come off and it could be a perfect white bed for a little girl. Kayla could hang a net over it for a princess effect when Ana was older.

"It's pretty."

Zach looked at the price tag. "It's not too bad. Do you want it?"

It was the prettiest one they'd seen yet. She'd seen similar on the web, though. "I think we could get it cheaper online."

"Maybe. But you'd have to wait for it to be shipped. We could have this one at home today. I can put it together and Ana can sleep in it tonight."

She loved the idea so much. But it felt wrong to let him buy everything. He must have sensed the direction of her thoughts because he frowned at her.

"Kayla, I want to do this. Let me get the baby furniture and you can create the room you want for Ana."

"I really didn't marry you so you'd pay for everything. I don't want you to think I expect it."

He came over and put his hands on her shoulders, rubbed up and down her arms. "Baby, I don't think you expect anything of the sort. But we're married now, and that means I get more money in my paycheck for you and Ana. The military knows it costs more for three people to live than one, so shouldn't I spend that money on both of you instead of me?"

Her throat ached suddenly. "I guess so."

"That's right, beautiful. I should and I will. Besides, you can show your appreciation later."

She arched an eyebrow. "Is there a particular way you want to be appreciated?"

He leaned closer, his lips brushing her ear. "Definitely. I prefer you to do it when you're naked, and it needs to involve my dick deep inside you. Aside from that, I'm open."

She blushed and laughed at the same time. "You've got sex on the brain, Zach."

"Don't you?"

A twinge of longing echoed through her. "Maybe."

"Then let's get this crib with the matching dresser and changing table. The sooner I get it put together, the sooner we can get naked."

"Okay, but let's skip the changing table. I don't need it when the dresser has that three-sided top— and I'd rather find something more functional for storage anyway."

"Whatever you say. You're the boss when it comes to baby furniture."

They bought the furniture, plus a sheet set, and loaded everything into the new SUV Zach had traded his car in for a couple of days ago. She hadn't been with him when he did it, but he'd called her from the dealership and described the interior, asking her if it would work. She'd been on the verge of tears as she'd told him he didn't have to do it. He'd said it was no big deal and asked again if the interior would work. It would and it did. Especially now as they loaded it up with baby furniture.

They stopped for something to eat on the way home. Kayla ordered a chicken sandwich while Zach ordered a burger, and they talked about Ana's room and getting the rest of their things over to his house. He planned to apply for base housing on Monday since there'd been no time Friday with all the other paperwork. He said it would take a couple of months or more to get a house. She kind of hated to move now that they'd painted Ana's room—plus having Chloe across the street was nice—but it was also the safest plan while the Kings of Doom were trying to start up again. She didn't know if they'd ever go away, or if she'd ever really be free of them, but being somewhere they didn't have access was a nice start.

It struck her that everything she'd ever wanted was within reach. But the part of her that was used to having the rug yanked from beneath her was still there, still waiting for the other shoe to drop. She loved Zach and there was no going back on that feeling. But he didn't love her. What if he never did?

She told herself it was silly to worry about his feelings for her when they'd been married for all of twenty-four hours. Maybe, with enough time, it would be true.

"I see those storm clouds in your eyes," Zach said softly.

Kayla blinked. How did he always know when she was letting fear and doubt creep into her thoughts?

"I'm fine," she said, taking a quick sip of her water. "Really. It's just a lot of changes in a short amount of time."

"Changes you wanted," he added.

"That's true. I'm happy. I'm not used to being happy. I keep waiting for disaster to strike. It's what always happens. My whole life, whenever we seemed to be settling in somewhere and life was going well, my mom or dad—or both—would fall off the wagon and disappear for a few days. Sometimes longer. And Bailey would be there to pick up the pieces for us. We ate a lot of mac and cheese, and she got us to school every morning. But then our parents would come back and we'd have to move because they couldn't pay the rent or bill collectors were after them. Sometimes we stayed anyway, and then the sheriff showed up to evict us or the bill collectors got so bad that we had to leave in the middle of the night. We didn't have much, but we left a lot behind during those times."

The memories hurt no matter how long ago they were. She didn't want that life for Ana. Not that she would ever do drugs, but the uncertainty of a life where bad people kept coming after you wasn't much better. Marrying Zach was supposed to change it.

Would change it. She believed that.

Zach took her hand in both of his. Cradled it like it was precious. Like she was precious.

"I'm sorry you went through that, Kayla. No kid should have their life turned inside out the way you did. No kid should have parents who don't care. But unfortunately they do. All the time. I can't change what happened to you, and I can't guarantee that disaster won't strike again." He hesitated. "I'm a SEAL, baby. I do dangerous things. It's possible I won't come back one of these days."

She trembled. He must have felt it because he lifted her hand and pressed his lips to the back of it. "That's not the plan," he added. "It's not ever the plan. But it's possible. For all of us. I promise you'll be taken care of though. You married me, but you've officially joined a family. You won't ever be alone again, Kayla. Neither will Ana. It's not just Bailey who'll be there for you, but the entire organization. HOT will be there if I can't be."

It was the first time he'd said the name of those he worked for. But she knew it because of what had happened when they'd gone to rescue Bailey from the Kings of Doom. She'd been told to never mention it, and she hadn't.

"I don't want HOT," she said, her heart throbbing. "I want you."

"And I want you." He smiled. "So we've got each other, and we've got Ana. And if it happens that I don't come back, which I intend to do my best to prevent, then you'll be okay. Nobody's taking your family away from you again, Kayla. Nobody's leaving you to figure out how to survive. I want you to know that. If we're living on base, then you'll have to move out. But you'll have enough money that you don't have to worry about how to pay the bills, okay?"

She hated this conversation. So much. Of course she understood why he was saying it to her, and she appreciated that he wanted her to feel safe. But life without him wasn't anything she wanted to imagine.

"I don't care about the money. I care about you. Please stop talking about what happens if you get killed on a mission."

He studied her for a second. Then he leaned forward and kissed her. "Okay, beautiful. We aren't going to talk about it anymore. I don't want to upset you. This is a good day for us. We've got Ana's furniture and we're going to fix her room. Then we're going to have sex before you call Bailey and ask her if we can get Ana. If Ana falls asleep in her new room, and we aren't exhausted, we're going to have sex again before we crash. Sound like a plan?"

Her heart still pounded with anxiety but she nodded and pasted on a smile. "Sounds like a delicious plan to me. But if it's going to happen, we'd better get that furniture put together."

———

NEO THOUGHT about her reaction to the topic of him not coming back from a mission all the way home. Then he thought about it while he was laying out parts to the crib and getting his battery-powered screwdriver ready to go.

He hadn't been trying to upset her, but considering how much she worried about stability, he'd wanted her to know she'd still have it. HOT would take care of her above and beyond what his military life insurance would provide. She wasn't ever going to have to uproot Ana in the middle of the night and whisk her away somewhere so they could start anew.

Not that he intended to bite the dust. He intended to be around as long as possible, but he also knew the reality of what he did and the possibilities, however remote, of something going wrong.

His phone buzzed and he picked it up from the window sill. Kayla had gone across the street to see Chloe because Chloe had called and said she had something to give them. He'd watched her walk over there and he kept an eye on the street so he could watch her walk back.

It wasn't Kayla though. It was Shade.

"Hey, man. What's up?" he said.

"Just got a call from my contact at the correctional facility."

Neo's neck started to itch. "Yeah? Anything good?"

"Depends on your point of view. James Dunn's had a regular visitor besides his attorney lately. His half-brother Steve, who was also in the Kings MC. Still rides a Harley, still wears the cut. He's probably ferrying messages between Dunn and Gentry. It's entirely possible Dunn is running the whole thing from prison."

"Fuck!" Neo shoved a hand through his hair and stared out the window at Chloe and Dirty's place. "Any news on his hotshot lawyer?"

"You aren't going to like it. He's managed to convince a judge to review the case next week."

Frustration hammered his temples. "It'll still take time to move through the system, but he could be out a lot sooner than we want him to be. He could be using Gentry to put the screws to Kayla now so it can't be connected to him when he's out."

But did Dunn really want money? Or revenge? What he knew of the man told him it could be either —or both.

"It's certainly possible. He's a lowlife according to my contact. He's running scams inside as part of a prison gang. Extortion, drugs, you name it. He sailed in there and took over in record time. If anyone can scam his way out again, it'll be Dunn." Shade blew out a breath. "I know that's not what you wanted to hear, man. I'm just repeating what I was told."

Neo's gut twisted. "We really need to find out where Gentry and his bikers are hanging out."

"We're working on it. You know that. Those fuckers are laying low, though. Money and Blade and I are at work now. Ghost is aware of what we're doing."

Across the street, Kayla stepped outside holding a

239

box. Chloe stood in the door talking to her. It was such a normal scene. Domestic. This was his life now. He didn't mind it. Except for the black cloud that the Kings of Doom created, everything was good.

"I'll come in and help," he said.

"No, stay with your wife. Whoa," Shade said with a laugh. "That sounded weird. Neo's got a wife."

"You're the only one left without a wife or a future wife," Neo replied. "Get used to it."

"Dude, I'm good. I don't need or want a wife. No way."

"That's what we all say," Neo said as Kayla started across the street. Chloe watched her go and didn't step inside again until Neo heard the door open. "I gotta go. Thanks, Shade."

"No problem. I'll let you know if we get anything else."

He put the phone down and got back to work on the crib while he considered everything Shade had said. There wasn't much they could do yet, but knowing that Dunn was involved certainly explained some things.

"How's it going?" Kayla asked as she peeked into the room.

"Great. Just about to starting screwing the parts together."

She stepped in and looked at all the pieces on the floor. "Wow, that's a lot of stuff."

"It is, but I got it handled. Don't worry."

She smiled. "I'm not worried."

"What did Chloe want?" he asked.

"She wanted to give us dinner. I brought home a pan of chicken and dressing. Oh, and she made strawberry pretzel salad for you."

Neo's taste buds started to water. "Damn I love that woman."

Kayla laughed. "So do I. I wish we didn't have to move. I'll miss being first on the list for Chloe's leftovers or new recipe experiments."

"Yeah, me too." That was a major bummer to be sure. Maybe Dirty would bring some to work. No doubt Chloe would continue to entertain and they'd be invited over.

"Maybe we'll get lucky and Dal will go away."

"Maybe so," he said, because it was what she wanted to hear. Even if Gentry went away, which Neo doubted, there was still James Dunn. If that lawyer got Dunn's conviction thrown out, the man could be back on the streets and looking for trouble within weeks. Maybe sooner. Neo didn't intend to tell Kayla about that unless it became a reality. By then, he'd have her and Ana on the base and out of reach.

"What can I do to help?"

"Go get my laptop and bring it in here so you can start shopping that Wayfair place for accessories."

"Oh no, I couldn't do that," she said softly. "I don't have a credit card yet and I can't get one because of my age and work history. I don't have enough stability for anyone to give me credit."

He made a mental note to add her to his credit

241

cards and bank account. He hadn't thought about her not having credit yet, but it made sense. He'd never intended for her to buy the accessories anyway.

"Kayla. Get the computer. You can give me cash if you want, or you can call it a wedding present and leave it at that."

She hesitated. Then she walked over and stooped down where he was kneeling and working on the crib. She put her hands on either side of his face and pressed her mouth to his. It was the lightest of touches, and it ignited a hunger deep in his soul.

"You're too good to me, Zach," she said when she broke the kiss.

He caught her to him when she would have stood and tugged her across his lap. He wasn't letting Dunn or Gentry get to her. He'd kill them both before they did.

"I'm not that good, beautiful. Because that one little kiss and I want to stop what I'm doing and eat your pussy so good you scream. Then I want to fuck you until I explode."

She put her arms around his neck and lifted her face to his. "You don't think I'm going to say no, do you? It won't take long to make me scream, I promise you."

He lifted her and carried her across the hall where they frantically stripped before falling to the bed together. It was crazy how much he wanted her, how much he needed to do this to her. Kayla matched him with her intensity in bed. For all that she seemed somewhat shy most of the time, she wasn't shy when it came to sex with him. He had every intention of pushing her back on the bed and spreading her legs wide, but she stopped him with a suggestion.

"I want to do you too. Let me turn the other way."

He wasn't about to say no, which is how he found himself on his back, Kayla's pussy in his face and her mouth and hands on his dick. Somehow, it turned into a contest about who would come first. Or so he thought because he was determined it would be her while she seemed to be attacking his cock with abandon, her tongue swirling over the head and down the sides before she put him in her mouth and took him as far as she could before doing it all again.

It took everything he had to stop the tingling at the base of his spine from turning into an inferno that raced through him and made him lose control. He licked the slick flesh of Kayla's beautiful pussy, swirling around her clit and pressing two fingers inside to find her G-spot.

More than once, he thought he was going to lose the battle—but then Kayla stiffened, crying out as she continued to stroke him. He'd thought the loss of her mouth would ease the battle, but it didn't. Especially when she licked the head while she was still whimpering from her orgasm.

Neo lost it then. He managed to warn her, but he

didn't know what she did because he nearly blacked out from the blinding pleasure. When he was done, he lay there blinking up at the ceiling and breathing hard.

What the hell?

Kayla rolled over, laughing softly. Her chest was covered with his semen. The sight made him nearly growl with male pride and possessiveness. What was it about marking a woman with cum that turned guys on so much? He didn't know, but damn if he didn't like it.

"I think I'm going to need a shower," she said. "That was amazing."

"Fuck yeah, it was," he agreed. "Shower with a pal?"

She climbed up to the head of the bed and sprawled on top of him, spreading semen on his skin as well. "I think we both need it. I'm a dirty girl and you're a dirty boy."

Fuck, and there was another turn on. Kayla saying the word *dirty*.

"So dirty. We need to get clean."

Her eyes sparkled. "I like getting dirty with you. You make me *want* to get dirty."

"How dirty?"

"*Very* dirty. As dirty as it takes to come like that every time."

He rolled them to the side of the bed. She stood and he followed. The bed was rumpled and the room smelled like sex. He liked it. He took her hand.

"Come on, beautiful. I want to run my soapy hands all over your pretty body."

"What a coincidence. I want to do the same to you."

They stepped into a hot shower together. By the time they got out, the water was running cold.

Chapter Nineteen

KAYLA WAS RELAXED AND HAPPY. HER LIMBS WERE loose and languid, and her heart was glad. She held the back of the crib while Zach screwed the slats down and attached the sides. They'd gotten a little side-tracked with sex and showering—and more sex while showering—but they were back to work now and Ana's crib was coming along.

The crib would be done soon and then it was time for the dresser. The furniture that had originally been in this room had been moved downstairs to Zach's old room to make way for the new stuff. It was so white and pretty, and it was going to look terrific when she finished decorating.

She'd gotten Zach's computer and shopped Wayfair like he'd told her to do. She'd showed him her choices, and she'd made sure to choose things that were good quality but not pricey. He told her to add it all to a shopping cart and then they could check out when they'd finished with the furniture.

She'd picked a blush and white rug, white sheers for the windows with a black curtain rod, some sweet little prints with bunnies and kittens and puppies, and block letters that spelled Anastasia. She'd also picked out a small bookcase for children's books when the time came and a wicker trunk where she could store blankets and pillows. Everything she'd picked was less than five-hundred dollars, and though she couldn't afford it in one lump payment, she could give Zach money toward it.

Or not, since he'd said to consider it a wedding present. Maybe she'd do something nice for him instead. Buy him something, though she had no idea what he might want or need. He'd been a single guy with a healthy paycheck for so long that he'd pretty much bought himself whatever he wanted.

She thought about how much he loved the dessert Chloe had sent over. What if she learned how to make it? Chloe would teach her. Kayla fought a sudden flush of embarrassment. It wasn't much of a present, really. Then again, as Chloe always said, her food was made with love and that's why it tasted so good. Kayla could put a lot of love in a dessert for Zach.

He fitted the front of the crib onto the sides and screwed everything in, then grinned up at her. "All done. Let's see what it looks like."

Kayla walked around the front of the crib and

over to the door so she could see the bigger picture. "It's so pretty. I think she'll love it. Later, I mean. I don't think she much cares at her age."

"Probably not. Where do you want it?"

"I think on the pink wall."

They moved it together. She'd put the sheets into the washer earlier. They weren't done yet, but they were in the dryer and soon would be.

"It's going to be great," Zach said. "Let's get the dresser together, then maybe we can reheat some of Chloe's food. Did you call Bailey yet?"

"Not yet. I got a little side-tracked." And not by shopping.

He grinned. He knew what she meant. "Yeah, that was fun, wasn't it?"

"Very. Just when I think you can't make me come again, you do."

He waggled his eyebrows. "You're welcome, beautiful."

Kayla laughed. "Full of yourself, aren't you?"

"I'd rather you were full of me."

"I like being full of you. But I think we'd better wait until later or we'll never get this furniture done. Or eat."

He picked up one of the long sides of the dresser and started to put the wooden pegs into place. "Probably right. Let's get this done, get some food, and get our little girl."

Kayla's skin prickled with hot emotion at how easily he claimed Ana and wanted her to be safe and happy. He said *our* little girl like he'd done it every day of Ana's life. She couldn't love him more if she tried, even though it scared her senseless to care so much about a man who lived every bit as violent a life as James had. More so, actually. Even if Zach was one of the good guys who made sure the world was a safe place for people, it didn't change the fact he might not come back one day.

She hadn't wanted to think about it earlier when he'd said what he did about HOT and being a family, but she knew it wasn't something she could completely ignore. It was something Bailey had to live with too. And Chloe. All the terrific women she'd met who were married or dating the men on Zach's team.

"Can you hold this for me?" he asked.

She went over and gripped one of the sides of the dresser. Zach connected it to the back piece, then gave her a grin. Her heart throbbed so hard. It was scary to love someone other than her sister and her baby so much.

"Thank you, Zach."

"It's no big deal. I've put stuff like this together before. But you're welcome."

"That's not what I meant. I was talking about Ana."

He tilted his head. "I'm not sure I follow."

Her throat was tight. "You called her *our* little girl. I can't tell you how much that means to me."

"Aw, baby, don't cry."

He put an arm around her and hugged her to his

side. That's when she realized a tear had spilled down her cheek. She swiped it away.

"Sorry. I didn't mean to cry. It's just that Ana's never had a dad. Not really. James never cared a thing about her, other than how much money she could bring on the black market. Alexei is the closest thing she's had to a dad, but of course he can't be more than a really great uncle. And now you've called her ours, and it makes me happy. That's all."

"I told you it was my plan to make you happy."

"You're doing a great job of it."

He pressed a kiss to her forehead. "Come on, beautiful. Let's finish the dresser. I've worked up an appetite between sex and this."

They finished putting everything together, placed the furniture and cleaned up the mess. Kayla retrieved the sheets from the dryer. Zach helped her put them on the mattress and they retreated to the kitchen to heat up Chloe's casserole.

Kayla called Bailey while the food was heating so she could arrange to pick up Ana. They were also going to get the rest of her things while they were there. Kayla didn't have much so it wasn't like she needed a moving van. She'd spent most of her life without a lot of stuff, and other than living in the in-law apartment for the past few months, she'd never had her own home before. As grateful as she was to Bailey and Alexei for providing that space for her, it had never felt like hers.

It was slowly sinking in that living here with Zach,

as his wife, meant this was her home too. Sure, it was a rental, but she could put up pictures and decorate the way she liked. She'd done a little of that in the apartment, but the furniture wasn't hers and she'd only done stuff like buy a few accessories here and there when she had money.

Here—and even when they moved—she had an entire house to play with. And a full kitchen in which to learn how to cook more dishes than she knew how to make right now.

"You're smiling, Kayla. I'm happy to see that."

Kayla met his gaze. "Was I? I didn't realize. I was just thinking about Ana's room, and about living here with you." She felt shy but she also knew she could say things to him. He understood. "I've never had a home where I didn't feel like I might have to leave it at any minute. I mean I didn't feel that way over at Bailey and Alexei's, but it's their house, not mine. And while this isn't my house either, it's the first time it feels like it is. Does that make sense?"

He nodded. "It's ours together. The house came furnished, but when we move on base we'll need our own furniture. You'll get to pick everything that you want because decorating's not my thing. All I want is a couch that feels substantial and not like I have to be careful sitting on it. Oh, and maybe it'd be nice if it's not pink. Not sure I'd like a pink couch."

Kayla laughed. "No pink. Got it. What about blush?"

"Blush?"

He looked adorably confused for a moment and she giggled. "It's another word for pink. I'm joking. We'll save the blush for Ana's room. And maybe our sheets."

He blinked.

"Kidding, Zach."

He laughed. "Damn, beautiful. I think you're actually relaxing a bit. For the record, I like it when you aren't worrying about everything."

She put her hand on his where it rested on the table and squeezed. "I like it too."

She hadn't stopped worrying, probably never would, but for now she felt safe and content. It was an amazing thing to feel. She only hoped it lasted.

———

NEO LIKED SEEING Kayla at ease. Her smiles were quicker, and there was a looseness to the way she moved that wasn't usually there. Kayla was always nervous, always uptight. She lived with one eye over her shoulder. He wanted to ease those storm clouds for her. Make her feel secure.

It was her insecurity that had made her run from him after the night they'd shared together a couple of months ago. And it wasn't all her fault. He knew that too.

He'd treated her carefully, like a friend more than someone he wanted to get naked with. He'd been attracted to her from the first moment he'd seen her at

Camel's place back when Bailey'd been kidnapped by the Kings of Doom. She'd been haunted, and he'd wanted to erase that fear from her eyes. He'd wanted to protect her. Fiercely.

But she'd had an infant, she'd been through a lot of trauma, and there was no way in hell he could date her like he would any other woman. So he'd treated her like a friend because it didn't raise any alarm bells for Camel or Bailey. He'd also known she wasn't ready for more back then.

As time went on and he saw her more often, they got comfortable together as pals, but always with that attraction simmering beneath the surface. Until the night it blew up and they got down and dirty together. God, what a night that had been. When he'd awakened and she was gone, a knot formed in his stomach that hadn't eased until the night she'd sat on his couch and told him why she'd run away from him.

One week ago and now they were married. It defied explanation, but there it was. He'd married her and he'd claimed her as his own. He wasn't done claiming her, either. Sex with Kayla was fantastic, better than anything he recalled with any other woman. He was twenty-seven, almost twenty-eight, and he'd had his share of sexual encounters, but none had ever moved him at a deeper level the way being with Kayla did.

He thought of Dirty and Chloe, the way his pal had gone from single and prowling to focused and committed seemingly overnight. Dirty had fallen hard for Chloe and they were still going strong.

After Kayla heated the food and they ate, Neo did the dishes. Then they went to get Ana, as well as the rest of Kayla and Ana's belongings. They spent time with Camel and Bailey first, sitting on the patio and chatting about how their day had been. Kayla showed Bailey pictures of Ana's room, with the furniture in boxes and then put together, and Bailey put her hand to her chest and sighed.

"That's so sweet. Perfect for our little Ana-Banana."

"It was Zach's idea to do it today," Kayla said.

Bailey's gaze swung to him. "That's wonderful."

"It was a good time to do it," he said. "She was here with you and we could get it done faster. Every little girl deserves a pretty pink room."

Bailey's eyes misted. She glanced at Kayla, and he knew she must be thinking about their childhood.

"Yes, they do," she said softly.

At one point, when Kayla and Bailey went inside to look at a new dress in Bailey's closet, Neo and Camel discussed what Shade had told him.

"Fuck," Camel said softly, keeping an eye on the door and his voice down. "Dunn's working this from prison?"

"Seems like it. He expects to get out soon, so now's the time to go after Kayla. Before he can be blamed for it."

"Yeah. I don't like it."

"Neither do I."

"Fucking bikers. Shouldn't be so goddamn hard to find. They wear distinctive jackets and ride noisy-ass Harleys." Camel blew out an angry breath. "But if they don't have a known clubhouse yet and they're laying low, then what's one more damned Harley in the metro area?"

Pretty much what Neo had been thinking. The Kings of Doom were keeping clean for the moment. If they hadn't been, there'd be some recent arrest records. They probably didn't have enough members left to support criminal activity just yet. If Dunn got out and took over, that would change.

"We need to find them before Wednesday."

Camel pinched the bridge of his nose. "Yeah. We still have a backup plan to deliver the cash and track them, but I'd rather find them first."

"Me too. If it comes to giving them cash, I'm not letting Kayla deliver it. That's a dealbreaker."

"Agreed."

They didn't get to say anything else because Kayla and Bailey came back outside. Bailey had Ana on her hip and the sisters were chattering about silk and sandals and some other load of feminine crap Neo didn't really care about. But Kayla looked happy and carefree, and he wanted more than anything to let her stay that way.

They were there for another hour, then they loaded up the SUV, put Ana into her car seat, and said their goodbyes. It was a chatty trip back home.

Not between him and Kayla, but between Kayla and
Ana. Kayla said something, and Ana responded with
babbling. It was adorable as hell which was why he
didn't interrupt.

He thought about his life just over a week ago
when he'd been going home alone, carrying takeout,
and eating in front of the television while watching
Netflix or YouTube. He'd looked forward to the nights
when the team went to Buddy's so he could eat with
other people he liked instead of by himself. He and
Shade had prowled the bars a couple of times, but
Neo never connected with anyone he wanted to take
home.

His life had been lonely since Dirty moved out, no
getting around it. He was an introvert at heart, though
an extroverted one, so he loved his alone time. But too
much time by himself made him miss what it was like
to have someone else to talk to whenever he wanted to
talk.

Now he had Kayla and Ana in his life. It was an
adjustment, but not one he minded making.

When they reached the house, he pulled into the
carport and turned off the engine. "Hang on and I'll
help you," he said to Kayla before she could open the
door.

She gave him a sweetly exasperated look. "I can
get out of this monster truck by myself. I'm not that
short."

"Monster truck? Cute. I know you can climb
down yourself, but let me do it anyway."

"You're adorable," she said. "Okay, I'll wait."

He went around to her side and held out a hand to help her. Then he opened the back door and unbuckled Ana from her car seat while she babbled in his face.

"Za!"

"You want pizza, baby girl?" he asked. "I think we're a little full to order pizza tonight, but maybe your mommy has something yummy for you."

He lifted Ana from the car seat and handed her to Kayla.

"Take her inside and I'll get the rest."

"Are you sure? It's a lot of stuff."

"It's not that much. I got it. Show Ana her room."

She shook her head. "Not until you're there, isn't that right, baby girl? Zach has to be with us. He put everything together for you, my love."

His chest tightened as two pairs of eyes stared at him expectantly. "Yeah, okay. Give me a few minutes and I'll join you. Can you get the door or do you need me to unlock it for you?"

Kayla smiled. "I've got it."

He watched her go over and put her key in the lock. Ana waved a chunky arm at him and he waved back, his heart cracking just a little bit at how trusting and innocent she was. Fucking James Dunn had wanted to sell her like she was a purebred puppy or something. What the hell was wrong with people like that?

And not just people like him, but the kind of

people who would buy a black market baby, no questions asked. But maybe they didn't actually know what was going on. Some people were so desperate for children that they didn't ask too many questions when faced with the possibility of finally having one. He couldn't blame everyone who found themselves in that situation, though he didn't doubt that some of them knew what was going on.

He shook his head, tamping down on the flare of anger, and unloaded the SUV. It took three trips before he had it all inside. He carried a load up to the main floor and found Kayla and Ana waiting for him. Both of them smiled when he walked into the room.

His heart skipped and his stomach knotted. Not in a bad knot, but the kind of knot that said he was facing something he'd never encountered before. The two faces smiling at him didn't change, but something had changed.

"You ready?" he asked them.

"We're definitely ready," Kayla said.

"Let's go then."

He let them go in front of him. It wasn't until they'd entered Ana's room with its pink accent wall and white furniture that it hit him what had changed. Kayla turned around, showing Ana the room, and Ana babbled and swiveled her head back and forth. Kayla fixed her eyes on him and smiled, and the thing that was different washed over him like a tsunami.

He was falling in love. Not only with Kayla, but with Ana too.

Chapter Twenty

Happiness was a bubble inside Kayla, lifting her up and making her float along like she was made of air. It was crazy to be so happy, especially when Dal Gentry was still expecting her to give him seventy-five thousand dollars in a few days. Money she definitely didn't have, though Zach told her not to worry about it because the SEALs would take care of everything.

But Gentry and the Kings weren't inside this house she shared with Zach and Ana, and they weren't inside her little girl's pink and white bedroom as she turned around and showed Ana her new space. Ana burbled happily, but she didn't really care about the room. She was still too young to care.

Kayla knew she'd love it when she was older. Especially once all the things Kayla had ordered came in and she placed the rug and accessories where she wanted them. This one small room was everything

Kayla had ever wanted when she'd been a little girl, and everything she'd never had.

Pink and white, her own little space with toys and books and soft textiles. A sanctuary where she could be a little girl without fear. She could play dress up and have tea parties and sleepovers. She'd never had a sleepover, but she wanted Ana to have them one day.

Zach stood in the door, watching her and Ana slowly turn. The expression on his face changed as she met his gaze, and her heart skipped a beat. He looked intense—and somewhat lost. Before she could ask him what was wrong, his expression changed again. He smiled at her, and love flooded her heart so fast that she felt as if it would burst.

"I think she likes it," he said as Ana tilted her head back and stared up at the ceiling before turning to look at the pink wall and her new crib.

Kayla laughed and bounced Ana up and down. "Do you like it, Anastasia-belle? My little Ana-banana-boo?"

Ana chortled with glee and Kayla laughed. So did Zach.

He came into the room and stood with them. Kayla leaned into him and he put his arm around her and Ana both and hugged them close to his side. She felt his lips on the top of her head, and then he kissed Ana's head too.

"Welcome home, Ana."

Tears spiked in her eyes, all prickly and hot. "I can't wait to get it finished," Kayla said, because she needed to speak or the emotions inside her would break.

"Lesley always says her stuff comes fast when she orders it online."

"I got an email. It'll be here by Tuesday."

He was still hugging her to him. "Great. We'll finish everything then."

Ana reached for Zach, putting her little arms out and holding them wide. He grinned. "You want to come to me, Ana-boo?"

Kayla let her go and Zach hefted her up higher than she'd been in Kayla's arms. She burbled some nonsense and then she laughed. "Za!"

Zach laughed too. So did Kayla.

"You don't really think she wants pizza, do you?" he asked.

Kayla shook her head. "No. She just likes saying it."

Zach tickled Ana's belly and she laughed. "Or maybe she's trying to say Zach."

"Maybe so," Kayla said. "She's a little young to start talking, but it's coming soon."

"She's eight months old, right?"

"Yes. Another month or so and she should say her first word. If the baby books are right," she added.

Zach looked at Ana. "That's only an average, right Ana-banana? You could be a little genius. Can you say mama? Ma-ma."

Kayla folded her arms and hugged herself, half wondering if this was real or if she'd fallen into a dream. Zach carried Ana around the room and let her look at everything. He kept talking to her, and Kayla's heart beat like a drum the whole time. It was sweet and special, and it made her hopeful for the future even while her natural inclination to prepare for disaster kept up a running commentary about how she shouldn't get too comfortable or too relaxed because everything could change in an instant.

Ana started blinking and yawning, and then she laid her head on Zach's big shoulder. He carried her over and smiled down at Kayla. "I think she likes me."

I like you. No, I love you.

"Why wouldn't she? You're pretty terrific, Zach."

Zach bent to kiss her. "You're terrific too, Kayla. Both of you." He straightened. "Do you think she's ready to go down for the night?"

"I think we're about there," Kayla said. "I need to bathe her and change her, and then put her in her crib. Oh—"

"What, honey?" he asked when she didn't continue.

"I left the baby monitor at Bailey's."

"We can leave the doors open. Will you be able to hear her then?"

She looked across the hall to the master. It wasn't a huge house and the rooms were close enough. "I should be able to. It's not that far."

"Okay. We'll get the monitor tomorrow—or we

can buy a new one and you can leave that one with Bailey for the times they watch Ana overnight."

She loved that he thought about Ana staying with Bailey and Alexei. It wasn't something she envisioned often, but it was nice to know the option was there.

He carried Ana into the bathroom and handed her over. Kayla stripped her down while Zach set up the baby bath tub. He took Ana from her like they'd been doing it together for months so she could fill the tub with warm water. He stayed to help, and when Ana splashed them both, they laughed.

When Ana was bathed and changed into her pajamas, they took her into the bedroom to put her into her new crib. Her eyes were wide open but they soon drooped as Kayla sung to her. Zach stayed with them the whole time, and Kayla looked up every once in a while. Warm green eyes stared back at her. He smiled, and her heart flipped every single time.

He was so handsome, so strong. She loved him so much, and she didn't know how to tell him. Didn't think she should, really. He'd had a lot of changes in his life this week. He didn't need another one, especially one as big as telling him how she felt.

He crept out of the room before Ana was asleep. When her eyes were closed and she didn't stir, Kayla followed. Zach waited with a glass of wine and a beer. It was still early, only eight o'clock, and she wasn't sleepy. She took the glass gratefully and they clinked her glass and his bottle.

"How did you know I wanted wine?" she asked.

"I assumed."

She took a sip and sighed. "I don't drink every night, I swear. But when I'm feeling uptight, it relaxes me. I know that's probably not a great thing."

"It's okay so long as you don't overdo it."

"I have the genetics to overdo it." She twirled the glass in her fingers, thinking. Remembering. "My parents didn't do anything unless it was to excess. Drinking, drugs, fighting. I like white wine, but I don't think it'll turn me into an addict."

"You don't have to explain. It's okay if you like wine."

"It worries me sometimes, but I try to be careful. That night when we did shots downstairs...." She shook her head. "That wasn't typical for me. I don't usually drink hard liquor."

"It wasn't typical for me either."

She cocked her head. "So why did you do it?"

He shot her a grin. "Why did you?"

"Nerves. Frustration with life. But mostly nerves."

"Nerves about what? Me?"

She rolled her eyes, but it was a mock gesture. "Duh. Of course you. I was so attracted to you, Zach. But you'd only ever been like a friend to me and I thought that's what you were still being. I wanted more, but I didn't think you did."

"Kayla, baby, believe me when I tell you this. I wanted to fuck you from the first moment I saw you. You were standing in Camel's house, lost and alone and worried for your sister, and all I could think about was getting my cock inside you."

Her insides melted with those words. Not only because he'd wanted her from the beginning, but because the carnal image of his cock inside her made her wet just thinking about it. "Really? I always thought you were being nice."

He snorted. "Nice? I wanted to get down and dirty with you from the start. And that wasn't a nice thing just then when you'd been through so much."

"I guess I wasn't in a place for that at the beginning, but it didn't take long before I wanted more from you. Which is why I did what I did that night. I hated that I needed shots to do it though."

"I don't hate what happened, beautiful. I only hate how we didn't talk for two months."

"I hate that too," she said, her heart aching with regret. "I shouldn't have run away like I did."

He put his arm up. She understood the message and scooted over beside him, pressing into his side. His arm settled around her. "It happened," he said, his breath warm and scented with beer. "But here we are anyway."

She sighed as she cuddled into him. "Here we are. It's only been a week. We're married and Ana has her own sweet room. I feel like I have whiplash."

He laughed. "So do I, Kayla. But that's okay. My job gives me whiplash on a regular basis. This is a good kind of different, not a bad kind."

She hoped it stayed that way. "I love what we did to her room. I'm going to hate to move out."

He kissed the top of her head again. "Yeah, I know. But we can do it again in the next place. Look at this like practice."

She would, but she still hated it. She hated that she never really got to settle down. Something always came along and she had to move on again. "I wish Dal Gentry had stayed in his sewer and never crawled out of it," she said with a growl. "Asshole."

Zach set his beer down and tipped her chin up so she could meet his gaze. The fierceness she saw there made her want to recoil, but this was Zach, not some nasty criminal biker who didn't give a shit about any rules but his own.

The fierceness in Zach's eyes, the utter violence leashed behind their green depths, was there for her. He would let it loose if he had to, but never toward her or Ana. He was their protector. Their safe place.

"I promise you they'll stop coming for you. One way or the other, I'll make it happen. I swear. The Kings of Doom are no match for a SEAL team."

———

NEO WOKE up during the night with that telltale prickling on his neck. *Trouble.*

He sat up with a start when he realized Kayla wasn't beside him. His gut twisted. Not with fear, but with something close to it. He reached for the weapon he kept on the nightstand and moved silently across the floor, ready to do violence if he had to.

He found Kayla in Ana's room, looking down at her baby who slept peacefully. She looked up when she heard him. Her eyes were glassy with tears. He didn't even think about it, he just went over and pulled her into his arms. Relief flooded him. The warning system was for her this time, not for any outside danger. She was crying, and he was attuned to her pain. So attuned that it woke him from a dead sleep in the middle of the night.

He didn't want her to cry, but he was glad he wasn't facing an intruder. Especially not one who'd come looking for her.

"What's the matter, beautiful?" he whispered. "Did Ana wake you up?"

He hadn't heard anything, but maybe his hearing wasn't dialed in to baby frequency yet.

"I woke up and couldn't go back to sleep."

She'd been tired when they'd gone to bed, her eyes drooping so frequently that he hadn't tried to make love to her again. He'd held her and listened to her breaths grow even before he'd finally fallen asleep too.

He rubbed his hand up and down her back. "Do you want to talk about anything?"

He wasn't typically a chatty, bare-your-soul kind of guy, but for her he'd listen and do his best to untangle whatever was causing her problems.

She put her arms around his waist and held on

tight. "No. It was a bad dream. That's all. But it scared me, and I had to make sure Ana was okay."

"You ready to leave her?"

She nodded, her head moving up and down against his chest. He ushered her from the room, pulling the door almost all the way closed but leaving a good five inches of space so they could hear if Ana woke and started to cry.

"Need anything from the kitchen?"

"No," she whispered.

He took her into the bedroom and pulled the covers back on her side. She didn't get in though. She stepped into him, pressing her palms to his bare chest and then down over his abdomen, tracing every ridge of his six-pack, exploring him. His dick hardened instantly. Need for her was a hot itch in his brain, a throbbing in his balls. But he didn't move. Instead, he let her explore his torso.

And then, when her hand slipped beneath the waistband of his athletic shorts, he hissed in a breath as her touch scalded him. She hadn't touched his cock yet, and he was ready to come unglued.

"Kayla," he groaned. "What are you doing, baby?"

"Touching you."

His laugh was rusty. "Yeah, I noticed. And I don't mind at all, but it's killing me to let it happen at this pace."

She tipped her head back—and wrapped her

hand around his cock. "Oh, you mean you want me to touch you like this?"

He couldn't think. Couldn't breathe. His balls were tight against his body and his dick was like iron. Her hand was soft and silky as she squeezed, pumping him deliberately.

"That's good," he said, out of breath, "but I can think of even better things to do with it."

She dropped to her knees and took his shorts down at the same time. Then she gazed up at him and curled her tongue around the head of his dick. "Things like this?"

"Yeah. Fuck yeah."

He saw stars. Kayla took him into her mouth, swirling her tongue around his cock while cupping his balls with one hand and pumping with the other. She made lust burn hard at the back of his brain, but there was another emotion crowding in there as well.

Mine. All mine. Always.

He let her keep going until he couldn't take another moment and then he lifted her up and tossed her onto the bed in one quick move. She squeaked and laughed at the same time, a sultry laugh that told him she was turned on and enjoying herself.

"You didn't let me finish," she complained.

"Nope," he said, putting a knee on the bed and reaching for her silky little robe. She'd wrapped up in a robe to go into Ana's room and he undid the ties and shoved it open. All she wore under it was a tank top that clung to her beautiful tits and a pair of lacy panties that did things to his brain. He dragged them off and tossed them aside, then wedged himself between her legs with his shoulders, shoving them open.

She was wet and ready for him. He tested her with a finger and she bowed up off the bed, hissing in a breath and gasping out his name. He grinned.

"Yeah, Kayla. Like that, baby. You are so fucking gorgeous."

He dropped his head and buried his face in her sweet wet heat, licking and tasting and teasing her as he attacked her clit and then retreated before she could explode. Eventually, she fisted her hands in his hair and growled at him. He laughed against her pussy, and the vibrations made her moan.

Then he gave in and let her have what she wanted, pushing her into a shattering orgasm that had her shoving a fist into her mouth to keep from waking the baby. When she was finished, when she flopped back on the bed utterly shattered, he climbed her body, licking and nipping and sucking her perfect nipples on the way up to her luscious lips.

He hooked a knee and curled it around his hip, then he did the same to the other knee. Finally, he sank into her balls deep, heart pounding, cock aching for release.

"You feel so good, Kayla. So fucking perfect wrapped around me."

"I love it when you're inside me," she moaned. "So much."

"I love it too," he said, heart twisting with emotion as the words wrenched from him. He loved fucking her, and he was pretty sure he loved her. He'd never felt like this before, but it was so damned new that he didn't think he could say the words yet.

But he felt them. He felt them with every thrust, every sizzle of pleasure. He felt them as he dragged another orgasm from her, and he felt them when he finally let go and found his own release deep inside the hottest, sweetest body he'd ever buried his cock in.

Chapter Twenty-One

"THERE'S FIFTEEN OF THEM," VIKING SAID, TOSSING A file onto the conference table in the SEALs' ready room on Monday morning. "We got a plate number for Gentry and tracked it to an address. He's not living there anymore. We also have a good shot of him, but not the car that Kayla saw because the street camera had already overwritten the footage."

Neo reached for the file and the others let him have it first. He flipped open the cover and scanned the contents quickly before shoving it toward his teammates.

"Fifteen," he said disgustedly. "They were prospects or junior members when we busted up the club."

"Now they've decided to take over and reestablish the organization," Dirty said as he read over the file after Neo shoved it at him. There were a lot of papers inside, but the ones that mattered to Neo were the brief on the number of current members and the information on Dal Gentry—a big, tattooed mother-fucker with a goatee and a mean look—and Steve Dunn.

Gentry was a petty criminal with busts for assault, disturbing the peace, passing bad checks, and domestic violence. He'd never done any significant time. Steve Dunn was a lot younger than James, the son of his father and second wife. He'd come into the club a few years after James, and he'd been working his way through the ranks. His record was clean, which was why he got to visit his half-brother in prison. He was the perfect conduit for orders passing between Dunn and Gentry.

"It was probably inevitable," Viking replied to Dirty. "They're a brotherhood. Like us in a perverse way, with their own rules and hierarchies."

"Except for the fact they're fucking criminals," Neo replied, his brain churning with anger and a determination to find and stamp out every last asshole who wore the Kings of Doom patch on their cut. They'd threatened his woman and child, and he wasn't letting that stand. He didn't care who was in charge or what their internal politics were. They all needed to go, and he was going to be the one who cut them down if that's what it took.

He'd left Kayla early that morning, still sleepy and soft in their bed, her lush body wrapping around his only an hour before as he'd stroked deep inside her and made them both come. Then he'd got up, showered, dressed, made coffee and wrote her a note that he'd left on the counter near the coffee pot. He'd decided to leave a note every single day he was with her. She needed to start each day with someone telling her how fucking awesome she was. If he didn't do it, who would?

When he had to deploy, he'd try to write them out beforehand and instruct her to read one every day he was gone. He might not write enough of them, because he never knew exactly how long he'd be gone, but in that case he'd tell her to start over at the beginning and reread them all until he returned.

The note he'd left this morning told her how amazing she was, and how much he loved her perfect body. Maybe it should have said that he loved her, but he wasn't completely comfortable with that thought yet. How did you tell a woman you'd been married to for three days that you thought you might be in love with her? Especially a woman like Kayla who was used to people bailing on her or not being what they'd purported to be in the first place?

"Yeah, they're definitely fucking criminals," Money grumbled as he flipped through the papers. "Assault, battery, passing bad checks, domestic violence, soliciting. Not as bad as the asswipes we helped collar a few months ago, but they just didn't have time to get there yet."

"They want to get there," Neo said. "And they need money to do it. Partly why they decided to target

Kayla." He frowned. "Dunn has to know she doesn't have that kind of money, so why try it?"

"If they've surveilled her at all, then Dunn knows she's lived with me and Bailey," Camel said. "We bought the house, so he might think we could get a loan for the cash if we didn't already have it."

Viking nodded. "That's a good guess. They don't care if she has it or not, just that she can find it."

Neo's belly tightened. "Yeah, but do any of us think all they want is 75k? They're a motorcycle gang with a code of honor, and Kayla is a traitor in their eyes. If not for her, their officers wouldn't be in prison. Dunn wouldn't be in prison."

"That's true," Camel said. "It's about more than money."

Neo jerked his head at the file. "Why don't we know where Gentry and his fuckwads are holing up yet?"

"Because they're fifteen douchebags in a crowd and this isn't our primary mission?" Viking said, turning it into a question that wasn't really a question. "They didn't leave a forwarding address, man."

Neo's fists clenched on the table. "We need to find them. Gentry and Steve Dunn at the very least. Find them and sweep them up."

Viking's eyes narrowed. "Ghost gave us permission to find out what we could, not to take anyone into custody. The military doesn't operate against domestic criminals on US soil. You know that, Neo."

Frustration and anger hammered at him. "I know,

but what are we supposed to do? Wait until he does something to my wife and kid? Call the police?"

Camel's brows climbed his forehead. Neo knew why.

Yeah, he'd called Ana his kid. Well, fuck, she *was* his. He'd claimed her mother and that meant he claimed her too. Besides, she was freaking adorable—and she seemed to like him. He'd walked into her room to have a peek at her this morning and she'd opened her eyes and smiled up at him. Then she'd opened her arms as if reaching for him. He couldn't say no. He'd picked her up, checked her diaper, then took her with him to the kitchen. Before he left for work, he carried her in to her mother, who smiled at them both, her face lit from within with so much love for her kid that it nearly blinded him.

He kind of wished she'd look at him that way. Maybe one day.

"We aren't going to let anyone do anything to them," Viking growled. "She's not driving herself to work, right?"

"Right."

He didn't want her going in at all, but the salon depended on her and she still needed her own income. She hadn't said that last part, but he understood it. Kayla was too used to things disintegrating on her and she wasn't going to let herself be without resources of her own. She wanted to work so she wouldn't fall on her face. Just like his sister in that regard, so he couldn't argue with her about it.

Since Chloe had been taken at gunpoint from the salon by her ex, Dirty had helped Avery get a deal on security cameras and silent alarms. The place was wired for trouble and the police were on call. Signs in the windows proclaimed that to be the case, so any criminal who wanted to test the system would have to be either dumber than shit or beyond caring.

Neo had to hope that Dal Gentry was neither of those things. He didn't think the biker would be with James Dunn pulling the strings. If Dunn had started this process while still in prison, then he had a bigger plan at work. He wasn't looking for instant grati-fication.

"I assume Ana isn't going to the salon with her anymore either," Viking continued.

"No, she's not. She's with Ella again today."

Chloe was driving them both to Ella's where they'd drop off Ana, and then she and Kayla were going to the salon. Kayla wasn't happy about not being able to drive herself, but she understood. She'd sworn she did when they'd discussed it last night, anyway.

"Soon, beautiful," he'd said. "We'll get Ana into base daycare and us into base housing."

He was applying for both as soon as this meeting and morning training were done. He didn't know how long it would take, but he'd know once they were on the list. Until then, they had to be vigilant.

"Why don't we lure him out?" Money asked. "Ella or Quinn can spare the cash. Like Blade said before, we can put a tracking device in the bag and Kayla can hand it over—"

Neo growled. "No. Not Kayla. I don't want her involved."

"Gentry probably isn't going to accept it from one of us and you know it," Money said. "It's better if it's her. We'd be there backing her up."

"Not acceptable. She's not an operator and I won't put her in danger. Would you let Ella make a drop like that when the fucker waiting for the money'd threatened her?"

"We haven't even gotten that far," Viking interjected before Money could respond. "One thing at a time here."

Neo twirled the pen he'd been holding and sent it skipping across the table as he leaned back and put his hands behind his head. His fury was tightly contained, but it simmered beneath the surface. And not really at these guys, but at the way some random-ass mother-fucker had showed up and wrecked Kayla's peaceful existence, sending her into a tailspin that ended with marriage and yet another move from one house to a different one in the space of days.

"I'm calling Ian Black," Neo said, shoving to his feet. "We can't operate inside US borders, but he can."

"That's true," someone said, and they all jerked toward the door. General Mendez walked out of the shadows and into the room. Everyone scrambled to their feet and snapped to attention. "As you were."

They relaxed, though Neo didn't think he'd ever relax fully. Not until he knew Kayla was no longer in danger from those assholes.

"Ghost tells me we've got a problem with the Kings of Doom," Mendez said. He dropped into a chair and propped his booted feet on the table, crossing them at the ankles. "Somebody fill me in on the latest."

————

"YOU LOOK MIGHTY HAPPY," Chloe said when Kayla opened the door for her that morning.

She'd been up for a couple of hours, since Zach had left, and yes, she was happy.

"I think married life agrees with you," Chloe added.

Kayla laughed and retreated to the kitchen while Chloe closed the door behind her. "So far, so good," she called out. "Do you want some coffee?"

Chloe sashayed in behind her, looking gorgeous in a pencil skirt with low-heeled sandals and a white button down. She wore a chunky bracelet on one wrist and sported a big diamond on her ring finger.

"Of course I do." Chloe took a seat at the table and started to coo at Ana, who sat in her high chair.

Kayla poured a cup of coffee for her friend and went back to fixing Ana's oatmeal. "Thanks for the casserole and the dessert," she said. "Zach loved it."

"I'm glad."

Kayla set the cup down in front of Chloe. It took her a moment to say what was on her mind. "Do you think you could teach me to cook?"

Chloe's grin was huge. "Of course I can, honey. I'd love to!"

Kayla took a moment to appreciate the relief and love washing through her. It was hard for her to ask for things sometimes, especially things she considered big, because she might get a no instead of a yes.

But not from Chloe, apparently. Kayla returned the smile. "Thank you. So much."

She'd originally intended to ask how to make the dessert he loved. But that wasn't big enough. Zach deserved more. He loved Chloe's food, so she would learn to make it.

Maybe. She might suck at it, but at least she could try.

"No problem." Chloe sipped the coffee. "So how much do you know how to do anyway? For reference."

Kayla laughed as she brought Ana's oatmeal to the table. "I can microwave a frozen dinner. Heat up a can of soup. Oh, and I can fix ramen noodles. And oatmeal. That's probably my greatest accomplishment."

She spooned some up and blew on it before offering it to Ana.

"Okay," Chloe said. "I can work with that. If you can follow the directions on an oatmeal packet, you can follow my directions. And those in a cookbook. It'll be fine, hon."

They chatted while Kayla fed Ana. When Ana was done eating, Chloe followed Kayla into the newly decorated baby room so Kayla could put Ana's dress on.

"Oh my goodness, this is so *sweet,*" Chloe said. "You and Zach did it this weekend?"

"Yes. I've got some things coming from Wayfair tomorrow and then I'll finish it up."

Chloe stood in the middle of the room and turned around, looking at the paint and furniture. "So adorable. I love it. I bet she will too when she's old enough."

Kayla frowned. "We won't be here then. Zach's applying for base housing."

Chloe made a face. "I forgot. Damn. But you'll fix her room up there! It'll be great."

Kayla looked at the pink wall, feeling wistful. She'd lived in this house for a few days. It shouldn't mean a thing to her, and yet it did. Crazy.

"I know. I'll hate leaving you though. I think it'd be so fun to live across the street from you and Ryan. Heck, I wish Bailey and Alexei were here too. One big happy family in the same neighborhood."

Chloe squeezed her hand. "Oh honey, I get it. But it won't be so bad. The base isn't too far away from any of us. It'll be fine."

It would, and she would get used to it. She always did.

"Are you ready to go?" she asked Chloe as she picked Ana up and propped her on a hip. "I think I have everything. Ana's diaper bag is by the door."

"Yep, let's roll. We'll get Ana-banana to Princess Ella and then we'll be at work in time for Mrs. Jenkins to roll in and demand I change her hair color yet again."

Kayla had gotten used to the idea that Ella was a princess by now, though it was always a little strange to be reminded of it since the woman was so normal. She snorted at the thought of Mrs. Jenkins. "She's a fun one, isn't she?"

"She sure is. I've told her that much color is going to break her hair off at the roots, but she keeps arguing with me. One of these days I'll give in and let her find out."

They grabbed everything and headed out the door. Kayla locked up, double-checked the lock, and they walked across the street and piled into Chloe's car.

"I'm sorry we have to do this every day," Kayla said as Chloe put the car in reverse. "It's such a pain in the butt to move the car seat all the time."

"It's fine, honey. Ryan and Zach and the others will take care of everything soon and life can get back to normal."

Kayla wasn't sure she believed life would ever be normal for her, but she fiercely wanted it to be.

They turned out of the neighborhood and Kayla's

phone dinged with a text. She thought it might be Zach, but it was an unknown sender.

Do you have my money?

Her heart throttled into high gear as she shoved her hair behind her ear and typed back: *I have two more days. I'll get it.*

Unknown: *Not sure I believe you. If you don't have it by now…*

Kayla: *I'm working on it. I swear.*

She sent the text with shaking fingers. When there was no reply, she set the phone on her lap and turned to look out the window, trying to pull herself together before Chloe figured out something was wrong.

They were chatting about work and Kayla was feeling almost normal again when Chloe slammed on the brakes. "What the hell?" she cried.

Kayla's hair had fallen in her face with the sudden stop and she dragged it out again so she could see what Chloe was looking at.

All she got was an impression of an object blocking the road before the glass beside her head shattered.

Chapter Twenty-Two

MENDEZ LISTENED ATTENTIVELY AS VIKING BRIEFED him on the situation. Tension crawled across Neo's forehead and down his spine. If Mendez didn't give them the go ahead to *do* something, then Neo was going to explode. Collecting intel was all well and good—and vital—but not acting on it was a fucking nightmare.

And yet the military didn't do shit like that because an act of Congress forbade it. Made sense when you thought about all the ways the military could be used against the citizenry by unscrupulous political leaders—and had been in other countries that didn't have such a law on the books. That shit was how you ended up with dictators.

Still, Neo wanted to go after Gentry and the Kings with all the considerable skill at his disposal and take them the fuck down. He didn't need military equipment to do it. Just his bare fucking hands.

Mendez rubbed his forehead as if he too felt the tension. "So what I'm hearing is these fuckers are extorting Kayla Jones—excuse me, Kayla Anderson —and threatening her child's life and well-being. They've given her until Wednesday to get the money. Correct?"

"Yes, sir," Viking said. As their team leader, he was the one who spoke for them all. Probably a good thing since Neo's gut roiled with impotent anger. No telling what he'd say if he were the one giving the briefing.

Mendez picked up his phone and casually scrolled through it, and Neo wanted to explode.

"Hmm, that's interesting. Looks like you boys have a team bonding day Wednesday. Not sure what Ghost has in mind for you, but I don't expect to see you around HQ."

Neo's heart soared. *Fuck yeah.*

Viking didn't miss a beat. He shot Neo a grin before answering. "That's right, sir. We're bonding."

"Make sure you don't use my equipment to do it," Mendez added as he stood. Before they could join him, he made a hand signal to keep them in their seats.

"No, sir, not part of the plan."

"If you'll excuse me, I need to call Mr. Black and discuss our training methods with him."

"Yes, sir. Thank you, sir."

Mendez strolled over to Neo's chair and stuck out his hand. Neo jumped to his feet and shook hands with the general.

"Congratulations, Neo. I hope you'll have a long and happy—and mostly uneventful—marriage to Kayla."

"Thank you, sir. Me too, sir."

The phone on the conference table blared to life. Viking picked it up.

"Lieutenant Commander Erikson," he said in cool tones. He frowned. "What? Okay, yeah, put her through."

He dropped the phone in the cradle and gave them a hard look. Neo's gut twisted. He didn't like that expression on his team leader's face. He didn't have his cell phone because of where they were in the facility, but he had a powerful urge to drop everything and retrieve it from his locker so he could call Kayla. The back of his neck started to itch like crazy as his stomach bottomed out.

"Chloe and Kayla didn't show up at Ella's," he said. "They aren't at work either. Ella called there when they didn't arrive with Ana."

The phone rang again. "That'll be your wife, Money. Talk to her and calm her down."

Money snatched up the phone and Neo stood there blinking in disbelief, his guts turning to ice.

"The Kings took them. But why?" he growled. "It's not Wednesday yet. What the fuck," he exploded. "We still had *two* days!"

His gaze met Dirty's. His teammate's face had gone white. He suspected his was the same. Kayla and Chloe and Ana. Missing. He loved all three of them. He'd kill for them, sacrifice himself—whatever it took. The look on Dirty's face told him that Dirty would do the same.

And Camel's. Camel had that dark cool look that meant he'd gone deep inside himself to a place of stillness. That place he used whenever he called on his skills to hit targets from afar. If they could get him a clear shot within a mile of the Kings, he'd take them out with deadly precision.

Mendez clapped a hand on Neo's shoulder and he started. He'd forgotten the man was there. "Easy, son. We got this." He headed for the door. "I'm calling Ian now. You boys get ready to roll. HOT equipment authorized for a joint exercise."

Neo and his teammates ran for their gear. They were grabbing pistols and dragging on assault suits when Ghost appeared in the entry. Motion ceased as they waited for whatever he was about to tell them.

"James Dunn is dead. Hanged himself in his prison cell this morning."

"Shit," Camel swore. "That means Gentry's in charge—and rewriting the rules."

That was exactly what it meant. But what did the fucker want? Revenge? More money?

It hit him in dark place that Kayla could already be dead. And Chloe. Maybe not Ana. Probably not Ana if Gentry intended to sell her to the adoption agency.

Neo's heart was a dead weight in his chest as his

mind raced through all the possibilities. He wanted to scream. Cry.

Kill.

He couldn't do any of it though. Not yet. He had to keep it together and operate on the assumption they were still alive. That he could rescue them.

Ghost's secure phone pinged. "Viper says Black's expecting you. Get moving, sailors. Find our family and bring them home."

Neo's eyes pricked with tears. He slammed his weapons in their holsters and headed toward the exit. Last thing he did was stop and grab his phone on the way out of the building. Two missed texts.

He opened them as the booted feet of his teammates echoed around him. He crashed to a halt and everyone else did too.

"What is it?" Dirty demanded, shoving his way to Neo's side. "Is it Kayla?"

"They've got her phone," Neo said as a tendril of cautious elation began to unwind itself inside him.

He didn't have to tell his teammates what that meant. They all knew that a cell phone meant tracking. Especially for people with the kind of access they had. He turned the phone so they could see the picture of Kayla holding Ana with Chloe sitting beside them. Dirty growled.

"What do they want?" Camel asked, sounding a million miles away. In his head, he probably was. Envisioning his shots. Watching biker heads explode as his rounds connected.

"The price has gone up," Neo gritted. "One million dollars by sundown."

————

KAYLA, Chloe, and Ana huddled together on a nasty bed in a nasty room in a nasty building, and Ana was crying. Kayla tried to soothe her, but Ana was hungry and Dal Gentry wouldn't let Kayla have the diaper bag that contained Ana's snacks.

"Shh, baby, shhh," Kayla crooned. Ana was having none of it. She wailed and threw her arms up and down and Kayla's heart was breaking.

"Let me take her for a second," Chloe said softly. "You need a break."

Kayla let Chloe pull Ana onto her lap and then scrubbed her eyes. She'd been crying too, out of anger and fear for her baby mostly, though also for them, and her eyes were swollen.

"I'm sorry," she said to Chloe again.

Chloe bounced Ana, who still cried, and looked over at Kayla. "It's not your fault, Kayla."

"It is. If you hadn't been with me, you wouldn't be here."

"I'm glad I'm with you," Chloe said fiercely, and Kayla believed she meant it. Her heart swelled with gratitude and love for her friend. "I've been through this shit before, and I *know* we're going to be fine. Ryan and Zach will find us, Kayla. They will. I have faith."

"I hope you're right."

She didn't have Chloe's faith, though she wanted it. But life was always a shit sandwich for her, at some point, and she'd been overdue. When the passenger window had busted in on her, she hadn't realized what was happening. But then she'd looked up and found herself staring at the barrel of a pistol. That was when the rumble of motorcycles finally registered in her brain. She'd heard them before Chloe'd slammed on the brakes, but she hadn't been on her guard like she should have been. She'd assumed it was a plane flying overhead and hadn't bothered to look.

She hadn't been diligent, and for that she couldn't forgive herself.

Come on, Kay-Kay! What could you have done even if you'd managed to figure out the sound was motorcycles? They already had you.

Her face stung with the cuts she'd gotten from flying glass, and the dried blood was beginning to itch. Chloe had ripped off one of her sleeves and dabbed at the cuts as best she could once they'd gotten thrown in here. None were deep, thankfully. Both Chloe and Ana were unhurt.

Kayla shot to her feet and paced back and forth, fear churning inside. The room was small and dingy and there was nothing they could use for a weapon. She'd looked. Chloe had looked. There was a dirty bed with nothing but a mattress, a table with a chair —they'd considered the chair, but it was too unwieldy —and one window high up on the wall. Chloe had already pushed the table over and stood on it to look outside.

"Woods," she'd said. "Nothing but woods."

The Kings had caught them on an isolated stretch of road where they usually took a short cut to the highway that would take them to Ella's place. They'd been surrounded, and someone had bashed in her window. Another of the brothers stood beside Chloe's door and motioned at her to open it. When she did, he'd yanked her out and shoved her into the backseat. Then he'd taken over the driving.

They hadn't cared that she and Chloe saw where they were going. A bad sign to her way of thinking. When they'd made it to this weathered building in the back of beyond, Dal Gentry parked his black and chrome Harley Fat Boy and swaggered over to yank her from the car.

"Hello, bitch," he'd growled in her ear. "Have a nice ride?"

"I said I'd get the money," she'd growled back because she knew better than to show fear in front of these men. "You're making a mistake."

He'd barked a laugh. "No mistake, bitch. The terms have changed."

Kayla rubbed her hands up and down her arms, shivering. She didn't know what the terms were because he hadn't told her, but he'd taken her phone away and forced her to give him the code. She'd debated lying about it, but he'd nudged his chin at one of the other men—yet another one she didn't remember—and said, "Gimme the brat."

Chloe started singing to Ana, but it didn't really help. Her little sobs were weaker now, but she still cried and slapped her hands at Chloe. She'd done the same to Kayla.

"Za!" Ana wailed anew, and Kayla's skin prickled with fresh heat as anger roared to life inside.

She stormed over to the door and started banging on it. "Gentry!" she screamed. "Bring me that fucking diaper bag you asshole! If I can't take care of Ana, then you won't get any money out of her at all! No rich bitch is going to pay top dollar for a damaged kid."

She was breathing heavy, ready to sink to the floor and sob, when the door jerked open. It wasn't Gentry who stood there with the bag though.

"Steve?"

He sneered. "Yeah, it's me. Shut that fucking kid up, Kayla," he said as he threw the bag at her.

He slammed the door and Kayla snatched up the bag, hurrying over to the bed to dig out one of the prepared bottles of formula. Thankfully she'd made a couple up so that Ella would have them ready to go. There were some snacks and pureed vegetables as well, though nothing that was going to get them through more than a day.

Kayla growled in frustration as she fumbled for the correct bottle since she'd included a couple of empties with powder so Ella could mix them if necessary. She still hated James for the fact she had to bottle feed and being imprisoned by his club only made her resentment worse.

"Slow down, honey," Chloe said softly. "Here, give it to me. You take Ana and I'll get it for you."

Kayla took Ana in her arms and Chloe got the bottle, shook it up, and handed it over. Ana took it greedily and the wailing ceased. Chloe and Kayla looked at each other, breathing easier for a minute.

"Thank God," Kayla said.

"Who was that guy? You knew his name."

Kayla snorted bitterly. "He's Ana's uncle. Not that you'd know it from the way he behaved, right?"

"Oh dear."

"Yeah, those Dunn men are real sentimental about their own flesh and blood. Asshole." Kayla rocked Ana while she ate. Her eyes were still swollen and her face was red, but at least she was quiet now. Maybe she'd have tired herself out enough to take a nap.

Kayla sniffed and wiped her nose on her shoulder. She stuffed her tears down deep, determined to stay strong for Ana. And Chloe, though Chloe didn't seem to need any help in that quarter. Her friend was so stoic. It amazed her.

"These guys are definitely assholes, I'll grant you that," Chloe said. "But they aren't as bad as Travis and his militia. They're downright welcoming compared to that group. Travis beat me within an inch of my life when he captured me. He'd planned to kill Ryan when he came to get me, and then he was going to rape me before killing me. Oh, and he threatened to let his militia have a go at me too."

"How did you survive it?" Kayla asked, horrified.

"Well, I was scared, I won't lie. But then I realized that I loved Ryan and he loved me and no way in hell was I letting him die because of me. I was going to fight and give him a chance to get to me." She smiled. "It wasn't easy, but that's what happened. I escaped but Travis caught me. Then I stabbed him. But Ryan was there before Travis could shoot me. He took Travis's gun away, and I got it. I was going to kill him, but Ryan talked me out of it. I wanted to kill him so bad, but Ryan was right that it would haunt me if I did. So I didn't. Then Travis pulled a pistol he'd kept hidden—and Ryan shot him before he could shoot me."

"Wow."

Chloe shrugged as if it was nothing, though Kayla could tell she was still emotional about the incident. "So you see, it'll work out. Ryan found me before. He'll find me again. He's searching for me, same as Zach is searching for you. They're pissed as hell, Kayla. They're pissed and they're coming. These guys should really be thinking about that. But they probably aren't based on the fact we're parked in a room with an outer wall and there's nobody in here with a gun to our heads just in case—and I'm not telling them."

Kayla hugged her baby a little tighter. Not so

tightly she set off any fussing. "I wish I had your faith, Chloe. I really do. But it never works that way for me."

"It will this time."

"How can you be so sure?"

"Love. Love moves mountains. And when your man is a lethal killing machine trained and sanctioned by the US Navy? Honey, nothing can stop him. Just do what it takes to stay alive until he gets here. Because he *will* be here."

Chapter Twenty-Three

THEY DIDN'T HAVE THE LUXURY OF WAITING UNTIL nightfall to raid the building where the Kings of Doom were keeping Kayla, Chloe, and Ana. The SEALs rendezvoused with Ian Black's security forces, otherwise known as the Bandits, and piled into a couple of high tech SUVs owned by Black Defense International. Jace Kaiser and Brett Wheeler were in one vehicle with half the SEALs while Colt Duchaine and Jared Fraser were in another.

HOT was liaising, which was permitted by the Congressional Act that prevented them from participating in law enforcement operations—even if this wasn't technically a law enforcement operation—and Ian and Ghost were sharing information on locations and cell phone tracking data.

Neo sat with his head back and his eyes closed, listening to the conversation around him but thinking about Kayla and Ana. Kayla, with her beautiful smiles and the underlying fear in her eyes that something would always go wrong, and Ana with her chubby cheeks and her enthusiasm for saying "Za!" at the drop of a hat.

If anything happened to either one of them, he'd go insane. He wanted to fix this for Kayla. To prove to her that it didn't always go wrong. That she could depend on him to be there every time she needed him.

I'm coming, beautiful. Hang in there.

His heart hurt and his brain whirled with hot anger. Dirty was in much the same boat over Chloe, and Camel wasn't far behind. The damage to Bailey if Kayla and Ana were killed would be irreparable, and Camel would have a long road to travel with her as he tried to pick up the pieces and keep her together.

Neo had texted Gentry back and agreed to meet him later. He wasn't going to keep that meeting because he and his team were blowing in like a fucking typhoon and taking Gentry down before it happened.

"Cell tower data indicates the women are in the same location," Jace Kaiser said. "We've got the coordinates. Heading there now."

Neo opened his eyes. They were gritty and he blinked a few times to clear them.

"You with us, Neo?" Shade asked, and Neo blinked at his teammate.

"Yep. Ready to kick some biker ass."

"If Chloe has one scratch—*one,*" Dirty growled.

"Somebody please tell me the assholes are sitting in the open," Camel added. "I'll pick every single one of them off before they even hear the first shot."

"Calm down," Remy "Cage" Marchand said. He was their team's second in command and he glared at them all now with steely eyes. "You assholes know that failure is not an option here. Concentrate on the task and worry about killing the fuckers *after* we have our objective."

"We aren't killing anyone," Brett Wheeler said. "*If* we don't have to. That's not the mission. Rescue the hostages. Capture the bikers and turn them over to law enforcement."

"You don't really think those assholes are going to surrender without a fight?" Neo said. "They demanded one million fucking dollars by sundown. Does that sound like a group of jerks that aren't looking for trouble?"

Brett grinned at him in the rearview. "Nope, but I gotta say what I gotta say."

"Okay, listen up," Jace Kaiser said, turning in his seat to look at them. He was holding an iPad and had a Google Earth map on the screen. Or what was probably a classified version of Google Earth. HOT had those too. "The terrain is wooded. There's one road in and it's probably being watched. The building they're in is an old tobacco barn that's been out of use for years and been converted into a storage facility at one point and a flea market at another. Most recently it was a garage. It's fallen into disrepair and hasn't been used in about ten years, but it has recently been leased to King Makers, LLC, which is supposed to be an auto repair and painting facility."

"Yeah, right," Dirty muttered.

"Hey, just telling you what it says," Jace replied. "We'll insert via the woods. Once we've got a visual on the place, and the heat map data, we'll proceed."

"No wonder there was no sign of those assholes," Camel said as he looked over Jace's shoulder. "That place is way out in the boonies."

"Yeah, but that's a good thing for us," Neo said. "It means nobody's gonna hear it when we start shooting."

"If there's a well, we can drop the bodies down it," Dirty said. "Toss some quicklime in after."

"Holy shit," Cage replied. "You crazy bastards are gonna get us booted out of HOT and into the darkest basement Mendez can find. Heads in the game. Now."

"I know, I know," Dirty said. "Just blowing off steam."

"All I want is my wife and daughter back," Neo said. "I don't care what happens to Gentry and his sick fucks so long as they never come after my family again."

Camel clapped him on the back. "Amen, brother."

Neo closed his eyes and thought of how good it would be to hold Kayla again. To spoon with her in bed, and to see little Ana's face light up when she held her arms out to him and wanted to be picked up. His stomach was in knots but that didn't matter. It wouldn't affect his ability to operate. He knew how to push that shit down deep and do what had to be done.

All he had to do was pray that Kayla was still alive and Ana was with her and not headed for someone's nursery. If either of them were gone, then he wouldn't be responsible for what he did to Dal Gentry. And he wouldn't care how dark a basement Mendez threw him in, because nothing would ever matter to him again.

———

WHEN THE DOOR OPENED AGAIN, Dal swaggered in with Steve on his heels. Kayla hugged Ana closer and tilted toward Chloe, who'd stiffened at the appearance of the two men.

"Well, well, well, what have we here?" Dal said. "Two bitches ripe for fucking and a brat that'll bring some good money from rich people who can't have kids."

"Fuck you, Dal," Kayla said, anger flaring bright. She'd spent a year with the Kings of Doom and she knew how they operated. How a biker wouldn't respect you if you cowered before him. Oh, he might still hurt you if you talked back—probably would in fact—but he'd take a bit more time to toy with you.

And time was what they needed. Kayla still didn't have Chloe's faith that Zach and Ryan would come, but if there was the slightest hope then she had to try and prolong whatever this was. Even if it ended up costing her more pain by the end.

"Go ahead and talk back to me, bitch. It won't save you. If that military dick of yours doesn't give me my money, then I'm sending you back to him in pieces."

"I would have gotten the money if you'd given me until Wednesday. You broke your word."

Bikers like him didn't like it when someone accused them of going against their word. Dal snorted. "That wasn't my deal, bitch. That was your fucking ex-lover's deal. But he's dead, and I'm in charge now."

Kayla's heart thumped. "James is dead?" Her gaze slewed to Steve. He didn't show any emotion, but she wouldn't have expected him to. He and James were related, not close.

"Hanged himself this morning. Damned shame, ain't it?"

Kayla processed that. James was dead and she felt nothing. Gladness maybe. Relief. He would never try to claim Ana, never show up one day and say he'd been deprived of being a father. But hanged himself? No, not James. He was too selfish and too scheming to ever give up.

"I can't say it's a shame," she said. "But I doubt it was his idea."

Dal laughed. "No, probably not. Can't say whose it was, but it's amazing what you can get done when you know folks on the inside."

"What are you going to do with us?" she asked. Chloe was silent because Kayla had convinced her that she needed to be the one to do the talking. She understood bikers, and she understood the complex systems which had dictated their lives. It was all about honor and duty and the club. These men were a feudal system, and their loyalty was to the king. And Dal was angling to be the king. James was dead, and he'd been a VP. The president of the club was in jail as well. How long before Dal greased the right palms and had him killed too?

"Well, doll, if I get my money, then I suppose I could let you go. Or, more fun, you and the swinging dick you've shacked up with could end up dead in a murder-suicide." His gaze shifted to Chloe and then back again. "Such a shame that you caught him with that bitch right there. Shot them both and then turned the gun on yourself. Though maybe the two of you are the lovers, and he'll be the one dead. You two can run away together."

Which was code for making them into sex slaves for the club's business and pimping them out to anyone who could pay. Kayla's heart throbbed and her belly roiled. She wanted to spit on him, but she wouldn't. That was carrying things a little too far. She met Steve's gaze. Glared.

"And you're okay with this? Your brother was VP.

You had a path to the top of the club laid out for you already. Hell, you're more likely to command allegiance than Dal simply based on who you are."

Dal stalked over and loomed above her. Her instinct was to put Ana down in case he attacked, but she couldn't risk doing anything that aroused his predator instincts toward her baby. It'd be like dropping blood in the water with a great white shark swimming nearby.

"Watch your mouth, whore. Stevie doesn't have the stomach for what it takes to lead, do you, boy?"

"Nope," Steve said. But he was standing behind Dal, which meant that Dal didn't see the venom in his eyes.

Kayla nearly laughed. Steve Dunn was no fan of Dal's, no matter what Dal thought. Given time, he'd turn on the hand that fed him and strike like a cobra. Too bad it wasn't going to happen right that minute. Not that she'd be any better off, but maybe she would. Maybe she could prevail on Steve's relationship to Ana to get him to let them go.

Probably not though. Dunns didn't care about blood family, only about their motorcycle family. And that only because it make them feel like something other than the lowlife douchebags they were.

Dal rubbed his crotch and eyed her up and down. Then he stepped closer, his crotch right in her face. "Let's see your game, baby," he said as he unzipped his dirty jeans. "Suck me off and maybe I'll be nice to you."

She'd rather stick a fork in her eye. He correctly read her militant look because he arched an eyebrow and fondled his cock. "You bite me or do anything aggressive, I'll throw that kid against the wall so hard she'll splat like a melon. You got that?"

"Yes," she said, trembling with rage and fear. Not fear for herself, but fear for Ana. For her baby, she'd do anything. Suck every dick in this place if she had to.

And Dal knew it. He dropped his pants to his knees and his dick sprang free.

"Now give the kid to this bitch and suck me good, Kayla. Suck me like the good little whore you are."

———

"FIFTEEN BIKES AND ONE CAR," Viking said over the earpiece. "It's Chloe's."

Neo gripped his gun and waited for the signal. They'd arrived in the area fifteen minutes ago and humped in from the drop zone to surround the dilapidated tobacco barn and the rusty garage. It was daylight, but the sun was starting to sink to the west and the woods were heavy enough that it made the area darker than if they were in the open.

Good conditions for a raid.

"Heat signatures in the building. There are eight people in the garage, five lying down in the upstairs part of the barn, and five in a room on the lower floor. Four adults and one baby. They're alive."

Neo's knees would have gone weak if he weren't so focused on what came next. One way or the other, he was holding his wife in his arms tonight.

"We're a go, men," Jace said in their ears. "Commence Operation Team Bonding. Over and out."

Chapter Twenty-Four

Kayla placed Ana into Chloe's arms. Chloe's eyes were wet and angry as she stared back at Kayla.

Kayla gave her head a little shake, warning Chloe not to speak or do anything to stop what was about to happen. She didn't want to do what Dal wanted, but she didn't have a choice. If she were lucky, she could close her eyes and think about Zach.

"Hurry up, bitch," Dal growled. "I got shit to do."

"You want this fast or you want it good?" Kayla threw at him as she wiggled on the mattress as if finding a better position.

Dal didn't say anything, just stepped in closer with his dick in his hands. "Open your fucking mouth and shut up."

Kayla's heart throbbed. She gritted her teeth hard. She would get through this. Somehow. Some way. She closed her eyes and started to open her mouth—

And the room exploded.

Instinctively, she rolled backward away from Dal. Chloe rolled too. Ana was still her in arms, wailing with fright. The walls shook. Around them, dust flew and splinters rained down on their heads. Kayla covered Ana's ears as explosions sounded in the distance.

Chloe's eyes met hers. Kayla realized with a shock that Chloe was grinning.

"Told you so," she mouthed.

Kayla's heart skipped and then soared. Was she right? Was it Zach and Ryan and the SEALs?

As the dust settled, a man in black military gear stalked toward them. He looked like something out of a futuristic movie with a helmet, goggles, a black vest, a rifle slung over his chest and a pistol in his hand. When he reached them, he dragged the face covering he'd been wearing down and pulled the goggles up.

Kayla cried out. Then she scrambled to her feet and threw herself into her husband's arms.

"Hello, beautiful," he whispered into her ear before he kissed the daylights out of her.

When they finally stopped kissing, she cried out again and turned to get Ana from Chloe. But Alexei was there, holding Ana and grinning. "Hey, Kayla. You looking for Ana-banana?"

"Yes. Oh god, yes."

"I checked her over quick. She's not hurt. We didn't use a flash-bang in here, so her hearing will be fine. I know it was loud though. Couldn't be helped."

Alexci handed her over and Ana clung to Kayla's neck. She was sniffling, not wailing anymore, which was a relief. Zach put an arm around them both. It was a little awkward with all the guns, but it's where she wanted to be.

"Za!" Ana cried when she looked up at the tall man standing so near.

Kayla blinked. Was this kid for real trying to say Zach? It wasn't just an attempt at pizza? Or maybe she associated Zach with pizza. Kayla laughed with wild love and relief and joy, and Zach hugged them close.

"Yeah, baby girl, I could use some pizza too. Maybe tonight, huh?"

Zach led them from the building and out into the fresh air. Chloe and Ryan were there, and a bunch of other men in black too. The SEAL team.

Emotion flooded her. She loved them. Every single one of them. She could never show them how much, but she was going to try. No wonder Chloe cooked for these guys all the time. She was still thanking them in the best way she knew how.

Fourteen men knelt on the ground with their hands behind their heads. Scalding fury roared through her at what Dal had tried to make her do.

"Where is he?" she growled. "I want to spit in his face."

"Too late, Kayla," Zach said softly. "He's dead."

Kayla hugged Ana tight and closed her eyes for a second. "Good. Saves me from having to kill him."

Zach led her over to a big black SUV that pulled into the clearing but he didn't open the door. Instead, he turned her. He searched her face, his green eyes filled with the kind of worry she hadn't seen there before.

"I'm sorry you suffered even a moment of fear, Kayla. I'm fucking pissed as hell that I didn't stop those assholes from taking you. I let you down, and it kills me that it happened—"

She put trembling fingers over his lips. Love swelled in her heart, in her soul. She couldn't let him think he'd failed her. It was the furthest thing from the truth.

"You came for me, Zach. You didn't abandon me. You told me you would protect me, and you did. Chloe was right. She had faith, but I have to admit that I wasn't sure. I've never been able to count on anyone but myself and Bailey."

"I didn't protect you the way I wanted to," he said.

She hated to see him this way. Hated the remorse in his eyes. Love was so huge inside her that it had no choice but to spill free.

"I love you, Zach. You're the best thing to ever happen to me, besides Ana. Without the two of you, my world wouldn't be the same."

He tugged her and Ana closer and kissed her swiftly. It was a hot kiss with tongues and desperate need, but it didn't last. He broke the kiss and then kissed Ana's forehead.

"I love you both. When I thought I might lose you —" He closed his eyes and shook his head. "I would have torn the world apart with my bare hands to get to you, Kayla. Nothing was going to stop me from finding you."

She smiled, and everything was right and perfect. Her whole world, for the first time ever, felt exactly the way it should. Full, beautiful, bright. Because of him.

"I can't wait to see what the future brings with you, Mr. Anderson. I'm thinking it's going to be amazing."

He opened the door for her and helped her inside. Then he climbed in beside her and drew her close. "It's already amazing, Mrs. Anderson. Because I have you and Ana-banana."

———

TWO MONTHS LATER...

NEO STOOD beneath a pergola crowned with white flowers, wearing his US Navy dress uniform, with a view of the Chesapeake Bay in the background. Beside him, Camel stood with the ring box that contained platinum wedding bands in his pocket. Camel and Bailey had gotten married a month ago, in a beautiful ceremony in a Russian Orthodox church, and now it was Neo's and Kayla's turn.

He'd asked her if she wanted the wedding like Bailey's, with the white dress and the big reception, but she'd said no, she really didn't. She'd wanted a princess wedding as a little girl, but she wasn't a little girl anymore. What she wanted was a ceremony with her friends and family, with a beautiful view and a catered reception, and here they were.

The music started, and Neo's insides twisted.

"Relax," Camel said. "You're already married."

"I know. But this is important to Kayla."

"Yeah, and you got it handled. She's happy. Bailey said so."

He was glad to know it, though he was still somewhat nervous. She hadn't talked about her dress, so he still didn't know what she'd chosen to wear. She wanted it to be a surprise.

Bailey came down the aisle carrying Ana in her arms. Ana could walk now, but not so well that she'd stroll the length of the aisle in anything resembling a timely manner. She liked to explore along the way.

Ana was dressed in pale pink and she threw handfuls of flower petals from a little basket that Bailey held as they walked. Everyone in the audience laughed softly as she passed by, chattering and tossing.

Her first word had indeed been Mama. She was working on Dada. And Neo was her daddy legally now because he'd formally adopted her. She still said Za sometimes, and they still didn't know if she meant pizza or Zach. They'd probably never know.

The music swelled and Kayla appeared. Neo went numb at how blindingly beautiful she was.

"Breathe," Camel said under his breath.

Neo sucked in a breath obediently and the stars he'd started to see faded away.

Kayla was wearing white. Not just white, but a traditional wedding dress with a train. It was simple and beautiful, clinging to her form like a caress. She walked down the aisle on General Mendez's arm, and Neo had a moment of envy for his commander.

Mendez's wife and child were in the audience, as well as all the SEALs and their women. Ghost was there, and the guys from the Bandits, including Ian Black, who'd tipped an imaginary hat at Neo when he'd first walked into Money and Ella's backyard. Some of the guys from Alpha and Echo squads were there too, including Jake Ryan and his talented tattoo artist wife Eva. Eva had covered Kayla's tattoo. Instead of a motorcycle tattoo, Neo got to look at the HOT logo with the globe and eagle and rifles every time he did his wife doggy style. It was fucking hot as hell.

There were too many other people to name, but suffice it to say if anyone stormed the property, they'd get a *very* unpleasant surprise when a shit ton of special operators descended on them.

Life had been better than he could have ever dreamed these past two months. He'd deployed twice, both short assignments, and come home each time to a beautiful wife and baby daughter he adored. Lesley and Kayla had talked several times and seemed to really like each other, and he and Kayla were planning a trip to Missouri soon.

Neo wrote Kayla notes every morning. He hadn't slacked off on that and never would. Almost losing her had affirmed to him how important it was to tell her every day how special she was and how much he adored her.

Dal Gentry was dead and the Kings of Doom were once more without a leader. Neo didn't think they'd be a threat to Kayla again. The ones who'd cared were done, and the rest didn't have the stomach for it. They'd been following orders without quite knowing what Gentry intended. Kidnapping Kayla, Ana, and Chloe had been a breaking point for them.

Gentry'd had scouts watching all the women at the salon. When he'd realized that Kayla and Chloe drove out of the city together to drop Ana off, he'd started making a plan to intercept them before they reached their destination.

In the end, Neo and Kayla had stayed in the house across the street from Dirty and Chloe. Kayla wanted to, and he didn't see why not at that point. It was a good thing too, because Kayla was learning to cook from the master. And so was he, because Kayla taught him what Chloe taught her. He wasn't too good to work beside his wife in the kitchen. In fact, he enjoyed it.

Kayla reached his side and the general put her

hand in his. Neo's skin leapt at her touch. It always leapt at her touch.

"You look incredible," he told her.

She smiled shyly. "So do you." Her gaze dropped over his chest. "So many medals. My goodness."

"I'll let you take them off me later," he told her, lowering his voice so the minister didn't hear.

Speaking of minister, Ian Black lifted his arms and began, "Dearly beloved...."

Neo grinned like a fool at Kayla. She grinned back.

It was so crazy, having Ian Black marry them, but among his many other talents, Black was ordained. Neo suspected it was the same kind of ordained that anybody could get on the internet, but who knew with Black?

That was life for you. Crazy, unpredictable, surprising—and fucking awesome.

And it was only going to get more awesome from this day forward...

Books by Lynn Raye Harris

HOT Heroes for Hire: Mercenaries

Black's Bandits

Book 1: BLACK LIST - Jace & Maddy

Book 2: BLACK TIE - Brett & Tallie

Book 3: BLACK OUT - Colt & Angie

Book 4: BLACK KNIGHT ~ Coming Soon!

———

The Hostile Operations Team ® Books

Book 0: RECKLESS HEAT

Book 1: HOT PURSUIT - Matt & Evie

Book 2: HOT MESS - Sam & Georgie

Book 3: DANGEROUSLY HOT - Kev & Lucky

Book 4: HOT PACKAGE - Billy & Olivia

Book 5: HOT SHOT - Jack & Gina

Book 6: HOT REBEL - Nick & Victoria

Book 7: HOT ICE - Garrett & Grace

Book 8: HOT & BOTHERED - Ryan & Emily

Book 9: HOT PROTECTOR - Chase & Sophie

Book 10: HOT ADDICTION - Dex & Annabelle

Book 11: HOT VALOR - Mendez & Kat

Book 12: HOT ANGEL - Cade & Brooke

Book 13: HOT SECRETS - Sky & Bliss

Book 14: HOT JUSTICE - Wolf & Haylee

Book 15: HOT STORM - Mal ~ Coming Soon!

———

The HOT SEAL Team Books

Book 1: HOT SEAL - Dane & Ivy

Book 2: HOT SEAL Lover - Remy & Christina

Book 3: HOT SEAL Rescue - Cody & Miranda

Book 4: HOT SEAL BRIDE - Cash & Ella

Book 5: HOT SEAL REDEMPTION - Alex & Bailey

Book 6: HOT SEAL TARGET - Blade & Quinn

Book 7: HOT SEAL HERO - Ryan & Chloe

Book 8: HOT SEAL DEVOTION - Zack & Kayla

Book 9: Shade's book! ~ Coming soon….

The HOT Novella in Liliana Hart's MacKenzie Family Series

HOT WITNESS - Jake & Eva

———

7 Brides for 7 Brothers

MAX (Book 5) - Max & Ellie

7 Brides for 7 Soldiers

WYATT (Book 4) - Max & Ellie

7 Brides for 7 Blackthornes

ROSS (Book 3) - Ross & Holly

———

Who's HOT?

Alpha Squad

Matt "Richie Rich" Girard (Book 0 & 1)
Sam "Knight Rider" McKnight (Book 2)
Kev "Big Mac" MacDonald (Book 3)
Billy "the Kid" Blake (Book 4)
Jack "Hawk" Hunter (Book 5)
Nick "Brandy" Brandon (Book 6)
Garrett "Iceman" Spencer (Book 7)
Ryan "Flash" Gordon (Book 8)
Chase "Fiddler" Daniels (Book 9)
Dex "Double Dee" Davidson (Book 10)

Commander

John "Viper" Mendez (Book 11)

Deputy Commander

Alex "Ghost" Bishop

Echo Squad
Cade "Saint" Rodgers (Book 12)
Sky "Hacker" Kelley (Book 13)
Dean "Wolf" Garner (Book 14)
Malcom "Mal" McCoy (Book 15)
Jake "Harley" Ryan (HOT WITNESS)
Jax "Gem" Stone
Noah "Easy" Cross
Ryder "Muffin" Hanson

SEAL Team
Dane "Viking" Erikson (Book 1)
Remy "Cage" Marchand (Book 2)
Cody "Cowboy" McCormick (Book 3)
Cash "Money" McQuaid (Book 4)
Alexei "Camel" Kamarov (Book 5)
Adam "Blade" Garrison (Book 6)
Ryan "Dirty Harry" Callahan (Book 7)
Zach "Neo" Anderson (Book 8)
Corey "Shade" Vance

Black's Bandits
Jace Kaiser (Book 1)
Brett Wheeler (Book 2)
Colton Duchaine (Book 3)
Tyler Scott
Ian Black
Jared Fraser
Thomas "Rascal" Bradley
Dax Freed

Jamie Hayes
Mandy Parker (Airborne Ops)
Melanie (Reception)
? Unnamed Team Members

Freelance Contractors
Lucinda "Lucky" San Ramos, now MacDonald
(Book 3)
Victoria "Vee" Royal, now Brandon (Book 6)
Emily Royal, now Gordon (Book 8)
Miranda Lockwood, now McCormick (SEAL Team
Book 3)
Bliss Bennett, (Book 13)

About the Author

Lynn Raye Harris is the *New York Times* and *USA Today* bestselling author of the HOSTILE OPERATIONS TEAM ® SERIES of military romances as well as twenty books for Harlequin Presents. A former finalist for the Romance Writers of America's Golden Heart Award and the National Readers Choice Award, Lynn lives in Alabama with her handsome former-military husband, two crazy cats, and one spoiled American Saddlebred horse. Lynn's books have been called "exceptional and emotional," "intense," and "sizzling." Lynn's books have sold over 4.5 million copies worldwide.

To connect with Lynn online:
www.LynnRayeHarris.com
Lynn@LynnRayeHarris.com

Made in the USA
Columbia, SC
01 July 2020

12920653R00195